PRAISE FOR ROBIN PAIGE'S VICTORIAN MYSTERIES

"I read it with enjoyment . . . I found myself burning
for the injustices of it, and caring what
happened to the people" – *Anne Perry*

"I couldn't put it down" – *Murder & Mayhem*

"An intriguing mystery . . . Skillfully unravelled"
– Jean Hager, author of *Blooming Murder*

"Absolutely riveting . . . An extremely articulate,
genuine mystery, with well-drawn, compelling
characters" – *Meritorious Mysteries*

"An absolutely charming book . . . An adventure
worth reading . . . You're sure to
enjoy it" – *Romantic Times*

D1336307

The Victorian Mystery Series by Robin Paige

(written by Susan Wittig Albert with
her husband, Bill Albert, writing as Robin Paige)

THE *Victorian Mystery* SERIES

4

Death at DEVIL's BRIDGE

ROBIN PAIGE

SOUTH
DOWNS
CRIME &
MYSTERY

First published in the UK in 2016
by South Downs CRIME & MYSTERY,
an imprint of
The Crime & Mystery Club Ltd,
PO Box 394, Harpenden,
Herts, AL5 1XJ, UK
Reprinted, 2017

www.crimeandmystery.club

ISBN
978-0-85730-019-5 (print)
978-0-85730-020-1 (epub)

Typeset in 11pt Palatino
by Geethik Technologies Pvt Ltd, India
Printed and bound in the UK by Clays Ltd, St Ives plc

ACKNOWLEDGMENTS

Our thanks go to Robin Barker, for the generous loan of the 1895–98 issues of *The British Journal Photographic Almanac*, and to Charles Albert, for his help with engineering details. We are also grateful to the many readers who have written to comment on the technical and historical authenticity of this series. We very much appreciate your interest and support.

Bill and Susan Albert
aka Robin Paige

MAJOR CHARACTERS

THE GENTRY

Sir Charles Sheridan, *of Bishop's Keep and Somersworth*
Lady Kathryn Ardleigh Sheridan, aka Beryl Bardwell, *of Bishop's Keep*
Lord Bradford Marsden, *of Marsden Manor*
The Honorable Miss Patsy Marsden, *of Marsden Manor*
Roger Thornton, *Squire, of Thornton Grange*

SELECTED EXHIBITORS, COMPETITORS, AND GUESTS AT THE ESSEX MOTOR CAR EXHIBITION AND BALLOON CHASE

Herr Wilhelm Albrecht, *German motorcar racer and driver of Lord Marsden's Daimler*
Mr. Arnold Bateman, *Cambridge, inventor and driver of the Bateman Electric Car*
Mr. Arthur Dickson, *Sheffield, owner and driver of a Serpollet Steamer*
Mr. Sam Holt, *journalist, of* Autocar *magazine*
Mr. Harry Dunstable, *promoter of the British Motor Car Syndicate*
Mr. Frank Ponsonby, *bill-broker and driver of a Benz*
The Honorable Charles Stewart Rolls *of Trinity College, Cambridge, aeronaut and owner of a Peugeot*
Mr. Henry Royce, *electrical engineer, of Manchester*

DEDHAM VILLAGERS

Dr. Braxton Bassett, *surgeon*
Harry Hodson, *the Crown's coroner*
Mistress Bess Gurton
The Widow Jessup
Young Jessup
Edward Laken, *Constable*
The Reverend Barfield Talbot, *Vicar of St. Mary's Parish*
Tom Whipple

SERVANTS AT BISHOP'S KEEP

Mudd, *butler*
Pocket, *footman*
Mrs. Sarah Pratt, *cook*
Amelia Quibbley, *housekeeper*
Lawrence Quibbley, *mechanic to Lord Bradford Marsden and photographic assistant to Sir Charles Sheridan*

1

"Far behind them, Mole, Toad, and the Water Rat heard a faint warning hum, like the drone of a distant bee. Glancing back, they saw a small cloud of dust with a dark centre of energy, advancing at incredible speed. . . . It was on them! The 'Poop-poop' of the horn rang with a brazen shout in their ears . . . and the magnificent motor-car, immense, breath-snatching, passionate, with its pilot tense and hugging his wheel, possessed all earth and air for the fraction of a second, flung an enveloping cloud of dust that blinded and enwrapped them utterly, and then dwindled to a speck in the far distance, changed back into a droning bee once more."

—KENNETH GRAHAME
The Wind in the Willows

THE SKY WAS darkening over Dedham Vale as Bess Gurton hitched up her woolen skirt, climbed the stile, and set off along the margin of Dead Man's Meadow. High overhead skittered an early and erratic bat, half-blind in the dying light. Higher yet, in the tops of the horse chestnut trees, a few rooks offered somber good nights.

Bess tightened her grip on her willow basket. The ominous voices of rooks frightened some, but not her. "Rusty death a'cawin'," her neighbor Sally would say, looking up from her knitting when she heard the birds shrieking. "Sittin' in judgment," she would add with a shudder, and get up to close the casement. "Passin' a death sentence on some poor lost soul."

But about rooks, Bess knew better. As a girl, some thirty years ago, she had kept a rook called Figwort, a sociable bird with a bright, inquisitive eye. She had raised Figwort from a fledgling, and while he grew up to be a mischievous thief, stealing the odd bit of this and that, he was never the least bit malevolent. No, if the melancholy calls of the sleepy rooks in the dying twilight brought anything to Bess's mind, it was an ancient longing that harked back to her childhood, a foolish, reckless wish, Sally would say, and surely quite wicked. Her neighbors in Dedham Village, Bess had learned long ago, were easily affrighted by what they did not understand and swift to suspect any impulse that seemed out of the ordinary.

And this wish was indeed an extraordinary one, at least by village standards. Audacious, intemperate as it might seem to those who did not dare think on such things, Bess wanted to fly.

"And why not, I'd like to know?" she would ask herself truculently. "Wot's wrong wi' it?"

And herself would respond, gently reassuring, "Nothing's wrong with it, Bessie, me girl. Birds do it, angels do it, yer gammer's done it. Now, stop shilly-shallying an' git on wi' it. If ye'r ever goin' to fly, let it be now!"

The desire to fly was not uniquely nor even originally Bess's wish. She had learned it from her grandmother, who had raised her from infancy in the whitewashed cottage on Black Brook which Bess occupied now, together with a company of cats, an ancient Jack Russell terrier named Fat Susan, and a milk cow named Patience. In those days, Gammer Gurton had had two cronies, both of whom could fly—or so Bess understood from the hushed stories she heard around the kitchen fire when she was quite a young girl. And Gammer herself had also flown, Bess was sure of it, for hadn't she seen her with her very own eyes one moonlight night, astride a hurdle, skirts and cape snatching at the brambles as she sailed low over the hedge and into the Great Wood?

Others might have thought it a dream, but not Bess. She had never forgotten the sight of her grandmother silhouetted against the bright, full moon, but she was not exactly clear about the details—just how Gammer and her friends managed to get off the ground, that is. The task seemed easy enough, however, and Bess was a brave, strong girl. So she tried it herself, taking a running leap off Black Rock with Gammer's ash broomstick under her. But all she gained from the experiment was a torn skirt and two badly scratched knees. Questioned at home, she confessed to her effort to get off the ground and begged Gammer to tell her how flying was done.

But Gammer, alarmed, sternly bade her hold her tongue. "Such un-Christian foolishness!" she cried. "Put it out o' yer mind this instant, Bessie. Flyin'! Why, I niver heard sich nonsense in all me life!" The two cronies vanished from the cottage fireside, Bess never again saw Gammer soar over the bramble hedge, and not one more word was spoken on the subject. When the old woman died at last, in Bess's thirtieth year, the secret of flight died with her.

During the next dozen years, Bess—who remained unmarried—was so busy with the work of supporting herself that she had little energy to spare for fanciful dreams of flying. Gammer had left her a dairy cow and some hens, and Bess made a small living from the milk, cream, butter, and eggs she sold in the village. She supplemented this income by peddling the asparagus, broccoli, and cauliflower from her garden and by harvesting the willows that grew plentifully along the River Stour, weaving the wands into baskets. She also raised bees, in neatly thatched wooden hives ranged on the sunny side of the wattle fence across the back garden.

Indeed, so bustling and busy and pleasantly earthbound was Bess's life that her childhood ambition lay like a forgotten memory in the bottom of her heart—until, that is, the day she noticed a loose slate in the hearth and raised it to discover a cavity beneath. From this hiding place she lifted a curious leather-bound book, printed in black letter and unquestionably ancient, its brown pages annotated with spidery handwritten notes.

Reading was reserved for the candlelit hour before bedtime, which Bess always spent with the newspaper supplied by her friend Sarah Pratt, cook at Bishop's Keep, several miles down the lane. Now, having discovered the book, Bess was so curious that she could scarcely wait until evening to read it. Unfortunately, however, the black-letter text and spidery annotations could not be deciphered by the light of her candle. So on the following day, Bess purchased a paraffin lamp, an acquisition she had deliberately postponed. She had an inborn distrust of modern inventions, such as the post-office telegraph which clattered so loudly that one could scarce make oneself heard, or Lord Marsden's new horseless carriage, which he drove with such reckless abandon. But the lamp proved quite useful, and Bess sat down in its circle of light to decipher the ancient text.

To her disappointment, though, the mysterious book turned out to be nothing more than a collection of ancient recipes. She was about to cast it aside, when she turned a page and found "A Receipt for Flying Ointment." Her eyes widened and, tilting the book to the light, she read the recipe with a swelling excitement. Some of the ingredients—honey, goose grease, thyme, basil, chicory—were familiar staples of her larder and garden. Soot (whatever could be the purpose of *that* ingredient?) could be had from her chimney, while plovers' eggs, pig's blood, and some of the less familiar plants (water hemlock, for instance) would have to be specially procured.

Breathlessly, Bess put down the book and considered. The ointment sounded perfectly odious, to be sure, but what did that matter if it got her over the bramble hedge and into the air, like Gammer Gurton? The biggest problem, of course, was gathering the more unusual ingredients without arousing anyone's suspicion. And it was not just the fear of ridicule that caused Bess to proceed with caution. The last witch burned to death in England had been set afire near this very village, scarcely ten years before Queen Victoria took the throne. Bess had no intention of giving her neighbors the slightest excuse for honing their tongues on *her* doings. Whatever she did, she would do in secret.

So it was that Bess was out and about with her basket on this late-summer night, just as the full moon began to rise over Dedham Vale. Following the recipe's instructions, she had scraped from her chimney the pinch of soot, gathered the required number of plovers' eggs, plucked the requisite wild herbs, and was at this moment on her way to Bishop's Keep to obtain the pint of fresh pig's blood Sarah Pratt had promised to save for her. The footpath was now almost completely dark, and she picked her way with caution, half-wishing she had not embarked upon this phase of her mission so late in the evening. But as the recipe specified that the monkshood should be gathered at moonrise and the spot where it grew was more than halfway to Sarah's kitchen, the journey was necessary.

The path dipped steeply through a narrow opening in the dense hedge. Clutching her basket in one hand, Bess half slid down the embankment and into the lane. Bishop's Keep was less than a mile away and Sarah would have a cup of hot tea and her pint of pig's blood ready and waiting, no questions asked, no answers required. She shook herself, squared her shoulders, and began to march briskly up the road.

She heard it before she actually saw it. The sound—a loud metallic clatter and clank—reminded her of the noisy threshing machines that had replaced the hand-harvesting of the fall corn. But because the lane was so deep and the tall hedges grew nearly together over her head, the horrible sound seemed to reverberate all around, and she could not tell from which direction it was coming, or which way she should run.

Her breath coming short and fast, Bess pressed her hands against her ears, standing paralyzed with fear in the middle of the lane. It was only when she saw the bright white lights bearing down upon her that she realized that she was about to be run down by that most dangerous of modern inventions, a horseless carriage. She flung herself off the road, landing with a mighty splash in the water-filled ditch. Drenched, mouth and eyes filled with mud, she sat up, hurling curses after the motorcar— Lord Marsden's motorcar—which had disappeared with a great clatter around the turn.

It took several moments for Bess to drag herself out of the ditch and scramble to her feet in the lane. She found her basket, retrieved what she could of its contents, and started off toward Sarah's kitchen, muttering. A half-mile farther on, as the moon was casting a pale light over the way, she stumbled onto Old Jessup's body, lying in the grassy ditch, at the gate to Bishop's Keep.

2

"The hour before dinner, while we wait for late-arriving guests and for the announcement that the table is ready at last, gives us time to tell our friends grand tales about our lives."

—JENNIFER LASHNER
Our Victorian Grandmothers

"LORD MARSDEN, THE Honorable Mr. Charles Rolls, and the Honorable Miss Patsy Marsden," Mudd announced from the drawing-room door.

Lady Kathryn Ardleigh Sheridan stood and took her husband's arm as they went out onto the terrace steps to greet their guests. The open windows had admitted the clackety-clank of Bradford Marsden's Daimler pulling up the gravel lane and his sister's fresh laughter as the trio alighted, and Mudd's announcement was entirely superfluous. But announcing guests was Mudd's job, and Kate did not interfere. When she had inherited Bishop's Keep from her aunt Sabrina Ardleigh several years before, she had determined that she would change only what was unjust or just plain unacceptable to her American sensibility, and would accommodate herself to the rest.

But when she and Charles Sheridan were married three months ago in a private ceremony in the village church, Kate discovered that she had much more to accommodate than she had reckoned with—a disconcerting discovery, to be sure, for Kate loved her new husband deeply. She *must* love him, she reasoned to herself, to be willing to give up her freedom, her hard-won independence, and become the wife of a man who (upon his brother's shortly expected death) would inherit his father's peerage, his family's estates at Somersworth, and the dependency of his mother and his brother's wife.

At the thought of her mother-in-law, Kate flinched. She had wanted Charles's family to attend their wedding, but he had dissuaded her. Kate was anxious to meet her new family, so a few days later, they traveled to Somersworth. But when the dowager baroness learned that her son had not only married without her knowledge but had chosen a wife who was both American *and* Irish, she became hysterical. Dinner that evening was an agony, and Charles and Kate had left the next morning.

"I'm sorry," Charles had said miserably, as they drove away in the carriage. "I thought she would take it with a better grace. I hoped—" He took her hand. "But she'll come round. She will come to love you, as I do."

Kate hardly shared his confidence, but she managed a smile. "Until she does, we have our home at Bishop's Keep."

"Then you don't mind staying there, my dear, until all this is sorted out?"

Kate thought of the moldy old pile that was Somersworth Castle and the angry old woman who ruled there, and nodded vigorously. "As far as I am concerned, we can live at Bishop's Keep forever. It suits me perfectly."

Bishop's Keep seemed to suit Charles, too. He had spent most of his time in the last few months modernizing the old Georgian house, installing water pipes and plumbing and gas lighting and an electric dynamo which (he claimed) would eventually power all manner of mechanical appliances. There was even talk of adding a telephone as soon as the Exchange came to Dedham.

Charles's innovations did not always work the way he anticipated, however. The pipes clanged as if a dozen smiths were pounding on them. And Mrs. Pratt was so afraid of the new gas cooker that she refused to touch it until Charles himself demonstrated its safety features. But Charles was so proud of these improvements that Kate scarcely had the heart to criticize, or even to remark that she herself was rather fond of paraffin lamps, however old-fashioned they might be.

Kate pushed aside these ungrateful thoughts and welcomed their guests, who were still goggled, capped, and coated. "Please," she said to Patsy, "let me help you with your things," and stepped forward to unwind her pretty young friend, the daughter of Lord Christopher and Lady Henrietta Marsden, from the heavy veil that covered her elaborate ash-blond coiffure. When the layers of motoring apparel had been removed, Bradford Marsden, Patsy's elder brother and a close friend of the Sheridans, introduced Charlie Rolls.

Unencumbered of cap and goggles, Rolls was revealed to be a darkly handsome young man of nineteen or so— just Patsy's age—with deep-set eyes, dark brows, and a rakishly devil-take-it air that owed something to the alertness of his look and the willful, almost arrogant lift of his firm chin. Kate had understood from Patsy that he had just completed his first year at Cambridge.

"He's the third son of the first baronet of something-or-other," Patsy had confided, revealing in those words his lowly social status. "But Charlie's position scarcely matters. I don't intend to marry him, or even to fall in love with him—just to enjoy his company. Whatever Mama says," she had added defensively.

Kate did not reply, although inwardly she applauded Patsy's independence. Several years before, Lady Henrietta had arranged the marriage of her eldest daughter, Eleanor, to a wealthy candy manufacturer—a marriage that had proved disastrously unhappy. Kate knew that Lady Henrietta intended her youngest daughter to wed Squire Roger Thornton of Thornton Grange, the stern, dry offshoot of an old county family whose extensive lands adjoined Marsden Manor. She would be aghast at Patsy's friendship with the brash young man from Cambridge, whose father, Lord Llangattock, had only recently been admitted to the peerage. Charlie Rolls might be handsome as a lord, but his lack of title and fortune made him practically unmarriageable.

However, Lord Christopher and Lady Henrietta had taken themselves (and Eleanor and her infant son) to the south of France on extended holiday, leaving their younger daughter under the watchful eye of Patsy's spinster great-aunt, Miss Penelope Marsden. Great-aunt Marsden was not the vigilant chaperon that Lady Henrietta imagined her to be, however, for she retired at an early hour with her lapdog and a box of sweetmeats, leaving her niece to her own entertainments.

Currently, Patsy was entertaining herself with the Honorable Charlie Rolls, who was the houseguest of her brother Bradford. She was also spending a great deal of time at Bishop's Keep, where Sir Charles was teaching her the craft of photography. He had instructed her in the fine points of darkroom practice and had ordered two cameras for her from the London Stereoscopic Company, in Regent Street: a lightweight, pocket-size Vesta folding camera and a Frena Number One, which took lantern-size plates. Patsy seemed talented, and Kate hoped the girl would pursue photography half as enthusiastically as she was pursuing the young Mr. Rolls.

21

The last guest arrived a moment later. He was Barfield Talbot, the vicar of St. Mary's the Virgin, a stooped, elderly man with pale blue eyes deeply set in an aquiline face, beneath a mane of white hair. The good vicar was dressed carelessly, his cravat askew, coat missing a button, and hair as wild as if he had just that moment dismounted from the safety bicycle that he rode on his parish rounds. He hadn't, of course; he had been fetched by Pocket in the pony cart.

"Ah, Kate, my dear," he said, with special affection, and bent low over her hand in an old-fashioned, gentlemanly way. "It is good to see you looking so well. Marriage clearly agrees with you."

Vicar Talbot, who had performed the Sheridans' wedding ceremony, had been a friend of Kate's Aunt Sabrina. He had generously made himself her friend since her arrival from America—a friendship Kate welcomed, for it made up in part for the family she had lost.

Kate's father, Thomas Ardleigh, and her Irish mother, Aileen O'Malley Ardleigh, had both died when Kate was a child. The orphan had been raised by her uncle and aunt O'Malley, he a policeman on the streets of New York, she the mother of six other children whom she fed, clothed, and educated, for Aunt O'Malley was determined that all her children should go to school. Kate expected to make her own way in the world and labored hard at her lessons. When she was old enough to seek employment she worked first as a governess, then as a private secretary, and then—a fate at which Kate still often marveled—as an author. To supplement her meager income, she had written a story, and then had been fortunate enough to find a publisher who was willing to gamble on her work. Before she knew what was happening, her fictions, written under the pen name of Beryl Bardwell, had been accepted by an enthusiastic reading public. Beryl's earliest stories were of the sensational variety, penny dreadfuls with such titles as *The Rosicrucian's Ruby* and *Missing Pearl*, suitable for *Frank Leslie's Popular Monthly*, in which they appeared. "Our readers take great delight in exotic murder and its detection," Mr. Leslie had remarked as he handed Kate the payment for Beryl's third thriller. "I advise you, young lady, to continue to dip your pen in blood, and you shall do quite well indeed."

For a time, Kate had been glad enough to dip Beryl's pen in blood, and to trade her lurid tales for the independence money brought. But as she became more skilled as a writer, she grew increasingly weary of the frenzied drama that Mr. Leslie and his readers demanded. She particularly objected to the succession of bloody killings that substituted for plot in such novels, for her own inclination was rather to the subtler violence of the heart.

Hence, when Aunt Sabrina Ardleigh (Kate's father's sister, hitherto unknown to her) had surprised her with an invitation to come to England as her private secretary, Beryl took a brief holiday from sensational fiction. When she returned to her pen—or rather, to the new Royal typewriter Aunt Sabrina had purchased for her—she began to experiment with a different kind of writing: detective stories of a more psychological bent, with a deeper exploration of motive and feeling, stories in which the female characters were portrayed not as victims or the objects of men's fascination, but as free and independent women who made their way in the world by their wits. Mindful that the greatest number of her readers were women, Kate took care to create adventuresome heroines fired with spirit and determination. And mindful that the most powerful fictions are those that portray life realistically, she began to incorporate real people into her plots, disguising them as necessary to preserve their privacy.

This new interest required Beryl Bardwell to yield up her place as the Queen of Sensation Fiction (as Frank Leslie had crowned her) and look for a more congenial publisher. About this time, though, Aunt Sabrina, and her sister, Aunt Jaggers, died in a truly horrible way, poisoned. Kate (who had been instrumental in discovering their killer, and in fact formed her attachment to Charles during his investigation of the deaths) discovered to her surprise that Bishop's Keep and a modest fortune were hers. No longer compelled by financial exigency to tailor her fiction to tastes not her own, she could now write exactly as she chose.

The change had fired Kate with a new kind of creative energy. Recently, several of her stories had appeared in *Blackwell's Monthly*, and had been widely praised. The pseudonymous Beryl Bardwell was being hailed as a "female Conan Doyle," a compliment that first brought Kate a great deal of amusement, to which was quickly added an equal measure of apprehension. She had not disguised some of her characters or events as thoroughly as she might have done. What would happen if the identities of these real people were discovered? What would happen if *she* were discovered?

Indeed, Kate's private life as a writer had nearly prevented her from marrying Sir Charles Sheridan. She had loved him with a growing passion for months but had been reluctant to admit her feelings even to herself, knowing that her Irish blood and American upbringing made her unattractive to a member of the landed gentry, and believing that her writing (which she fully intended to be her life's work) would make her positively undesirable to any man.

But Sir Charles, when he learned of her covert occupation, was warmly supportive—all the more, perhaps, because his fascination with the new sciences of criminal detection coincided with her interest in fictional crime. In fact, their engagement had occurred in the midst of his investigation of several murders at Easton Lodge, during a weekend house party where the Prince of Wales was also a guest, and their hostess, the Countess of Warwick, a chief suspect. Together, Sir Charles and Kate had brought the inquiry to a successful conclusion, to the grateful relief of His Highness and the countess.

With a flourish, Mudd opened the double doors to the stately dining room and stepped through. "Dinner is served," he announced.

Charles turned to Kate, a smile crinkling the corners of his sherry-brown eyes. "Well, my dear," he asked, "shall we see what surprises from the kitchen await us this evening?"

The vicar raised his shaggy white eyebrows. "I do hope you have not lost your cook," he said earnestly. "Sarah Pratt is among the finest in the county."

"Mrs. Pratt is still with us," Kate replied. "Charles has presented her with a new challenge, however, and she has not quite mastered it. Last night's dinner," she added to the vicar, in a low voice, "was a culinary catastrophe. I hope we fare better tonight."

"A new challenge?" the vicar asked, and chuckled. "You cannot be suggesting that there is something in the line of cookery that confounds Mrs. Pratt."

Kate gestured at the gaslight that illuminated the drawing room. "You noticed, perhaps, that we are modernizing Bishop's Keep. Charles has piped water to the kitchen and installed a gas cooker. The water is welcome, but Mrs. Pratt is in mortal fear of a gas explosion."

She glanced down the mahogany table, which was covered with damask and decorated with clusters of green smilax interwoven with stephanotis and rosy-pink lapageria. The silver gleamed, the crystal epergnes sparkled, and the new gas wall sconces cast a golden glow over the room. But Kate shook her head with all the apprehension of a hostess who has good reason to fear the worst.

"I do hope," she said prayerfully, "that things are going well in the kitchen."

3

"God sends meat and the devil sends cooks."
                                    —THOMAS DELONEY
                                    Works, 1600

BUT IN THE kitchen, things were not going well at all. Sarah Pratt was rushing to assemble the lobster *bouchées*—cooked lobster and mushrooms stirred into a Mornay sauce and piled into delicate pastry cases. The sauce had scorched, in consequence of the gas jet being turned too high. Worse, Mrs. Pratt's hand was trembling so violently from nerves (the gas, after all, might explode at any moment) that she had snipped a great deal too much fennel into it. And there was Harriet the kitchen maid, standing beside the cooker, weeping, her finger in her mouth. She had carelessly stuck it in the gas flame when she attempted to remove the kettle.

"I don't care tuppence fer yer finger, Harriet," Sarah Pratt snapped. "The soup's already gone up an' the lobster must follow without delay. Put these pastries into that miserable oven to brown. Five minutes only, not a minute more."

Sarah spoke with greater certainty than she felt. Five minutes would have been quite adequate in her steady, predictable coal range with the capacious oven, which had been a fixture in her kitchen for over two decades. But the new gas cooker, which Sir Charles had installed in place of the dependable iron range, was of an unknown temper. Perhaps the cases should be browned for seven minutes, or ten, or even more.

"Watch," she commanded. "Don't let 'em burn on their bottoms!"

"Yes, mum," Harriet said, eyeing the cooker as if it were the devil. Sarah turned to the next task, preparing the hollandaise sauce that would go up with the salmon, after the joint. Then there were the carrots to cream and the peas to be cooked with lettuce and tiny onions, and the sweet to send up—a gooseberry fool, ready and waiting in the galvanized box under the ice tray. And then the savory—ham croquettes wrapped in bacon and fried—and to finish off, the blackcurrant ice, which had been worked in the ice-pail that afternoon by Harriet and Nettie. It was a menu of which Sarah might be proud. And yet she trembled, remembering the charred roast pork of the previous evening and the cheese soufflé that had emerged, cratered, from the gas oven.

Disaster was doomed to be revisited on Sarah Pratt's kitchen, however, for the bottoms of the lobster *bouchées* turned black, rather than brown. The hollandaise curdled, the vegetables were cooked to a pulp, and the savory was as soggy as old sponge. When the blackcurrant ice went up and Sarah could at last lower her stout frame into her chair, she was near tears.

" 'Tis that cursed cooker," Bess Gurton said darkly. "A tool of the devil himself." She spoke from the opposite side of the fire, where she sat with her injured ankle propped on a stool, the cat on the floor beside her, and her wet and muddy cape spread over a chair.

"We both bin cursed," Sarah said. "If 'twould of bin a carriage instead of Lord Marsden's motorcar that come round the corner, ye could've got out o' the way wit'out mishap."

"An' pore Old Jessup," Bess Gurton muttered, reaching down to stroke the cat. "Give me quite a start, y'know, findin' 'im like that, face up i' the ditch. Stark starin' dead, 'e was."

"But it wa'n't Lord Marsden's motorcar that kilt 'im," Harriet reminded her, wringing out the washing-up cloth. "Ye said 'e di'n't bear a mark."

"Ye-es," Bess replied slowly, "but it might still of bin the motorcar. Say 'e died o' fright at bein' near run down. 'Oo kilt 'im then, I'd like to know? Young Jessup, 'oo come along not two minutes after I found 'is old dad, 'e was askin' that question. ' 'Spose me dad died o' fright,' e sez. ' 'Oo kilt 'im then?' "

" 'Twere drink an' the devil that did fer Old Jessup," Sarah remarked. "The way 'e beat 'is pore ol' wife, the man had it comin' to 'im, I say. I doubt Tilda Jessup'll grieve overlong."

Bess frowned down her long nose. "All the beatin's in the world don't give folks the right to act like maniacs. No regard fer anybody. Mad fer speed they are. That motorcar was flyin' faster'n a bullet!"

Harriet drew close, her eyes large with excitement. "Faster'n a bullet!" she marveled. "Oh, Bess, ye'r lucky to be alive!"

Bess nodded. "Would of bin dead as mutton 'f I hadn't flown into the ditch. But they'll git wot's comin' to them," she added, with grim satisfaction. "I laid one o' Gammer Gurton's best curses on that motorcar, I did. They'll find out it don't do to treat Bess Gurton oncivil-like. Sooner er later, they'll go smash."

"Ye better watch out, Bess Gurton," Sarah cautioned. "Ye don't want to go layin' curses on the gentry's motorcars.

ROBIN PAIGE

Curses come home to roost, same as chickens." She heaved
herself out of her chair. "Ye'r probably wantin' to git home
an' put that wrenched ankle to soak. Pocket kin take ye
i' the pony cart, an' come back fer the vicar. I'll git the
blood."

She paused, looking down at her friend, hoping to hear
Bess's reason for walking out on a dark night to acquire
a pint of fresh pig's blood. But Bess, still stroking the cat,
was staring into the fire with such concentration that she
didn't notice. So Sarah went to the pantry and fetched the
glass container of blood, along with a packet of cake and a
small crockery pot that had until recently contained a fine
Dijon mustard. It was now full of quince jam. The cake
and jam were a gift from Sarah to Bess, in honor of Bess's
recent birthday.

"Here be some cakes and jam," she said, handing the
packet to Bess, "and the blood. Put it in yer basket an'—"

At that moment, disaster struck again. Sarah's fingers
slipped, the jar dropped to the stone floor, and smashed.
The pig's blood, no longer as fresh as it had been, showered
the cat, splashed the hem of Bess Gurton's woolen skirt,
and puddled, stinking and greasy, on the stones of the
hearth.

The cat jumped off Bess's lap and streaked for the door.
Bess cried out and leapt up, knocking over a jar of vinegar
and herbs that had been set to steep near the warmth of
the fire. The sharp tang of vinegar mingled with the heavy
stench of blood.

"Ooh!" Harriet moaned, backing away superstitiously.
"Spilt blood comes from the divil!"

"Stuff an' nonsense," Sarah snapped. " 'Tis just blood
an' vinegar. Git the mop, Harriet, an' clean it up."

But Harriet's face had gone white and her teeth were
chattering. She clasped her hands under her chin. "Oh,
please, Mrs. Pratt, I beg—"

"Oh, git on wi' ye," Sarah said disgustedly. "*I'll* do it." She had just fetched the mop when Mudd entered the kitchen, his jaw set, his glance lowering.

"Well, now, Mrs. Pratt, ye've gone an' done it," he said, in the tone he reserved for pointing out Sarah's errors. In his late twenties, Mudd was young for a butler's position. He compensated for his youth by imitating an authority he could scarcely claim from experience.

Sarah turned, mop in hand. "Done wot?" she growled. "An' I'll thank ye to stay away from the hearth, Mr. Mudd. We've 'ad a bit of an accident."

"There 'as been an accident above stairs too," Mudd said. "The blackcurrant ice was tart as may be."

"Tart?" Sarah cried, disbelieving. "Not my best ice!"

"It 'pears that ye left out the sugar, Mrs. Pratt." Mudd shook his head sadly. " 'Er ladyship was mort'ly embarrassed."

And Sarah Pratt, now completely overwhelmed by tragedies, burst into tears.

4

"He showed me his bill of fare to tempt me to dine with him; poh, said I, I value not your bill of fare, give me your bill of company."

—JONATHAN SWIFT
Journal to Stella, 1711

HAVING RETIRED TO the library with his friends, Charles Sheridan sat back in his comfortable leather chair, an after-dinner brandy at his elbow, and began to tamp his pipe. In his bachelor days he had abhorred dinner parties, but now that he and Kate were married and settled (at least for the time being) at Bishop's Keep, he found that he enjoyed playing the host. He also found that he much preferred the comfortable library with its shelves of well-thumbed books to the coldly opulent magnificence of the library at Somersworth, where his ancestors' gilt-edged volumes gathered dust. He had never taken any particular pride in his baronial heritage, had only been grateful that his elder brother, Robert, had taken the family duties off his hands. But now Robert was dying, and the entire burden—Somersworth, his brother's seat in the House of Lords, the care of his mother—was about to fall on his reluctant shoulders. He pushed the thought away and glanced tenderly in the direction of Kate's alcove, where a green velvet drape concealed her desk and typewriter. Perhaps it was her lingering presence which imbued the room with such a comforting warmth, or the memory of their many lively conversations and spirited debates. The company of his wife was a fine thing, her intellect keen, her interests vast and diverse, her insights penetrating, if sometimes illogical.

But tonight's company of men was excellent, as well. Charles was fond of the elderly vicar, who dined regularly at Bishop's Keep, and his friend Bradford Marsden. And tonight, he had particularly enjoyed Charlie Rolls, a handsome, fine-featured lad with flashing dark eyes under thin dark brows, amazingly mature and self-possessed for nineteen, if a trifle conceited. While Rolls was at Eton (as Charles himself had been), he had specialized in practical electricity, and was presently working toward a degree in mechanical engineering at Trinity College.

The young man's greatest passion was not for his studies, however, but for motorcars, and his exuberant, school-boyish report of "larks" with his French-made Peugeot—at three and three-quarters horsepower, the most powerful automobile yet manufactured—had held the rapt attention of the entire dinner company. His listeners had been enthralled by the story of Rolls's breakneck journey from Victoria Station to Cambridge, which he completed in eleven hours and forty-five minutes, at an average speed well above the legal limit.

In fact, Charles thought, listening to the quick, impulsive Rolls, the boy was a daredevil, a rebel bent on challenging human limits by every possible means. He raced his father's yacht, he rowed in competition, he had just won his half-blue for cycling, and he was an avid balloonist. "If there's a record of any kind, on land, sea, or in the air," he had boasted at dinner, "I intend to break it."

But for the moment, Rolls's activities were land-based. He and Bradford were organizing a grand motorcar exhibition involving the leading proponents of motoring from all over England, the planning of which had occasioned his stay at Marsden Manor. Charles had remarked to himself that while Rolls was not gifted with a notable fortune, he obviously had a keen eye for profit and an even keener relish for competition. In combination, these two motives might in the end propel him to great wealth—although that was not likely to happen soon enough to satisfy Lady Marsden's requirements of a suitor for her daughter. Charles suspected that Patsy's infatuation with young Rolls would lead nowhere, except, most like, to their mutual unhappiness.

The vicar relaxed on the sofa, stretching his feet to the fire. "Well, Charles," he said comfortably, "you seem to be progressing quite well with your modernizing—although not necessarily in the kitchen."

Charles grimaced wryly. "I fear I have overestimated the staff. One would think that one's cook, of all people, would be anxious to relieve the kitchen maids of the coal-carrying. But she, and the maids too, are afraid that the new cooker will explode—and I'm not at all sure that Kate doesn't share their apprehension. Tell you what, Vicar—why don't you go down to the kitchen and reassure them as to its safety? They'll trust you."

Bradford Marsden glanced up at the gas chandelier, which spilled a warm glow over the room. "You've gotten that coal gas plant of yours operating successfully, then?"

Marsden was a fair-haired, handsome man in his mid-thirties, with a blond mustache and haughty, angular features, as impeccably groomed and dressed as any gentleman of high breeding and good birth. But his mouth wore a cynical half-smile, and his restless glance seemed to see into a future that held greater excitement than the tedious present. He suffered from a consuming and expensive passion for motorcars, much to the chagrin of his elderly father, whose only passion was his horses. Indeed, it was well that Lord Christopher Marsden was absent on holiday, Charles reflected, for the old man would certainly object to the motorcar exhibition that Bradford planned to hold on the Marsden estate a fortnight hence. Not only would the motorized vehicles frighten the stud, but the exhibition itself would suggest to his lordship's horse-loving friends that the Marsdens had gone over to the enemy camp.

"There's a bit of fine tuning to be done," Charles said, pulling on his pipe. That was another of the benefits of life at Bishop's Keep. There was leisure for scientific and technical experimentation. "So far, we have been operating only one of the three retorts, but I daresay—"

"Excellent," Bradford said hastily. He looked at Rolls, who was smoking a Turkish cigarette and sipping a cordial. "In that case, Charlie and I have a small favor to beg of you."

"Actually, it's a rather large favor," Rolls said. He grinned easily at Charles, his eyes sparkling, and spoke with an almost schoolboy eagerness.

Charles raised his eyebrows. "You need coal gas to power a combustion engine at your motorcar exhibition?" The thought that coal gas might serve as engine fuel had already occurred to him. Perhaps he might use it to power the single-cylinder stationary engine that now drove an experimental dynamo, which he hoped would soon electrify Bishop's Keep. If, that is, he could overcome the servants' concerns about what Kate termed "his explosive activities."

Rolls laughed. "We'll need a great deal more gas than that. We'll be lifting about a thousand pounds."

"Lifting?" Charles asked, surprised. "You want me to fill a balloon, then."

"I told you he's quick," Bradford said to Rolls, with satisfaction. "Never misses a clue."

"I fear *I* have missed something, though," the vicar said. "I thought we were to have a motorcar exhibition. And now we're to have a balloon?"

"The idea is to attract the public's attention," Rolls explained. "We thought it would be jolly to have a balloon chase—hare and hounds, d'you see? The balloon sails off across country and the motorcars pursue it. The first to reach the balloon's landing spot wins."

"Are you sure *any* will reach it?" Charles asked. "The lanes in this part of the country are atrocious. And the vehicles themselves are not dependable enough to—"

"But that doesn't matter, don't you see?" Rolls exclaimed. "It will be a glorious race, however it goes. And it will attract an enormous amount of attention," he added happily.

"Already has," Bradford muttered.

Charles went to the shelf and took down a thick chemical reference work. He opened it to a table of gas properties, then pulled out his ivory slide rule. After a moment's calculating, he said, "It appears that you'll need between twenty to thirty thousand cubic feet of gas."

Rolls frowned. "That's vastly more than we'd anticipated. Can you do it?"

"We don't normally produce anything like that amount here," Charles replied, "and my storage reservoir is quite small. But if we put the other two retorts into service, I daresay we can produce it in a day or so. And if the weather remains reasonably calm, the gas can be discharged directly into the balloon." He looked from

Bradford to Rolls. "I assume you have already procured one."

At Bradford's nod, the vicar leaned forward eagerly. "Ballooning has long been a dream of mine. I knew a man who lived in Paris during the Prussian siege of '70. He was one of the aeronauts—oh, fortunate men!—who carried mail and emissaries out of the city." His pale blue eyes shone. " 'I'll leap up to my God! Who pulls me down?' as Faust says. What a glorious excitement! *I* should like to have escaped Paris by balloon."

"Or flown over the Alps," Rolls returned warmly, "like that Frenchman, Francisque Arban, in '46. He ascended on the French side, during a storm that lifted him to a height of fifteen thousand feet and carried him over the mountains, and set down near Turin." His face was eager. "A great adventure. But myself, I should like to fly heavier-than-air aircraft."

"Like that German chap, Lilienthal, who was just killed in some sort of glider?" Bradford asked.

"Or like the American, Langley," Charles said, "who is testing mechanically propelled flying machines."

"*I* should prefer balloons," the vicar said. "Just think of achieving Glaisher and Coxwell's altitude record." He was transfixed. "Twenty-nine thousand feet! What an achievement! To soar like the Archangel, to see the world as God sees it . . ." He began to hum the refrain of "Nearer My God to Thee," then broke off. "But I don't suppose I shall ever have that opportunity," he said in a more practical tone.

Rolls grinned. "You certainly shall, if you wish, sir."

The vicar's eyes widened. "Oh, my goodness," he breathed incredulously, and lapsed into contemplation of his good fortune.

"So the gondola is large enough to carry a passenger," Charles remarked.

"Indeed, and the balloon itself is large enough to support several, depending on the degree of inflation," Rolls replied. He gave Charles a speculative look. "Marsden tells me that you're a photographer."

Charles smiled. "I suppose you would like me to ascend in your balloon—with my camera?"

"Exactly so!" Rolls said. "Yours will be the very first photographs of motorcars taken from the air. And you will photograph the winner as well. Can you imagine the newspaper reportage?" His hands sketched a banner headline. "MOTOR CARS RACE BALLOON ACROSS ESSEX! The idea was Harry Dunstable's. He is quite excited about it."

"Harry Dunstable!" Charles exclaimed.

"That's right," Rolls said. "And it's a stroke of genius, in my opinion. People will come from miles around. Why, we may even be favored by a visit from one of the Royals!"

"And what do you think, Bradford?" Charles asked.

But Bradford, nervously, changed the subject. An hour later, as the company was about to make its departure, Charles discovered why. His friend pulled him aside and said, in a low voice, "I say, old chap, I am afraid I must ask another favor. This exhibition, you see—" He smoothed his mustache nervously.

Charles waited, hoping that Bradford was not about to ask him for another loan. The last was being partially repaid in the services of Bradford's manservant, who was married to Kate's housekeeper and had a natural talent for tinkering with machinery. It was not a bad method of repayment, as it turned out, but Bradford's airy attitude toward his obligations disturbed Charles, and made him wish that his friend had a stronger sense of fiscal responsibility.

"It's Father!" Bradford burst out at last. "I received a telegram from him today, from France. Roger Thornton— blast the bloody beggar!—wrote him that I planned to make Marsden Manor the site of a motorcar exhibition, and he is in a raving paddywhack. He instructs me to cancel . . ." Bradford frowned petulantly, like a schoolboy reprimanded for being out of bounds. "He has forbidden me to hold the exhibition at Marsden," he said, in a low voice. "I haven't yet told Rolls, hoping that I might be able to make another accommodation and thus spare him and the other organizers any anxiety."

"So you are looking for a new site."

"I fear so," Bradford said. "It's not that I am afraid of the pater, but—" He looked uneasy, as well he might, Charles thought, for Lord Christopher had more than once threatened to reduce Bradford's allowance. "I don't suppose . . . that is, I shouldn't like to ask . . . oh, dash it all, Sheridan! Would you consent to holding the damn thing here at Bishop's Keep?"

Charles frowned. This request was scarcely easier to answer than a request for another loan.

Bradford spoke hastily, as though he feared Charles was about to refuse. "This exhibition will not be as large as that at Tunbridge Wells last spring—only four motorcars are entered in the chase, and a half-dozen others in the exhibit—and I can't think that there'll be any *real* unpleasantness." His smile was thin. "This one favor, please, Charles. I shall not forget it."

"Unpleasantness?" Charles asked.

Bradford gave him a quick glance. "Oh, you know," he said, shrugging lightly. "Motorcar enthusiasts are an opinionated lot. Tempers run high from time to time."

"Well, if Dunstable is involved, I can see why," Charles said grimly. "Most thinking people consider him a charlatan. He clearly has no plans to exploit those Daimler patents of his, and yet he's enticing investors with wild promises—" He broke off at the stubborn look on Bradford's face. It would do no good to chide his friend for falling in with the promoter's schemes—he had plenty of company. "Well, with Dunstable here, things should be interesting," he said. "And I'm intrigued by the challenge of filling the balloon and flying in it."

"Then you'll do it?"

Charles considered. The exhibition was scheduled for the same weekend Henry Royce was coming from Manchester to have a look at the dynamo. Royce, an able inventor, would certainly be interested in the motorcars. It was also the weekend of the village's annual Harvest Fete, which for fifteen years had been celebrated in the Park at Bishop's Keep. The villagers would enjoy the added excitement of motorcars and the balloon.

"If Kate agrees," Charles replied.

Bradford let out a long breath. "Thanks, old man. You don't know how grateful I am."

"I believe I can guess," Charles replied dryly.

5

"Poor fellow! His was an untoward fate."
—LORD BYRON
Don Juan

"**I** AM SORRY TO trouble you with this request, Charles,"
Constable Edward Laken said apologetically. "But
the villagers are quite up in arms. And the poor fellow
died outside your gate."

"I quite understand, Ned," Charles said, regarding his
old friend with a sober affection. "The servants here are
unhappy, as well. It was an unfortunate occurrence."

Charles and the constable had known one another
as boys in neighboring East Bergholts, across the
River Stour, where Charles had come to holiday with
his aunt and uncle. The two had ranged up and down
the Stour, climbing across the locks, snaring birds,
rafting on Jacques Bay. Now, Laken was the local
constable, and Charles had had occasion to renew their
friendship over the course of one or two recent criminal
investigations.

"I don't know that there's anything to be done, since the
man apparently died of natural causes," Laken said. "But

it might quiet wagging tongues if I could speak with your servants."

"By all means," Charles said. "Speak with whomever you please, although I fear you will hear only rumor." The death of Old Jessup, a tenant of nearby Thornton Grange, had been on the servants' lips since breakfast—a dozen different versions of it. "It is not true, then—I hope it is not—that the man was struck and killed by Marsden's Daimler?" Charles had heard that version from Thompson the gardener this morning, although he had not believed it.

Laken shook his head. "There were no marks on the victim's body, but Dr. Bassett will conduct an autopsy. Old Jessup was fond of his pint or two, and Bassett suspects apoplexy. But that aside, another of the village residents reports that she was nearly run down by a motorcar a few minutes before she discovered Jessup's body beside the road. That would have been at a few minutes before eight." He eyed Charles. "Lord Marsden was here last night?"

Charles frowned. "He and his sister and their houseguest arrived here just before eight, by motorcar. I cannot think, however, that they could have struck someone and concealed that fact for the entire evening. If they were involved, it must have been unwittingly."

"Young Jessup, the old man's son, is insisting that the Daimler was involved. He says that he himself saw the car, and that it was driven by Marsden's houseguest. Quite recklessly, he says."

"That would be Charlie Rolls," Charles said. "The Honorable Charles Stewart Rolls."

"Thank you," Edward said, and made a quick note. "Young Jessup saw the car traveling at a high rate of speed, and without a walking attendant—spewing great clouds of dust, he said, and making an intolerable noise." He paused. "He says he wants the driver charged."

"With what?" Charles asked. "Breaking a law that Parliament has already repealed?" The old law imposed a speed limit of four miles an hour in open country and required that a man (wearing a hat with a red band marked "Locomotive Attendant") should walk twenty yards in front of any self-propelled vehicle. Under the new law, the attendant was no longer required and the limit had been raised to twelve miles an hour.

"The old law has been repealed, indeed," Laken said, "and although the new statute does not go into effect for thirty days or so, I doubt that the magistrate would impose a fine. Even under the old law, the maximum penalty is ten pounds for breaching the speed limit and an additional ten pounds for failing to provide an attendant." He sighed. "But these are not the charges Young Jessup has in mind."

Charles raised his eyebrows. "What then does he want, Ned?"

"He wants the driver charged with murder," Laken said.

"Murder!" Bradford Marsden rose from his chair so abruptly that it fell over backward. "That is patently ridiculous, man! Why, we never laid eyes on that poor old fellow! We certainly did not strike him."

"I agree that making such a charge appears irresponsible," Edward Laken said quietly, "at least at the moment, and I doubt that a coroner's jury would bring a true bill on it. I tell you because that is the way feeling is running in the village with regard to your motor vehicle, and I thought you should like to know."

"Yes, yes, of course," Bradford muttered, feeling that he wanted to know nothing of the sort. "But the villagers must be made to understand—" he pressed his lips together. "Do you know yet how the old man died?"

"Dr. Bassett believes that he may have suffered an apoplectic stroke. If such is the case, his son, I understand, intends to assert that it was occasioned by a great fear—fear of being run down by your motorcar. He seems to hope for a verdict of manslaughter through the reckless operation of a speeding vehicle." The constable paused. "I understand that the Daimler was driven by your houseguest, the Honorable Charles Rolls."

Bradford nodded numbly. What if his father, already furious about the exhibit, should hear of this latest affair and come storming home? Bradford was over thirty, but he still had a healthy fear of the old man's anger, especially since the senior Lord Marsden controlled the family purse.

"Then I should like to speak with Mr. Rolls," the constable said.

Bradford stood. "I believe you will find him with my sister in the conservatory." He rang a bell. "Peters will show you the way."

"Thank you," the constable said. "I trust you will be prepared to answer the coroner's summons, should you receive it, Lord Bradford. The inquest will take place early next week."

"Of course," Bradford said. When the constable had gone, he sank back into his chair, trying to think what to do.

"Murder!" Sally Munby said to Bess Gurton, thumping her churn with great energy. "I'll *say* 'twas murder! Pore Ol' Jessup, mean as 'e was to 'is Tildy, didn't deserve to be run down like a dog. Next ye know, it'll be me, or you."

"But 'e weren't run down," objected Sally's daughter Martha, who was peeling potatoes for the noon meal. "There weren't a mark on the old man."

"Well, then, 'e was scarit t'death," Sally said, with an air of having the last word. " 'Tis all one to 'im now, pore fellow."

Bess Gurton sighed heavily. " 'Twas *almost* me," she said, recalling the event with a shuddery thrill. "If I 'adn't dove into that ditch—"

"Lor', Bess," Sally said, "ye must've bin *some* frightened. That motorcar, bearin' down on ye out o' the dark wi' eyes—"

"Like a dragon," Martha prompted helpfully.

"Like a great mad dragon," breathed Sally. "An' a roar like a—"

"Like a steam locomotive," Bess said.

"A run'way steam locomotive, barr'lin' down the tracks." Sally rolled her eyes and thumped her churn again. "Lor'! Ye'r a brave wooman, Bess. A brave wooman! If ye 'adn't dove into that ditch, ye'd'a bin murdered too!" The thumping paused, and Sally's voice took a different tone. "Bye the bye, Bess, 'ave ye seen the Widow Jessup's new black bonnet, with all the ribbons?"

Bess acknowledged that she had.

"Very strange," Sally mused, shaking her head. "Ve-ry strange, i'deed. It come from Colchester, I 'eard, an' cost at least a guinea. Don't ye think that's strange? Why, Tildy Jessup 'asn't 'ad a new bonnet since she were a bride, an' that was more'n twenty years ago. Wot I wants to know," she added in a conspiratorial tone, "is where that guinea come from. Wot d'ye think, eh? Where'd she get it?"

The conversation having shifted from her own narrow miss to the widow's new bonnet, Bess lost interest. She took her leave and walked up the High Street toward the Rushton house, which served as the village post office. Along the way, she received the best wishes of several acquaintances, who (like Sally Munby) expressed their pleasure to see her among the living. Crazy Mick, sweeping the steps in front of the Marlborough Head, called out to her in a voice like a grating mill-wheel, "Lucky ye'r alive, Bess Gurton, an' not murdered, like Ol' Jessup, pore fellow!"

And Rachel Elam, coming out of the apothecary shop with a bag on her arm, remarked with a dark look on the imminent danger in which they all stood at every moment, with horseless carriages and steam lorries snorting like wild devils down the High Street, charging into the very houses, "murtherin' innocent wimmen an' childern in their sleep."

And when Bess reached the steps of the post office, she encountered another and far grander personage, Squire Thornton, who also had views upon the subject.

"Mistress Gurton, is it not?" the squire asked. He was a tall, lean man with graying hair and thick gray eyebrows. His eyes were sharp and clear and his nose straight, but a mean mouth and thin lips robbed these features of their nobility.

Bess, astonished to be so greeted by such a man, dropped a faltering curtsey. "Good mornin', Squire," she croaked.

The squires of Thornton were the first commoners of the district, and the estate of Thornton Grange had been a mainstay of the parish of Dedham for several hundreds of years. In a time when the Marsden baronets had found it necessary to sell outlying parcels of land in order to protect the central holdings of the Marsden estate, Thornton Grange remained intact and well managed, and the Squires Thornton, thoroughgoing Tories who had passed the landholdings from father to son, from uncle to nephew, without subtracting so much as an acre, gained much respect thereby. This respect had been enlarged over recent generations by the ascendancy of the Thornton stables, which commanded the esteem of knowledgeable men beyond the bounds of the district.

But respect did not equal affection, and the Thorntons in their various generations had never been greatly loved in the parish. To a man, they had been unyielding and hard, just only by the lights of their own justice, prone to having their own way and rising to sudden and impetuous ire when thwarted. Yet it must also be said that they were not ungenerous, for they did their part and more in parish charity and supported their tenants in times of difficulty. And when they chose, they could be considerate and thoughtful. At this moment, it seemed, Squire Roger Thornton so chose.

"I understand that you very nearly suffered injury in a motorcar incident, Mistress Gurton."

"Ay, sir, that I did, sir," Bess replied earnestly. " 'Twas a 'orrible thing, sir. The fright o' me life."

"I can well imagine. The motorcar is a dangerous invention." The squire's tone was grave and solicitous. "The incident occurred on the same road where Old Jessup lost his life, poor fellow?"

"Ooh, yessir. Very near, sir. To tell truth, sir, I was the one 'oo found 'im dead, jes' after."

"You reported to the constable that you were nearly run down?"

Bess lifted her chin. "Yessir, an' so I wud say to anybody 'oo asked."

The squire's thin lips shaped themselves into a smile. "Very good," he said. He inclined his head, opened the door, and passed into the post office, where Bess heard him inquire as to the feasibility of sending a telegram to Nice. Then he turned and left again, but not before nodding once more to Bess, who returned the nod with another curtsey.

With respect to automobiles, the postmaster, Mr. Rushton, took a more judicious, but no less prejudicial, point of view. "The lanes are no longer safe for any of us," he pronounced, frowning down his long nose as he moistened the stamp and placed it precisely in the corner of the envelope Bess was sending to her cousin in Ipswich. "I wonder at Lord Christopher, permitting his son to own one, indeed I do." And with that, he took Bess's penny and deposited her letter in the canvas mail sack, which would be carted to Colchester, in time for the night mail train to Ipswich. "Poor Jessup," he added sadly. "Poor old fellow."

Mr. Rushton was a fussy little man with an exaggerated sense of his own importance. He kept the post office, which occupied the small front parlor of the Rushton home, with punctilious care, making sure that Mrs. Rushton inserted each piece of mail into the proper pigeonhole of the oaken cupboard, marked A to Z with gleaming gold plates. But Mr. Rushton permitted no one but himself to dispense the penny- and half-penny stamps from the official cardboard-leaved book, and no one else was allowed to count out the change, or even to open the cash drawer, with its three wooden bowls for gold, silver, and copper. It was also (and only) Mr. Rushton who sent and received telegrams, for he had passed the Post Office examination in Morse code. With this grasp of technology, he was respectfully regarded as the most up-to-the-minute person in the village, the only one in constant contact with developing events in the outer world. It was therefore quite something, Bess felt, to see him shake his head and hear him say that motorcars were dangerous inventions, and not to be trusted.

And while Bess believed that Mr. Rushton put too fine a point on most things, she fully agreed with him (and with Rachel Clam and Crazy Mick and Sally Munby and Squire Thornton) with regard to the dangers of motorcars. What if, instead of herself alone, there had been schoolchildren in the narrow lane? Or Dr. Bassett and his fat gray pony, or the vicar wobbling along on his safety bicycle, or the baker's boy with a load of loaves? They could *all* have been killed by the rampaging motorcar, and what then would have been the charge? Hardly murder, but mayhem, certainly, or massacre! Bess could scarcely wait until the day of the coroner's inquest, when Harry Hodson would call her to testify, and she fell to wondering how she might add a bit of lace to her best dress to make it fit for such a momentous event. In fact, she was so intent upon this addition to her wardrobe that she almost stepped out in the lane in front of Young Jessup, who was driving a shiny new gig.

Coroner Harry Hodson was a great, burly bear of a man who had for some years served as the Queen's coroner in the rural district encompassing Dedham and a dozen other small villages. He had been a country physician in the earlier part of his career, but had married a widow of substantial means and promptly retired. Harry enjoyed his office and competently upheld the oath he had taken when he assumed it: "I will diligently and truly do everything appertaining to my office after the best of my power for the doing of right and for the good of the inhabitants within the district." But he was a peaceful man at heart, and much preferred having nothing particular to do after breakfast and lunch.

On the afternoon of Old Jessup's funeral, Coroner Hodson met with Dr. Braxton Bassett, Constable Edward Laken, and Sir Charles Sheridan at the square deal table in Dr. Bassett's consulting room at the rear of Mr. Crosby's apothecary shop. Around them were the accoutrements of a village doctor: a glass-fronted case of leather-bound medical books, a grinning skull upon the windowsill, a table of chrome-plated surgical implements partially covered with a folded white cloth, a small stove topped with a steaming kettle. It was a convenient room, one oaken door leading to Mr. Crosby's apothecary, the other to Dr. Bassett's surgery. All that was needed was close at hand.

When all four men were settled in their chairs, teacups and biscuit plates before them, the coroner turned to

Dr. Bassett and, in a formal tone, asked for his opinion in the matter of Old Jessup's death.

The doctor, a man of middle age, with sharp, clear eyes and regular features, cleared his throat and announced that it was his belief that Old Jessup had suffered an apoplectic stroke. "It is scarcely surprising," he added, "since the man was much given to drink. Had he died at The Lamb, where he spent so much time, or in his garden or his bed, there would be no mystery about his death, poor old fellow, and no commotion."

Harry Hodson shifted his bulk in his chair. "But he died in the vicinity of a motorcar," he said, tenting his fingers under his chin. "An untoward event."

"I have examined the motorcar and found no damage consistent with its striking a pedestrian," Edward Laken said. "I have also questioned the driver, the lady passenger, and Lord Bradford, the owner. All three seemed genuinely surprised to learn of the incident. I do not believe they saw the old man."

"They were guests at Bishop's Keep that evening," offered Sir Charles. "If they had been involved in any way with a fatality, I am sure they would have spoken of it. In fact, I daresay we would have spoken of nothing else."

Harry Hodson drained his cup. "They did not see Bess Gurton, either, but she claims to have been nearly run down by the vehicle shortly before she discovered Old Jessup's body."

"That's neither here nor there," said the doctor, getting up to fetch the kettle. "There was not a mark on him, Harry. Jessup died of a stroke, and that's all there is to it."

Harry Hodson suppressed a belch. "It would be, Brax," he said sourly, thinking of the work required to collect and impanel a jury, "if it were not for the dead man's son."

"Yes," said the constable. "He has made a deal of noise." He sighed. "And the villagers—even those who did not particularly like his father—are greatly upset about the old man's death. Most believe that if the motorcar did not strike the old man, it frightened him to death."

While the doctor filled his cup, the coroner turned to Sir Charles. "You have looked into the matter with the constable, I take it. What do you think?" Harry had had occasion to call Sir Charles to testify in an inquest into the death of a constable and had a high regard for his opinion.

"I think," Sir Charles said gravely, "that it is a great pity— both the old fellow's death and the villagers' reaction. But I do not think that anyone is responsible, under the law."

"You are suggesting that there might be some other sort of responsibility?" the doctor asked, sitting down once again with an expression of interest.

"We do not understand the impact of the changes that are occurring in these modern times," Sir Charles said, "and neither, for that matter, does the law. But that, as you say, is neither here nor there. The fact is that the old man died of natural causes, and there are no eyewitnesses or physical evidence that would suggest either a motoring accident or foul play."

If Harry had had a gavel, he would have struck it smartly on the table and declared the meeting adjourned. "Thank you, gentlemen," he said. "I see no need for further consideration of this matter. I shall exhort Young Jessup not to make unfounded allegations."

The doctor chuckled. "Better you than me, Harry, old chap. I'm afraid your work is cut out for you, the way he's roaring round." He took the lid off a tin canister. "Would anyone like another biscuit?"

But if the coroner had expected the victim's son—a dark-complected man in his early twenties, with dark hair and flashing eyes—to resist his exhortation, he was a good deal surprised. Young Jessup heard the doctor's opinion, the constable's report, and the coroner's conclusion, and nodded his head slowly.

"You agree, then, that there is no need to convene an inquest?" the coroner said, much relieved.

Young Jessup nodded again, briskly this time, and the business was concluded. There would be no inquest, no jury, and no allegations of murder.

Which was not, of course, the end of the matter. For what Coroner Hodson and the others could not know and would not discover for some days to come, was that Young Jessup's agreement to a finding of Death by Natural Causes had been encouraged (some might even have said that it was purchased) by the payment to his mother of a substantial sum of money. Who paid this money and what the motive might be, only Young Jessup would be able to tell. But when Harry Hodson bade the boy a cordial goodbye and congratulated himself upon bringing this disagreeable affair to such an agreeable conclusion, he was deceived.

There was more to come. Much more.

6

" 'Tis not wise to change a cottage in possession for a kingdom in hope."

—English Proverb

IT WAS A Thursday evening late in September and the sun was dropping westward. Lawrence Quibbley, on his way home from his evening's work at Bishop's Keep, thought to himself that the next few days—the weekend of the annual Harvest Fete *and* of the grand motorcar exhibition and balloon chase—looked to be fair.

As he came up the dusty path, the kitchen door opened and Amelia stepped out. "Ooh, Lawrence, look at the sunset," she cried. "Isn't it beautiful?"

Lawrence turned to look over his shoulder, then turned back to his wife, her skin the color of a ripe peach kissed by the sun. "An' so be you, Amelia," he said, almost shyly.

Amelia blushed and half-smiled, and then bit her lip and her eyes brimmed. "Yer supper is ready," she said with a heavy sigh, and brushed a tear from her cheek. "Come an' eat, dear."

Lawrence's heart wrenched. "Don't cry, Amelia," he said, putting his arms around her. "It'll all come right i' the end, dear. Truly it will."

"I'm sure," Amelia said, with a sad lack of conviction. She pushed Lawrence away and returned to the task of cutting the steak-and-kidney pie she had baked in the kitchen at Bishop's Keep while she finished up her day's work. Lady Kathryn made it possible for the Quibbleys to sup together at home by giving Amelia the freedom of her evenings, except for special occasions.

To Lawrence Quibbley, it might have seemed that life held many promises. Only two short years ago he had been a junior footman at Marsden Manor, required to carry coals to the grand Marsden bedrooms, trim the many Marsden lamps, and serve as valet to any Marsden guest who was without a manservant. It was on such a temporary assignment that he had first served Sir Charles Sheridan, who had recently married the lady who employed Lawrence's wife (once her personal maid) as her housekeeper.

His wife! The word still struck Lawrence with a feeling akin to awe. He and Amelia had been married only six months, scarcely long enough for him to have become accustomed to lying in a bed warmed and scented by her lovely body, or rising to the sunshine of her morning kiss. Lawrence had never imagined himself a married man, and certainly not a married man living in such a palatial cottage, with a magnificent Daimler motorcar stored in the barn.

For such were Lawrence's living arrangements. The Quibbleys lived in Lady Kathryn's gate cottage, only a short walk from Bishop's Keep and a fifteen-minute bicycle ride from Marsden Manor. Lawrence was no longer a mere footman, but was Lord Bradford Marsden's chauffeur and mechanic. Unfortunately, Lawrence's automotive responsibilities had to be concealed from the senior Marsden, Lord Christopher, whose hostility toward motorcars was so unreasonable that the junior Marsden found it politic to deposit his Daimler (with Sir Charles's consent) in the barn at the gate cottage, where Lawrence maintained it. To complicate matters even further, Lord Bradford, as payment for an outstanding note, had arranged to loan Lawrence to Sir Charles for a time. Hence, Lawrence and Amelia lived in the rose-covered gate cottage and Lawrence divided his time almost equally between Lord Bradford's Daimler and Sir Charles's various improvement projects.

With this arrangement, Lawrence's prospects had risen substantially. Last winter, Lord Bradford had sent him to the Daimler Works in Germany, where he observed every stage of the motorcar's manufacture and assembly, from the casting of the block to the packing of the bearings. He had assembled and disassembled every part until he could do it blindfolded, learning how each part worked and why, and what one did when things went wrong, as they inevitably (and often catastrophically) did. Lawrence could look to the future with confidence, for men with such skills would be in great demand once the automobile came into its own.

But of equal advantage to Lawrence was his work at Bishop's Keep. Sir Charles, an amateur photographer of no small reputation, had shown him how to load and unload plates and cut films into dark slides and slide boxes. He learned to mix gold, silver, and uranium into developers and toners, and he spent hours under the dim light of the ruby lamp in Sir Charles's darkroom, fascinated by the photographic images that gradually appeared on negatives and prints—and then more hours washing, enameling, and varnishing prints to preserve the images.

But even that did not describe the full scope of Lawrence's duties. Sir Charles and Lady Kathryn had been married scarcely a month when Lawrence oversaw the installation of a water system. Then it was the gas plant, an outdoor coal-burning furnace that heated three long ovens and a large copper reservoir in which the gases were stored, necessitating gas pipes, valves, and lighting fixtures in the main downstairs rooms and a gas cooker in the kitchen. This was no sooner completed than two wagonloads of machinery arrived and Lawrence and Sir Charles set to work on the Otto stationary engine. In their hands the machinery came to life, the great piston popping irregularly in the enormous cylinder, the flywheel whirring, the leather belts creaking as they turned the dynamo shaft, magically producing electricity. Lawrence could be forgiven a certain smug pride in his feats. And considering Amelia's recent promotion to housekeeper in Lady Kathryn's household, Mr. and Mrs. Quibbley seemed justified in believing that life could scarcely be improved.

But a few days ago this happy situation was jeopardized. Lord Christopher Marsden, who had been away for the greater part of the year, was soon to return. Young Lord Bradford, whose relationship with his father was not of the best, planned to take up permanent residence in London and intended that Lawrence should come and bring the Daimler. "Bring Amelia, too," he had added brusquely. "My housekeeper can put her to work, and you may have rooms in the attic."

Lawrence had received this news with a stunned silence; Amelia with a torrent of tears. While some country folk might consider going up to London a step in the right direction, the Quibbleys knew better. Amelia was heartbroken at the thought of abandoning her new position as Lady Kathryn's housekeeper, Lawrence did not want to leave his interesting work with Sir Charles, and neither of them wished to trade their rose-covered cottage and garden for cramped rooms in a London attic.

Avoiding Amelia's tearful look, Lawrence drank his tea and ate his steak-and-kidney pie, wishing he had not told her about the summons to London. After a bout of tears, she had brightened and suggested what was, on the face of it, the simplest and best solution.

"Why don't ye ask Sir Charles to take ye on? Lord Bradford cud surely find somebody else to work on the motorcar. 'Twud be the best thing, seein' as we've the cottage." And she had cast a fiercely possessive look around the snug kitchen, with its cheerful blue teapot and the red geranium blooming brightly at the gingham-curtained window.

" 'Tis not as simple as that," Lawrence said testily. Lord Bradford had invested a substantial sum in his training at the Daimler Works and would not happily let him go. Nor did Lawrence feel that he could ask it.

"I still don't un'erstand why ye won't tell Lord Bradford ye'r not goin'," Amelia said now, pouring herself another cup of tea. "It's not like ye'r a slave, y'know, Lawrence. Ye'r free to work where ye want." She thumped the teapot onto the table with a stormy look. "Where *we* want. Mark me, Lawrence Quibbley, I will *not* leave me cottage an' me duties as 'ousekeeper to live in Lon'on."

Lawrence sighed. He loved Amelia, but she had a certain independence of spirit that sometimes made it difficult to deal with her. In this instance, her protective instincts toward home and hearth—a woman's deepest and truest instincts—were reasonable, and hardly to be denied. And yet, on the other hand, his employer's request was reasonable as well, indeed, many would say, more than reasonable. He had but to tell his wife to pack their belongings, and that would be the end of the matter.

Poor Lawrence. His happy and simple life had become wretchedly muddled, and he could not think how to unmuddle it.

7

"In the late 19th and early 20th centuries, a fierce debate raged over whether gasoline, steam, or electricity was the most efficient motive force for the automobile. It is difficult to say precisely why the gasoline-powered spark ignition engine, with all the engineering problems it posed, became the engine of choice, especially when one acknowledges that it offered no clear intrinsic advantage over steam or electricity. It is likely that many agents other than efficiency—social, political, and economic factors—were responsible for the primacy of the gasoline engine."

—Ira Piston, Jr.
The History of the Infernal Combustion Engine

IT WAS A pleasant Friday morning, the day before the Harvest Fete and the motorcar exhibition, and Kate was seated at her Royal typewriter in the sunlit library at Bishop's Keep, trying to keep her attention focused on Beryl Bardwell's current fiction. She was having a hard time of it, though, for she was distracted by the memory of an encounter that morning with Amelia. Her new housekeeper, it appeared, might be compelled to follow her husband to London, which would be a great pity.

"I *told* 'im I wudn't go," Amelia had said dramatically, twisting her hands, "but I fear the worst."

Kate put down Amelia's list of household linen replacements. "Would you like me to speak to Sir Charles about a permanent position for Lawrence? I count on you for so much, Amelia. And now that you're settled in the cottage—"

"The blessed cottage!" Amelia cried, clasping her hands at her breast. "Oh, the cottage, wi' all its roses! 'Tis the dearest thing in my life, besides you, mum, an' this post— an' Lawrence, o'course." This proclamation heralded more tears. "But it's not Sir Charles 'oo must be spoke to, yer ladyship," Amelia managed at last, wiping her eyes. "It's Lord Bradford. 'E's the one 'oo's determined as we'll go to London."

Kate said nothing to Amelia, but she determined to speak to Bradford on the subject. And to Charles, too. When the exhibit and the balloon chase were over, she would corner both men and see what could be done.

Having concluded this much, Kate felt better, and went back to her typewriter. Her current story featured two intrepid women who adventured around the world by motorcar and balloon, solving various mysteries en route. This ambitious narrative was to be climaxed with a display of forensic virtuosity in which a certain evil genius was discovered through the use of fingerprints.

Beryl Bardwell, however, had a tendency to create plots that demanded more technical knowledge than the author herself possessed. In the matter of fingerprints, Kate thought she had found a way to test Beryl's assumptions. But where balloons were concerned, she needed help.

She turned to her husband, who was seated in the leather chair beside the window, reading *The Times*.

"Charles," she said, "I need some information."

Charles scowled. "The Kurds are killing the Armenians again," he muttered, "with the connivance of the Turkish authorities. What a bloody corner of the world!"

"I need your advice about a *balloon*, Charles," Kate said. "Can you tell me how big it is? What it is made of? How it is controlled?"

Charles spoke in a lecturish tone. "The aeronaut uses bouyancy to ascend or descend until he locates an air current that will take him in the direction he wishes to fly." He put down his paper and looked at her. "Why are you asking?"

"She," Kate said.

Charles was blank. "I beg pardon?"

"Beryl is working on a new story, and her character is an aeronautess. *She* uses bouyancy to etcetera etcetera."

"Of course," Charles said, a smile hidden in his brown beard. "What a dunce I am." He went back to his paper.

As he read, Kate studied his face. The close-cropped brown beard, rising to the high cheekbones. The well-shaped nose, the broad forehead, the nearly invisible scar on the temple. The laughter lines at the corners of the firm mouth, the droop of the brown mustache, the questioning quirk of the eyebrow. It was a face she had come to love, although she had not plumbed all the mysteries behind it.

There was a rattle of gravel in the drive outside. Charles looked up, caught her eye, and smiled. "As to size and fabrication," he said, standing and going to the window, "come and see for yourself, Kate. Charlie Rolls has arrived, and brought a balloon."

A freight wagon pulled by a team of horses had stopped outside. The wagon was covered by a canvas tarp and topped with what looked like a giant-sized wicker picnic basket, turned upside-down. Charlie Rolls, nattily attired in tweeds and a golf cap, was dismounting from a horse.

"That basket is the gondola," Charles said, pointing. "That's where your aeronautess will ride."

Kate frowned, thinking that it looked very small and fragile. Tomorrow, Charles would be shooting thousands of feet into the air in that flimsy thing, with nothing to break his fall should the balloon spring a leak and the whole contraption fall to the ground—as had on occasion occurred, and recently too. But that was not something she cared to think about. She spoke instead of Rolls.

"That young man," she said. "I wish I knew him better. There's something about him—"

"He's a charming chap, but rather a daredevil," Charles said. "Knows no limits." He frowned. "I saw him driving that Peugeot of his at something close to fifteen miles an hour."

"The villagers think he frightened Old Jessup to death with his careless driving," Kate said. "And Lady Marsden would certainly accuse him of behaving recklessly with her daughter." She smiled. "Although to give the devil her due, Patsy is equally reckless. And neither Great-aunt Marsden nor Squire Thornton can do a thing about it." Patsy's great aunt was of virtually no use as a chaperon. Patsy did exactly as she pleased, without regard to her aunt's objections.

"Roger Thornton?" Charles asked in surprise. "What does he have to do with Patsy Marsden?"

Kate raised her eyebrows. "Why, didn't you know, Charles? The Marsdens have virtually promised Patsy to him." It had to be the antiquity of the Thornton line and the extent of the Thornton lands—and perhaps the reputation of the Thornton stables—that made the squire a suitable son-in-law. It certainly was not his person, or his personality. A sterner man Kate had never met, nor one so prone to sudden ire.

"But Thornton is twice the girl's age," Charles objected. "And a man of violent temperament."

"And jealous, into the bargain," Kate said. "I saw him last Sunday at church, positively glowering at Rolls, who was down from Cambridge for the weekend and had escorted Patsy to the service. I can't think what Lady Henrietta will say when Squire Thornton tells her that her daughter has lost her heart to an itinerant balloonist." She had spoken lightly, but sobered as she added: "He will, too. He is the sort to carry tales."

Charles smiled. "Throughout all my life, Kate, I have missed these little nuances of human behavior that you notice so readily."

"It's Beryl Bardwell," Kate replied modestly. "*She* notices things like that."

Charles laughed and held out his hand, his sherry-brown eyes warm. "Shall we give Beryl something to do besides worrying about Patsy Marsden and her suitors? Rolls's balloon is about to be unpacked and inflated. Perhaps Beryl would like to observe."

"More than observe," Kate said. "She intends to *fly*."

"Truly?" Charles asked, and when Kate nodded, he smiled. "That's my brave wife!" he said approvingly. "We shall arrange a flight for you."

Outside, Kate watched while Charles and Rolls directed the men to lift the gondola from the wagon and pull back the tarpaulin, revealing a neatly packed silk envelope striped red, yellow, and blue. They carried the silk bundle to the croquet lawn adjacent to the back garden, where Charles's gas-generating plant was located. When the balloon was laid out in its web of hemp rope, they connected it to a canvas tube, in turn connected to Charles's plant, and began the long process of filling it. Nearby lay the rest of the apparatus: the metal ring that would support the gondola, the ballast bags, the mooring lines and trailing rope.

Kate was on her way back to the library when she heard a great clatter of motorcars and turned to see a parade of them—four, she counted—coming up the lane. They stopped, and the drivers alighted and came toward her, led by Bradford Marsden.

"Ah, Kate!" he exclaimed. "I should like you to meet the drivers for tomorrow's chase. Gentlemen," he said to the accompanying men, who were pulling off their motoring caps and goggles, "your hostess, Lady Kathryn Sheridan."

Hostess? thought Kate in surprise. When she had agreed to holding the motorcar exhibition at Bishop's Keep on the same weekend as the Harvest Fete, she had not considered that she might have additional duties as a hostess. Charles had already invited one guest—a Mr. Henry Royce, who was expected to offer some ideas on the electrical system—and they were planning a Saturday night dinner to which the drivers were invited. Now, it seemed that today's luncheon must he provided, as well. Oh dear, she thought to herself, wondering how Mrs. Pratt would take the news.

But it was of no use to worry about Mrs. Pratt. Kate put on a gracious smile and was led down the line of waiting motorcars, polished and gleaming and ready for the grand day.

First was Bradford's familiar gasoline-powered Daimler, to be driven by a tall blond German named Wilhelm Albrecht, who wore a handsome Kaiser mustache and a monocle. The German clicked his heels and bowed over Kate's hand with a smile of supreme self-confidence. Kate wondered why, if the competition were so important, Bradford wasn't driving his own car. The arrangement seemed rather peculiar to her, and so did the mocking glance that Albrecht bestowed on the rest of the drivers.

The man obviously felt himself much superior to the others.

Second in line was an elegant-looking Benz, with a Union Jack fluttering from a staff fixed to the side. It was to be driven by its owner, Mr. Frank Ponsonby, an excitable-looking man in motoring garb—khaki dust coat, goggles, and knee-high boots—with a cigar, a high, white forehead, and almost no hair. Bradford and Mr. Ponsonby did not appear on friendly terms, and Kate remembered the talk she had heard about the fierce competition between proponents of different automobiles. Perhaps there was more at stake in this event than she had realized.

The third automobile looked to Kate rather like a high-wheeled gig. In the back, barely visible above the rear axle, was a boiler, topped by a short smokestack. The vehicle was a French steam car called a Serpollet. The driver was Mr. Arthur Dickson, a very tall, painfully thin man with a delicate air, from Sheffield. "I am here to prove that steam is the best propellant," he said, with a disdainful glance at the other cars. "And I shall do it, I promise you, or die in the attempt."

Frank Ponsonby gave an unpleasant laugh. "Just see to it that nobody else gets killed when that flash boiler of yours explodes, Dickson, old chap."

A vein began to throb in Dickson's temple but when he spoke, it was with only mild scorn. "The tubes are over three-eighths of an inch thick, engineered to withstand several times the operating pressure. They cannot possibly rupture. And as you well know, Ponsonby, where there is no accumulation of steam, there is no possibility of an explosion."

But Ponsonby was not to be put off. He bestowed an ingratiating smile on Kate. "You are wearying our hostess, Dickson. Ladies hardly care to hear technical details. It wearies their intellects."

"My intellect," Kate replied loftily, "is not at all wearied." She smiled at Dickson. "You believe the steam car to be superior to the petrol-powered vehicle, then, Mr. Dickson?"

Dickson spoke fervently. "Oh, *absolutely* superior, Lady Kathryn! The engine generates far more torque at low speeds, and hence there is no need for a transmission system. What's more, speed control is accomplished by this single lever." He pointed. "In a gas-explosion car, one must simultaneously regulate the throttle, fuel mixture, spark advance, and gearing—a task for a four-armed genius." He glanced at a glowering Ponsonby. "That surface carburetor of yours, Ponsonby—has it caught fire yet?"

Bradford took Kate's arm and steered her to the fourth motorcar. "May I present Mr. Arnold Bateman, and his Bateman Electric?"

Mr. Bateman, a short, athletic-looking man with dark hair and a thin scar across his nose, made an elegant bow. The vehicle which he had designed and built was an electrified dog cart with yellow-spoked wheels. "The virtue of the electric car," he explained briskly, opening a hatch to demonstrate the large battery, "is its simplicity and quiet operation."

"Ah, but vot happens ven it runs out of electricity?" Herr Albrecht inquired, adjusting his monocle with a superior look.

"Then Bateman must go looking for a lightning bolt," Mr. Ponsonby said, and laughed raucously. Even the autocratic Mr. Dickson condescended to a glacial smile.

"Of course, with the ponderous weight of that battery," Ponsonby added, *sotto voce*, "our friend will probably stick in the mud long before his power is gone."

Bateman lifted his chin. "You may have your fun, gentlemen. But when a primary battery is developed, as you may shortly expect, we shall have only to mix the appropriate chemicals to gain a reliable, continuous, and inexpensive source of electricity. And then—" He raised his voice. "And then, sirs, this lightweight, quiet, odorless Bateman Electric will leave your noisy, odoriferous, cantankerous gasoline machines in the dust. Mark my words, gentlemen. Mark my words." And he gave them a supercilious smile.

The other three glared at him and then at one another, and Kate, amused, almost expected to see the four of them, like two pairs of Tweedledees and Tweedledums, come to blows. But Charles walked up at that moment and greeted the drivers, and the tension dissolved. Kate took her leave, pleading the necessity of consulting her cook about luncheon.

"You will join us for lunch, won't you?" she asked the men, with more enthusiasm than she felt. They were so openly antagonistic to one another that she wondered whether they could be trusted to dine together in a civil manner.

But Charles seconded her invitation, Bradford accepted for all of them, and Kate went off to break the news to Mrs. Pratt.

8

"We live in an age of balloonacy."
—*The Daily Telegraph*, 1864

"He must needs go that the devil drives."
—WILLIAM SHAKESPEARE
All's Well That Ends Well

"WELL, WHAT DO you think?" Bradford asked, as he and Charles left the group of drivers and walked toward the balloon.

"Who invited the contestants?" Charles asked. "You?"

Bradford shook his head. "Dunstable. He thought a bit of rivalry would stimulate them to their best performance."

"A *bit* of rivalry?" Charles raised his eyebrows. "Bateman and Ponsonby have been at each other's throats since the exhibition at Tunbridge Wells. Dickson despises both of them for reasons that have little to do with racing. And all three are amateurs. They're no match for Albrecht, who has been winning races in Europe for the last two years. What is *he* doing here, Bradford? And why is he driving your Daimler?"

"Dunstable is looking for publicity for his Daimler patents. He thought Albrecht would attract the attention of the newspapers and motoring magazines. He plans to ride with Albrecht, and share in the glory when he wins. And Albrecht is driving my Daimler because it is fast and well maintained, thanks to Lawrence."

"Well," Charles said mildly, "with Albrecht in the race, there is no contest. But with regard to the exhibit, there's something else I need to mention to you, Bradford. The villagers are still quite upset about Old Jessup's death. According to the vicar—"

"I wish the vicar would stop his infernal gossiping," Bradford burst out angrily.

"The vicar is only reporting the villagers' concern. They cannot understand why there was no inquest into the old man's death, and many resent the fact that their annual Harvest Fete has been turned into an automotive exhibit. In retrospect, I wish we had not combined the two events. Some are likely to stay away—and some of those who come will bear a grudge, and may cause trouble."

"But we have already combined them," Bradford said with a dark frown. "And should any please to stay away, they are certainly welcome. The many gentlemen who will come from Colchester and Ipswich to see the motorcars will more than make up for the few villagers who might have come to toss a coconut or dance a country jig." His voice became half-mocking. "We are here to introduce the men of the future to the machine of the future, Charles, and to invite them to seek a share in the coming wealth of an industry yet unborn."

"You mean," Charles observed, unsmiling, "that Dunstable intends to sell them shares in his enterprises. I hope that you have not become his agent."

Bradford's frown became a scowl. "And is there something wrong with that arrangement? I cannot believe that you, of all people, agree with my father's antique notion that a peer's son should hold himself above business and industry. Or that a man, simply because he will inherit a title, should refuse to participate in the industrial growth of the country. Whatever you think of Dunstable, you must admit that security no longer lies in lands and rents, but in a portfolio of commercial shares."

"Of course I don't hold with the old view," Charles replied. "But *you* must admit, Bradford, that Dunstable's patent monopolies are clearly fraudulent. They are not the sort of—"

But Charles's objections to Dunstable's schemes were drowned out by the sound of an approaching carriage. It proved to be a hired gig from the railway station, driven by a red-haired, ruddy-faced young man in a Norfolk jacket and golfing cap. His companion, a square-jawed man with deep-set eyes, a high forehead, and a serious expression, was formally dressed in morning coat, wing collar, cravat, and hat and carried a leather portmanteau.

The young man jumped down from the gig. "I say there!" he cried exuberantly. "Is this where the motorcar hexhibition is bein' 'eld tomorrow?"

"It is," Bradford said. "I am Lord Marsden, one of the organizers of the event, and this is Sir Charles Sheridan, whose estate this is. And you are—?"

" 'Olt, of *Autocar* magazine," the younger man said loudly. He stuck out his hand. "Sam 'Olt. 'Ere to cover the hexibit an' chase."

"Indeed, Mr. Holt," Bradford said, shaking the other's hand. "I have been expecting you." He turned to Holt's companion. "And this gentleman is—"

"Mr. Royce," Charles said warmly. "Had I known the time of your arrival, Henry, I should have sent someone to the station." He turned to Bradford. "Mr. Royce is an electrical engineer with a reputation for manufacturing electric cranes of quality and reliability. When I told him of my plans to use electric power at Bishop's Keep, he offered to stop in, have a look, and offer his suggestions."

Royce bowed slightly. "Actually," he said, "it was your report of Lady Kathryn's miniature roses that caught my interest, Sir Charles. I am rather keen on gardening. But I seem to have come on a busy weekend," he added, glancing around. "There is to be a motorcar exhibit tomorrow?"

"Indeed there is," Bradford said genially. "Do you have an interest in motorcars, Mr. Royce?"

"I inspected both the Daimler and the Benz at the Crystal Palace Exhibit," Royce replied. "But I must say that while the concept of the petrol engine is intriguing, the machines I saw were flawed by careless workmanship." He spoke with a quiet authority that did not invite challenge.

Bradford darkened, and Charles smiled. "Mr. Royce has an eye for engineering detail," he said, "and a passion for mechanical perfection. If you and Harry Dunstable really want to improve the Daimler, you could do no better than to consult him."

"Dunstable!" snorted Royce. "I hardly think so."

Holt's head turned toward the line of vehicles along the gravel drive. "Those're the motorcars that'll run in the chase? I say, dev'lish good, gentlemen! Smart, smart. Bound to get notice."

Bradford relaxed. "We expect several other vehicles for the exhibit. Charlie Rolls's Peugeot will be here, of course, and a Panhard newly imported from France, a

De Dion steam tractor, an Offord Electrocar, and a motor bicycle—all available for inspection." He gestured. "After the event, you will be provided with aerial photographs of the chase. The four drivers are willing to be interviewed, of course. You will especially want to talk with Herr Albrecht, who will be driving a Daimler— *my* Daimler, in fact."

Holt stroked his chin. "Aerial photographs, eh? Now, that's a novelty. Well, yes, I cert'nly shall obtain hinterviews from the drivers, specially 'Err Albrecht, and from Mr. Rolls, too." He grinned. "Maybe 'e'll take me for a flight in that balloon."

"Where do you predict the balloon will land?" Royce asked with interest.

"If this westerly wind holds," Charles said, "it will carry us toward the coast, fifteen miles to the east." Unfortunately, the boggy terrain was likely to complicate their landing, and beyond was the Channel. If he and Rolls were not careful, they might find themselves on their way to France.

The landing wasn't the only worrisome thing, actually. The chase itself now struck him as a precarious scheme. If the wind increased, the balloon would rapidly outdistance the motorcars. And even under ideal conditions, the drivers would have to pursue in a roundabout way, through lanes that were little more than cart tracks. It would be a lucky thing if *any* of the vehicles were to finish.

Royce seconded his unspoken doubts. "The balloon might arrive at the coast, but the flimsy, ill-engineered contraptions I see here are not likely to go so far."

"Perhaps, Mr. Royce," Bradford said glacially, "*you* could build one that might fare better." His tone suggested that the possibility was remote.

Royce did not appear to notice the sarcasm. "At the present moment, I am fully occupied with more productive engineering work. If I were to become interested in automotive design, however, I can assure you that the Royce motorcar would be vastly superior to those here. Take the steering, as an example."

"The tiller serves perfectly well," Bradford said.

"Rather too well, as I understand it," Royce replied. "There is a problem with oversteering. I should think a wheel might offer better control, as on a yacht."

Bradford gave an involuntary "Ha!" of disbelief, and Sam Holt's eyebrows went up under his gingery hair. "Sure of yerself, are ye, Mr. Royce?" he asked.

"I shouldn't be so quick to doubt," Charles said. "As a matter of fact, some European racing drivers are experimenting with that very concept. I predict—"

"Damn it all, Marsden!" cried an angry voice. Charles turned to see a tall, stern-looking man in riding clothes striding toward them. "Have you any idea the ruckus those deuced motorcars have caused this morning?"

Charles was not surprised by the violence of Squire Thornton's speech. His neighbor was a man of passionate temperament, and it appeared that he had been tried beyond the limits of his endurance.

"Ah, Thornton," Bradford said, in a placating tone. "Mr. Holt, Mr. Royce—I should like you to meet Squire Roger Thornton, of Thornton Grange. The Thornton stables have a reputation that is known to all—"

"Damned right," Thornton snapped, ignoring all but Bradford. "You've thrown my horses into a state of nervous exhaustion, you and your bloody motorcars." He glowered. "I should think you would have better sense, Marsden, after what happened to Old Jessup. The entire district is still in an uproar. Harry Hodson and the doctor may call it what they like—the people believe your motorcar frightened the old man to death. They call it murder. And what your father will say—"

"I think we should take a turn in the garden, where we can discuss the matter privately," Bradford said, and taking Thornton by the arm, walked away with him.

Holt turned to Charles, his eyes gleaming with journalistic curiosity. "Murder? 'Oo got murdered?"

"No one," Charles said firmly, raising his voice over the clatter of another arriving vehicle. "No one at all."

"Ah, Mr. Holt!" a loud voice exclaimed. "Glad to see that you could come and review our little event!" A solid-framed, fresh-cheeked man alighted from a barouche. He wore the air of a Swiss admiral, sporting elegantly grizzled side-whiskers and dressed in a blue uniform coat and yachting cap with an elaborate insignia: an allegorical female in flowing garments brandishing a sheaf of lightning-flashes in one hand and steering a self-propelled chariot with the other.

"Mr. Dunstable, sir!" exclaimed Holt, running to shake hands. "Mr. Simms sends 'is greetin's fer a most successful hexibit, sir."

Charles knew that Mr. Simms was the editor of the new *Autocar*, and that the journal was as speculative as Dunstable's ventures. In fact, it was clear from the issues he had read that the journal was strongly biased in favor of Dunstable and his promotions—a not altogether surprising fact, since the bulk of the journal's advertising came from Dunstable's concerns. More to the point, Simms was the director of one of Dunstable's manufacturing promotions. It was hardly an arrangement, Charles thought, that fostered independent reporting on the emerging motorcar industry.

But the arrangement clearly suited Dunstable, who pumped Holt's hand, then turned to Charles. "Sir Charles," he said in a mellifluous voice, "I cannot tell you how grateful I am, sir, for your magnanimous offer of your fine estate for our humble event. You are truly a generous man, and I am in your debt. In your debt, my very dear sir!" Sweeping the yachting cap from his head to his breast, he bowed low.

"The estate is Lady Kathryn's, Mr. Dunstable," Charles said quietly, "and the loan of it was to Lord Bradford, who asked it as a favor to a friend."

Dunstable beamed, undismayed. "Very good, sir, very good! My compliments to Lady Kathryn. And of course, the affair is entirely Lord Bradford's from beginning to end, and wholly in his capable hands. And he will get all the glory when Mr. Holt writes of the event in *Autocar*, all the glory. Isn't that so, Mr. Holt?"

Holt's head snapped up. "Just so, Mr. Dunstable," he said, and whipped out his notebook. "Lord Bradford, all the glory," he muttered, scribbling busily.

Dunstable replaced his cap, straightened his jacket, and turned to Henry Royce. "And you, my dear sir," he said smoothly, "you are a prospective motorcar owner, I take it? You have come to the right place at the right time! Oh yes, indeed! Indeed, I must say, sir! Tomorrow, you shall be privileged to see a most amazing performance. I believe I can add, without fear of serious contradiction, that the Daimler will exceed every expectation for speed and road performance. Should you wish to purchase this exceptional machine—"

"I think, Sir Charles," Henry Royce said, turning his back on Harry Dunstable, "that I should very much like to see Lady Kathryn's roses. And then perhaps you will show me your electric generator and your new gas plant."

"I am sure Mr. Dunstable will forgive me," Charles said thankfully. "Lady Kathryn will be delighted to walk with us through the rose garden."

"Ah, yes," Royce said, with a sidelong glance at Dunstable. "That would be most . . . refreshing."

It was nearly ten that night before Kate could speak privately with Charles in their bedroom. She had spent the afternoon outside, watching the lively panorama with a great deal of interest, taking notes for Beryl's story. By dusk, a half-dozen other vehicles had driven up the lane, with a great clatter of pistons and odor of burning petrol. Workers were preparing for tomorrow's fete, as well, raising the Flower Show tent, hanging bunting and banners, and erecting amusements and a bandstand. And all the while, the tethered balloon was rising gently, a rainbow-hued mushroom, out of the center of the green croquet lawn.

"Your luncheon was quite successful, I thought," Charles said, wrenching off his tie.

Kate smiled as she brushed her long russet hair. Sarah Pratt had assembled a tasty soup, a cold joint, a jellied fowl, a cucumber and tomato salad, two pâtés, and a substantial pudding—all on an hour's notice. It had been nothing short of a miracle.

"Mrs. Pratt certainly distinguished herself," Kate remarked, "but the luncheon itself was terribly uncomfortable. The tension around the table was enough to ignite a flambé." She glanced at Charles in the mirror. "It wasn't just the four drivers, either," she added, "although they behaved badly enough, taunting one another like schoolboys."

"There's a great deal of competition among them," Charles replied. "They're convinced that the entire future of the British motorcar industry rests on the outcome of tomorrow's chase. It would be a wonder if they didn't bait one another."

"I suppose," Kate said thoughtfully. "And then there was that *awful* Harry Dunstable."

Awful, indeed. An amply upholstered man with elaborate side-whiskers, dressed like a coach driver. "He tried to sell me a package of shares in his Daimler company. Or, failing that, a Daimler itself. The man is a peddler, pure and simple."

Charles unbuttoned his shirt, looking grave. "Ah, yes," he said. "The distasteful, disgraceful Harry Dunstable. If we get through the weekend without murder being done, I shall be very surprised." He glanced up with a crooked grin. "Only joking, my dear."

Kate put down the hairbrush. "Who *is* he?"

Charles sat down on the bed to pull off his shoes. "A promoter with a reputation for questionable dealings. He snaps up promising patents and licenses, then uses them to lure investors to buy stock. He has floated the British Motor Car Syndicate for a million pounds—a million pounds, Kate! Mark my words, the man will end in jail—if someone doesn't kill him first. He's a dangerous man."

"Dangerous because—?"

"Because he now has control of virtually every major automotive patent," Charles said grimly. "He has cornered the market, so to speak, but his companies are simply bubbles. When they burst, and they will, there will be nothing left to do but import motorcars from France and Germany." Charles's voice had become angry. "Dunstable is hated far and wide, and for good cause. He will kill the British automotive industry before it is born."

"But isn't there a British inventor who could design a *British* car?"

"I have encouraged Royce to enter the field, but he is currently otherwise engaged. And he hates promoters. If he could develop a partnership with someone he liked, someone who could sell the motorcars he developed—" Charles shrugged. "But that's not going to happen for some time."

"And this disreputable man—Dunstable, I mean—is a friend of Bradford's?"

"One of Bradford's creditors," Charles said. "Bradford bought stock in an earlier speculation, and is still paying the piper." He looked up and saw Kate's face, and smiled. "But my own dear, why are we bothering ourselves with such a sour subject?" He held out both hands. "I shall have to go out at eleven and see to the inflation of the balloon, which will continue all night. But come to me now, love, and let us see if we can find another, sweeter business to occupy us for the hour until then."

A few moments later, they discovered it.

9

"A man in the world must meet all sorts of men, and in these days it did not do for a gentleman to be a hermit."

—ANTHONY TROLLOPE
Framley Parsonage

A T TEN THAT same evening, in the Marlborough Head in High Street and Mill Lane, Lord Bradford was hosting a late supper. The Head occupied a half-timbered building that had been constructed by a wool merchant in the 1430s, Dedham Village (which lay on the King's Highway between the trading towns of Ipswich and Colchester) having once been the site of a thriving colony of weavers. The building's term as a wool market ended when the Civil War dealt the local wool trade a death blow. For a time it was taken over by the village apothecary, until, after the Battle of Blenheim in 1704 it was transformed into an inn and named for the first Duke of Marlborough.

The Head's large parlor, its plank floor covered with a red carpet and its plaster walls hung with engravings of hunting scenes, was furnished with comfortable chairs. The room was reserved for the select society of the village, while the rest were relegated to the common room, with its straight-backed wooden settles and rickety stools. The parlor was low-ceilinged and dark, but large enough to seat Bradford's party of seven at a long plank table before the fireplace. On this September evening, the blazing fire warmed the air to a considerable degree more than comfort might have required. Mr. Crawley, the publican, was red-faced and sweltering as he ran to and fro carrying dishes and replenishing wine glasses.

A Londoner used to dining at Claridge's or the Carlton might have complained that Mrs. Crawley's substantial repast (which opened *con brio* with a brown Windsor soup; proceeded with flourishes to poached mackerel with gooseberry sauce, pigeon pie, steak and onions accompanied by creamed potatoes and a dish of boiled carrots; and concluded upon the lighter notes of custard tart, a local cheese, and apples) was more suited to a robust rural appetite than to a refined urban taste.

Still, the food had been hot and ample and the wine adequate, and as Bradford sat back with a cigar and surveyed the company, he could congratulate himself that he had fulfilled his social obligations. Inviting this unruly crew to Marsden Manor was out of the question, and he could not impose further on Charles and Kate Sheridan. As far as Bradford was concerned, his friends could content themselves with poached mackerel and pigeon pies and be glad of it.

Except that they were not his friends, if by that word one intended to designate gentlemen with whom one was intimate. Bradford glanced down the table, reflecting somberly that there was not a man present whose company he would willingly have chosen. Taken individually, each member of this roguish fraternity suffered from certain defects of character; taken as a group, the defects of each amplified the defects of every other. Bradford knew something scandalous and unsavory about most of them, and during this momentary lull in the conversation he allowed himself the caustic amusement of reflecting on it.

The Honorable C. S. Rolls sat at the far end of the table smoking a Turkish cigarette. The most debonair of the lot, he was fast becoming notorious for his unrestrained recklessness. Charming, witty, and handsome, Rolls had a reputation among women of all sorts (including Ivy Thompson's girls of the Colonnade in Regent Street), and it was rumored that he had recently been seen at White's, where he had lost a large sum at the tables, the beautiful wife of a certain sporting gentleman at his side.

It was that dare-devilish womanizing that troubled Bradford, and he frowned when he thought of Rolls's casual familiarity with Patsy. That she was a willing partner in this romantic escapade was no justification, for in Bradford's estimation, his younger sister had scarcely a brain in her pretty head. Bradford's frown became a scowl. He should have to caution Patsy about Rolls before anything more serious than a flirtation occurred between them—except that cautioning his sister was like dropping a red flag before a bull. In that regard, she and Rolls were quite alike. If it were not for the fact that a liaison would mar her chance of marrying into the Thornton property, Bradford would say that the two deserved one another.

But Rolls's wasn't the only disreputable character in the lot. Occupying the left side of the table were three of the drivers, none of whom would take prizes for virtue. Nearest Rolls sat Wilhelm Albrecht, suave and confident as he carried on a conversation across the table with Harry Dunstable, who looked like a Liverpool haberdasher with his fat cigar and vulgar red-and-green checked vest. Albrecht caught Bradford's eye, raised his glass in a mocking salute, and smiled, his monocle glinting mockingly in the candlelight. Albrecht knew very well that Bradford had wanted to drive his own car in the chase—would have done so, in fact, had it not been for his debt to Dunstable—and the knowledge amused him.

At the thought of the money he owed, Bradford felt his stomach lurch. It was that debt, that hateful, despicable debt, that gave Dunstable the right to insist that Bradford host this affair. If it had not been for the money, Bradford thought bitterly, he would have told Dunstable to go straight to hell with his damned exhibition and balloon chase. The wretched affair was only another of Dunstable's promotion schemes. It had brought Bradford nothing but grief and expense, and yes, shame, a miserable shame that made him feel vile and dirty, knowing that he was forced to be civil, to be a suppliant, even, to a vulgar scoundrel.

Sitting next to Albrecht, stoking his pipe, Frank Ponsonby gave him an insolent glance, and Bradford winced. Ponsonby imported the Benz motorcar, but his chief trade was as a bill-broker who bought and sold discounted notes—a form of money-lending that enabled men of little capital to engage in undertakings that they could not otherwise afford. Ponsonby, who also traded in gossip, no doubt knew precisely how much was owed by every man in this room, and to whom. He certainly knew of Bradford's pecuniary difficulties and would make whatever use he could of the knowledge.

Ponsonby drew on his pipe. "Ah, Marsden," he drawled, "a worthy repast. Must have cost you a quid or two." His unpleasant chuckle showed yellowed teeth, and Bradford saw with some surprise that he was very drunk.

Bradford marshaled what was left of his civility. "You enjoyed it, then, Frank?" It paid to be civil to a man, drunk or sober, who knew as much about one's private business as did Ponsonby.

The bill-broker lifted his glass, his high, white forehead gleaming like polished ivory. "Here's to success tomorrow." His eyes narrowed as his glance went to

Dunstable. "Success to those who deserve it," he amended in an acid tone.

Bradford knew that Ponsonby hated Dunstable almost as much as he did, although from a different motive, and one having nothing to do with money. Dunstable had gotten into a pretty mess with Ponsonby's married cousin Aurora Vickers (with whom Ponsonby himself was said to have been in love), and Ponsonby had undertaken to scare him off. But the matter had ended badly. Dunstable had dropped Mrs. Vickers, her husband had cast her off as well, and she had meanly retaliated against both by slitting her wrists in the bath while a guest at Ponsonby's home. Nasty allegations had been raised against Ponsonby, and although they were somehow hushed up, they surfaced every now and again. An ugly story, Bradford reflected, as he motioned to the perspiring Crawley to bring another bottle of port. It was a wonder that Ponsonby and Dunstable could bring themselves to occupy the same room.

On the other side of the table sat Arthur Dickson, his lean face gaunt, his cheeks hollowed, a ghost of his former self. Dickson, who had made a great deal of money in steam locomotives, had recently been charged by a competitor with having stolen a patent and stood to lose most of his fortune. A pity, because Dickson was in Bradford's opinion a bright man with a promising automotive future—if only he would abandon the steam car. But he quite naturally (as a locomotive man) preferred steam. He detested the entire petrol industry, and had made enemies of most of the men around the table.

"Success only to the deserving?" Dickson asked dryly, taking up Ponsonby's remark. "What are you hoping for, Frank? That you will reach the balloon, and the rest of us will end in the ditch? You know that's ridiculous. Petrol cars are no match for steam."

Ponsonby was drunkenly contemptuous. "It won't be the ditch for that rusty teakettle of yours, Arthur. It's more like to blow up like a bomb."

"At least my Serpollet will finish the race," Dickson said, "which is more than can be said for that unreliable Benz you're driving. And it is far less dangerous than a Daimler piloted by a German." His eyes went to Dunstable, whose portly stomach was shaking as he laughed at something Rolls had said, and back again to Ponsonby. "Or a man with a passion for a certain kind of loose woman," he added with ungentlemanly malice.

Ponsonby's face darkened and he rose, knocking his glass over. Beside him, Arnold Bateman put a hand on his arm. "Leave off, Ponsonby," he growled. "The woman is dead."

Damn, Bradford thought. Now we're in for it.

Ponsonby whirled on Bateman. "Who are you to defend Dickson, Arnold? Wasn't it he who reversed into your electric car at the Crystal Palace Exhibit and disabled it? How much were the damages? How much did Dickson pay?"

Bateman frowned doubtfully. "It was not intentional."

"Nonsense," Ponsonby snapped. "Arthur Dickson does nothing except by intention. If he can't prove the superiority of steam by any other means, he will do it by disabling his competitors."

Dickson stood, gray-faced and snarling. "If you care to step outside, Ponsonby—"

The German's mocking laugh rang out. Dickson swallowed and sat down.

Harry Dunstable rose to his feet. "What's this? A quarrel?" he asked affably. He shook his head in exaggerated rebuke. "Gentlemen, gentlemen, harness your competitive energies until tomorrow, when you will use them to prove the worth of yourselves and your machines! We must not allow inconsequential animosities to get the better of us when we stand poised on the brink of infinite opportunity and unrivaled fortune." His voice rang. "Opportunity and fortune, gentlemen! Riches and glory! Ours for the taking in the motorcar industry!"

"Ours, Dunstable?" Bateman asked fiercely. "Don't you mean *yours*?" Like Bradford, Bateman had sunk more than he could afford in one of Dunstable's earlier speculative enterprises and had been left with nothing but a parcel of worthless stock. The disgrace was too much for Mrs. Bateman, whose death left her husband with two young daughters. Bateman hated Dunstable even more passionately than Ponsonby did, if that were possible.

Cheerily, Dunstable lifted his glass. "Gentlemen, I propose a toast. Let us drink to the success of the exhibition, and to its underwriter and our host, Lord Bradford Marsden, who has brought us all together tonight under such grand circumstances. And to the winner of tomorrow's competition, whoever he may be." And he glanced pointedly at Albrecht.

The room resounded in silence.

"Drink to your damnation, Dunstable!" Ponsonby shouted, and threw his empty glass. It sailed past Dunstable's nose and smashed against the plaster wall.

"I say, old man," Dunstable said amiably, "your aim is a bit off."

Ponsonby stood for a moment, weaving back and forth. As Bradford watched, his eyes closed and he fell heavily forward across the table, face down in what was left of Mrs. Crawley's custard tart.

A half-hour later, having settled the bill and bid good night to those of the supper-party who were sleeping at the inn, Bradford went out in the street to wait for the stable boy to bring his horse. He had intended to drive the Daimler, but the group had decided to leave all of the vehicles at the exhibit site, ready for tomorrow's race. And to tell the truth, he welcomed the horseback ride home through the cooling dark, along lanes he knew and loved. In the Daimler, reflection was an utter impossibility. One had all one could do to manage the damned controls and stay in the road, and the rattling and bouncing and noise jarred thought right out of the brain.

Bradford had collected his horse and was waiting for his companion, Charlie Rolls, when he heard loud voices from the direction of The Sun, a nearby inn.

"I say, Marsden!" It was Roger Thornton calling, in an angry, injured tone. "Hold on there. I'll have a word with you!"

Bradford swung up on his horse and turned it in Thornton's direction. Some sort of meeting had apparently been taking place at The Sun, for a dozen or more men had spilled out of the lamp-lit interior and were hurrying away through the dark of High Street, their voices loud in the quiet night. Bradford recognized a few of them, villagers and farmers from the neighboring area, dressed in rough jerkins and corduroy breeches. The meeting must have been a citizens' assembly, gotten up to discuss the maintenance of the local bridges or some such. But what the devil was Thornton doing there?

"Good evening, Roger," he said gruffly. The memory of the supper-party's sour ending was still with him, as was the recollection of his unsatisfactory encounter with Thornton that morning. He knew very well that his mother intended the squire to be his brother-in-law, and while he did not anticipate the relationship with any particular joy, or envy his sister her prospective bridegroom, he thought he ought not do anything to jeopardize the plan. He lightened his voice, gesturing to the departing villagers. "I say there, old man, you're in strange company tonight."

"It's on your account, if you must know," Thornton said grimly. "I'm looking out for your interests."

"For my interests?" Bradford asked in surprise. "And how are my interests at stake in a village assembly?"

"I'll tell you," Thornton said. "Or better yet—" He turned, speaking to a man who stood in the shadows. "Come out here, Whipple, and tell his lordship what is troubling you and your friends."

"As ye say, Squire." Clutching his hat in his hands, Whipple came into the light. He was a sturdy, thickset man, with a wide face the color of brick dust, fringed with red whiskers. His eyes were red-rimmed and angry. "I'll tell yer lordship wot 'tis, since I'm bid," he growled. " 'Tis that balloon. An' the motorcars, too."

"Oh, it is, is it?" Bradford snapped. This had the look of trouble and he knew he should speak softly. But the evening had been long, and he was coming to the end of his patience. "And what is it about the balloon and the motorcars that distresses you? To my certain knowledge, many of your friends are planning to come tomorrow. There will be fine entertainment."

"Fine entertainment it may be to see a balloon go up," Whipple said with scorn, "but comin' down is another matter. We've seen balloons come down, the drag ropes wreckin' fences an' tearin' 'oles in 'edges." He paused, and added, in a meaningful tone, "We've also seen motorcars racin' in the lanes, sir, an' we've seen old men kilt. I speak fer all when I say we don't like it, m'lord. Not one whit."

Bradford drew himself up. "I trust you are not accusing me," he said stiffly.

Whipple's face grew darker, his tone more scornful. "I don't accuse nobody, sir. All I'm sayin' is we don't like it. An' 'ere's wot we done about it, sir. Every farmer an' 'ouse'older wot wants one of these kin git it." He held up a printed proclamation. "Wi' all due respect, m'lord," he added, touching his forelock with a mocking gesture.

Bradford took the proclamation and held it to the light that came through the window of The Sun. In stern black letter were printed the words "Balloons and Motorcars Strictly Prohibited," with the accompanying terse directive: "Aeronauts, motorcar drivers, and all such trespassing on this land will be prosecuted to the fullest extent of Her Majesty's Law."

"That means," Whipple interpreted, "that any leaseholder's got the right to summon the constable if yer balloon er any o' them motorcars comes on 'is land."

Bradford handed back the proclamation without comment. He glanced gravely at Thornton. "How are you involved in this business, Squire?"

"Some of those in attendance tonight are my tenants at Thornton Grange. I happen to share their concerns. I fear for the horses, as do other owners and breeders in the area." Thornton lowered his voice. "I shall say to you what your father would say, were he here, Bradford. The horseless carriage is a threat to the horse, and to the horse trade: stud stables, harness and carriage manufacture, even farming itself. You are bringing catastrophe on our heads."

"Oh, come now, Roger," Bradford said with a dismissive wave of his hand. "You cannot seriously argue that—"

"I can certainly so argue," Thornton said fiercely, "and others agree. I tell you, Bradford, every leaseholder in the district intends to post one of those proclamations. What's more, they plan to gather at the launch site tomorrow morning. There's going to be serious trouble."

Bradford controlled the expression on his face, but he could not keep the anger out of his voice. "You are collaborating with these men!" he exclaimed. "You are encouraging them in their lunacy!"

Thornton's stern face was dark, his frown fixed. "And just who is the lunatic here? What will your father say when he returns home and learns how you have betrayed his beliefs? What will your mother say when she discovers that you have encouraged your sister in her foolish flirtation with—" His eyes began to blaze with the flame of the Thornton squires. "I warn you, Marsden. You and your heedless friends and your motorcars and balloons are wreaking havoc. I won't stand for it."

"Excuse me, gentlemen," said a quiet, firm voice. "Is there anything wrong?"

Bradford turned and squinted into the darkness. "Oh, good evening, Constable Laken," he said. He laughed uncomfortably. "No, nothing wrong. A lively exchange of views on a controversial subject, that's all."

"That's fine, sir," Laken said evenly. "But perhaps, in view of the lateness of the evening and the proximity of residences, you would not object to exchanging your views in a lower tone."

"Agreed," Bradford said with a careless laugh, "although I think we have had our say."

"Marsden?" called Charlie Rolls, coming around the Marlborough Head with his horse. The young man sounded a bit sozzled, not surprising, since he had done more than his share of the drinking. "I say, Marsden, old chap, are we ready to leave?"

"I'm ready," Bradford said to Rolls. "Good night, Constable." He turned to Thornton. "I wish you a good night, Squire—and better company."

"You'd best mind what I said," Thornton snapped, "or you'll be sorry."

Bradford leaned over his horse. "I hear you, Squire," he said. "But it is much too late to change anything, even if I wanted to."

"Then I pity you, Bradford," Thornton said bitterly, "for you have called up the very devil, and you shall have the devil to pay."

10

"'But I always want to know the things one shouldn't do.'

'So as to do them?' asked her aunt.

'So as to choose,' said Isabel."

— HENRY JAMES
The Portrait of a Lady

WHEN THE IDEA came to her, Bess knew immediately that she should not act on it. If she were caught, it would go hard with her, for there was no possible explanation she could make. But having reflected on the matter while she was milking her cow and feeding the chickens and gathering willows for her baskets, she discovered that the idea was now firmly lodged in her head, and she could not choose *not* to do it.

So on Friday night, after it had grown dark, she gathered what she needed, tucked the bundles into the pocket of her skirt, and wrapped her black shawl around her. Then she set off in the direction of Bishop's Keep.

It was unlikely that motorcars would be out and about at this late hour, but Bess still throbbed with angry resentment at Lord Bradford and she did not care to be knocked into any more watery ditches. So instead of following the road, she took the footpath into the Bishop's Keep Park. The land lay in darkness, but the moon was bright enough to see the cars lined up near the road under a large banner that proclaimed GRAND MOTOR CAR EXHIBITION AND RACE! She shuddered when she saw them, swift, steel-clad monsters, out to devour quiet lanes and destroy sleepy villages and run down pedestrians. If what she read in the newspaper was true, soon every county family would have its horseless carriage, steam tractors would replace wagons, and even the vicar's bicycle would be motorized. The way of life she loved would soon be gone forever.

Beyond the exhibition area, illuminated by a gaslight so bright that it turned the night to day, was the balloon's launch site, whence Bess was bound. The night was still, and so quiet that she could hear the low voices of the two men tending the balloon well before she reached it. Bending low, clutching her shawl around her, she kept to the shadows of the trees.

The balloon was a pale ghost that quivered, half-filled with gas, within its net of confining ropes. In just a few hours, it would rise from the earth and go soaring, sailing away through the bright air, to land who knew where. If she could go with it—but that was a vain hope. No, her only expectation of flying lay in the secret formula in the leather book tucked into its secret cache before the fireplace, where Gammer Gurton had hidden it after *her* successful flight.

The balloon, moored to the ground, its gondola attached, was secured to a canvas hose, through which gas passed with a slight hissing sound. The fragile gondola was draped with hempen lines and ballast bags, and a five-pronged metal anchor hung from its side. Bess crept forward through the darkness, one eye on the two men. After a few moments, the pair turned their backs and walked away, sharing quick nips from a brown bottle.

Sure now that she was unobserved, Bess darted to the gondola and swiftly did what she had come to do. Then she slipped into the shadows, and hurried back along the wood toward the exhibition area. Here, there was only moonlight, flickering like a candle as thin clouds moved across the face of the moon, and she was less fearful of being seen. Scanning the line of mechanical monsters, she easily singled out the one that belonged to Lord Bradford. Going to it, she knelt down in the shadows and spent several moments completing her mission. Then she stood and brushed herself off, feeling strong and powerful and vindicated. A moment later, confident of having achieved success without detection, she stepped out boldly into the lane. She had tripped along only a few paces, however, when she was suddenly brought up short by the sight of a stout figure on the road in front of her, and a familiar voice.

"Bess Gurton!" Sarah Pratt demanded, hands on hips. "Why in 'eaven's name are ye skulkin' through the dark?" Sarah's voice became suspicious. "Wot're ye doin' that ye shudn't?"

The day of the balloon's arrival had been a long one, and the night dragged on longer still. By dawn, Lawrence Quibbley was fagged. Understandably so, since Mr. Rolls had put him in charge of inflating the balloon and Sir Charles had made him responsible for the plant that was producing the gas—two not-inconsiderable tasks.

Since yesterday, Lawrence and Thompson, the gardener, had tended the gas plant's three retorts, fueling them in rotation. Every nine hours, they opened the iron door of one of the ten-foot-long brick chambers, stepping back from the flash of flame and the pop! of the remaining hydrogen and methane igniting in the air. The intense heat of the furnace had reduced the coal to a bright orange-red layer of coke, which they scooped with long-handled shovels into the combustion-chamber below. They reloaded the retort with fresh coal and closed the door, retreating to a cooler spot to wipe the sweat from their faces, Thompson complaining mightily that he had hired on to tend roses in the sunshine, not to stoke a gas-plant by moonlight. It had taken a half bottle of whisky to soothe the man's ruffled spirit.

Thompson hadn't been Lawrence's only problem. There had been one or two difficulties with the Daimler, which he'd been required to attend to. Then the balloon—that unfamiliar and rather unwieldy object—had caused him some concern when one of its seams had sprung a leak.

But for all his bone-weariness, Lawrence was exhilarated. Looking up into the misty predawn sky, he could see that the balloon was already tugging at its mooring lines. By ten A.M., the scheduled time of ascent, the fog would have burned away, the balloon would have reached its functional capacity, fully capable of lifting its team of aeronauts into the heavens.

On the other matter under his consideration, Lawrence was not quite so pleased. He had thought of several possible ways of persuading Lord Bradford to abandon his motorcar project, so that he would no longer require Lawrence's services as a mechanic. The difficulty was, however, that each scheme Lawrence had come up with involved some sort of damage to the Daimler. This would not be difficult for him to execute, knowing every nut and bolt of the motorcar as he did. But if any mischance befell it, Lawrence himself would be the first to be blamed. More importantly, he was reluctant to damage the motorcar, for he had come to care for it in almost the same way that his father had cared for the family draft horse.

But after hours of deliberation, a glimmer of an idea—not yet a full-blown scheme—had come to him. It did not solve the basic problem, of course, but it would get him past it, and allow him to fulfill both Amelia's desires and meet his own obligation.

As the dawn broke, Lawrence's plan began to take a clearer and brighter form.

Lady Marsden's letter arrived by the Saturday morning post. Kate, opening it, read the following:

> Nice, France, September 20, 1896
>
> My dear Lady Kathryn,
>
> I take up my pen as a concerned mother, to appeal to you. It has come to the attention of Lord Christopher and myself that Patsy has become unwisely involved in a dangerous liaison with a young man, a guest of my son's at Marsden Manor, and that this reckless relationship has been supported, indeed, even furthered, by you. I believe I need not say that my son has acted injudiciously in the extreme to bring such a person into close acquaintance with his sister, and that it was quite irresponsible of my husband's aunt to allow the young man into my daughter's company. I must ask you to withdraw your support of this foolish intimacy and persuade Patsy (who is, for all her cleverness, an inexperienced and headstrong young girl who can do much damage to herself and her family through unwise associations) to abandon her injurious friendship with this person. I am confident that now that you have been informed of the facts, you will do as I bid, and withdraw your unwise sponsorship of this association.
>
> Yrs.,
>
> Henrietta Marsden

Kate sat with the letter in her hand for some time. Lady Henrietta's imperious voice spoke clearly and offensively, but she could see the mother's predicament. It was true that Patsy was a headstrong, impulsive young woman, unlike her more compliant sister, Eleanor, who had married at her parents' wish. (Never mind that Eleanor was already quite wretched.) And it was true that Patsy's relationship with Charlie Rolls was probably a dangerous one, at least in the sense that it would lead to her eventual unhappiness.

But unhappiness, in Kate's opinion, was relative, and might even be balanced out by moments of great happiness. She also felt very strongly that marriage was a matter of the heart, and that daughters should not be the victims of their mothers' matchmaking. Lady Henrietta obviously feared that Patsy's friendship with Rolls threatened the family's plan to marry Patsy to Squire Thornton and link the Marsden estates to Thornton Grange. After thinking about it for a time, Kate decided that she would say nothing of the mother's letter to the daughter, although she would do what she could to encourage the girl to think carefully about what she was doing. A little later that morning, she had her chance.

"You can preach all you like," Patsy Marsden remarked loftily, in response to Kate's question, "but I shan't change my mind. I intend to marry Charlie Rolls."

"You *have* changed your mind, you know," Kate replied, and poured her guest another cup of tea. Outside the window of the drawing room, she could hear the noise of the crowd gathering for the fete—the cries of children, the thwacking of the coconut shies, the shouts of a vendor hawking hot pies. "Only a fortnight ago, you said you didn't intend to marry Charlie Rolls, or fall in love with him either, for that matter. You had set your heart on becoming England's premier female photographer. What has happened to that ambition? I thought it a fine one, for which you have a great talent."

Patsy pouted. "You don't like him."

"My liking or disliking the young man has nothing to do with it."

Patsy's pout deepened. "You think I should be a dutiful daughter and marry Roger Thornton."

Kate picked up her cup, drank, and set it down again. "I think," she said deliberately, "that you should stop allowing your mother to push you into doing things you know you will regret."

Patsy's cornflower-blue eyes, the same shade as her elegant silk dress, opened wide. "Then you are saying I *should* marry Charlie! Goodness, Kate—why can't you make up your mind?"

"I am saying, Patsy, that you should neither marry to please your mother, nor marry to spite her."

"To spite her?"

"Yes. Either will make you dreadfully unhappy, and inflict a world of harm not only on yourself, but on the man, as well." Kate leaned forward and put her hand on Patsy's arm, speaking with all the earnestness she could summon. "Marry no one unless your heart—not the heart of a daughter nor that of a rebel, but your true woman's heart—leads you to it, Patsy."

Patsy was silent for a moment, and Kate wondered whether her words had struck so deeply that they offended, or whether they had merely glanced off an impenetrable surface. But at last the girl sighed and spoke. "No one but you will talk honestly about such things, Kate. I fear you understand me too well."

"I have learned to understand myself," Kate said with a small smile, "and we are rather alike, you and I."

"I think we are," Patsy said, "in spite of your being—" She stopped and bit her lip, coloring.

"Being an American, and Irish? Perhaps, Patsy, that is what makes us alike, you and I. We do not always think or feel or behave as those around us expect. It is hard for us *not* to do as we choose, even though we might not know exactly what that is."

"And yet you married." Patsy spoke almost accusingly.

"I married when I knew that my heart had chosen well. And I have not regretted it." To herself, but not aloud, she added, *in spite of the difficulties.*

For there *were* difficulties. She and Charles were enjoying a temporary reprieve just now from the burdens of his family. But when his brother was dead, and Charles should become the Baron of Somersworth, those burdens would have to be shouldered. There would be a move to Somersworth, so he could manage the family estates; and months in London, when Parliament was sitting; and social obligations in a society that would be forever foreign to her. She had known all of this when she married Charles, of course, but that did not make it any easier to bear.

Patsy clasped her hands. "I should so much *like* to be married to Charlie. He is handsome and charming and free-spirited, and he loves me—or at least he says he does. With him, every minute would be filled with excitement, with *freedom.* He would take me flying in his balloon, motoring across England, climbing in the Alps—and all the while I should be taking photographs. Mama should have to give way, and I should never have to suffer Roger Thornton again."

Kate heard the longing behind Patsy's words, and understood it. "I am sure Charlie does care for you," she said gravely. "You are a beautiful young woman with courage and wit, and you have every bit as much free spirit as he does. I can easily imagine your ascending in a balloon with your camera, or touring Europe in your own motorcar."

"But that's not what *Mama* wants for me," the girl said. She twisted her gloves in her hands. "And if I do not marry Charlie, I shall have to agree to marry Roger Thornton."

"Not so," Kate said sternly. "I grant you, it might be easier to defy your mother as someone's wife. But you may confront her with equal success as *yourself*. All it takes is the courage to know what you want and the strength of will to choose."

Patsy pressed her lips together. "If I refuse Squire Thornton, Mama would be sure you put me up to it. She doesn't like you, you know. Ever since Bradford determined to marry you—"

"Your brother wanted to marry me because he was in one of his dreadful fixes and thought it would be convenient to have a wife with a fortune. Your mother quite properly convinced him that it was not a good idea—and if she had not, I myself should have had to refuse him. Anyway," Kate added with asperity, "the point is not what your mother likes or dislikes. You are a woman of independent mind, Patsy. You must make your mother understand that you mean to exercise it."

On that heresy, the French doors opened and Charles looked in. "We shall be ready to launch in half an hour, Kate. Are you coming to see us off?"

"Of course," Kate said.

"And I shall be there too," Patsy said. "With my camera."

"Good," Charles said. "We shall want a great many photographs." As he shut the door again, Kate wished that she had had a moment alone with him before he flew off into the blue. Not that she feared for his safety, of course. Bradford had assured her that Rolls, despite his youth, was an experienced balloonist, and Charles himself was an extraordinarily capable man. Still, there were hazards, and many people had been killed in ballooning accidents.

"Well," Patsy said, returning to their subject, "I am not *absolutely* determined to marry Mr. Rolls." She frowned. "I am resolved against Roger Thornton, however." She gave a dramatic sigh. "Poor Roger is likely to suffer a great deal. He has his heart set on marrying me. I fear that he may do something . . . unwise."

"I doubt that," Kate replied lightly. "It is only in novels that lovers die from a broken heart."

A moment later, though, Kate wondered whether she had been mistaken. She heard loud shouts and cries and thought that the balloon must be going up before its scheduled departure. But as she and Patsy, with her camera, hurried to the terrace, she saw Roger Thornton. He was marching at the head of a group of shouting men, and his expression was murderous.

11

"The Essex farmers had become all too familiar with balloon descents on their property. Crops were trampled, hedges damaged and stock terrified. Hence the natives became decidedly unfriendly. Passengers who had paid handsomely for the privilege of a place in a balloon car and had sailed into the sky . . . with the cheers of the crowds ringing in their ears came down to earth with a vengeance when they found themselves looking down the business end of a blunderbuss.

— L. T. C. Rolt
The Aeronauts: A History of Ballooning, 1783–1903

Vicar Barfield Talbot could hardly contain his excitement as he contemplated the balloon flight. He arose in the misty dawn on the day of the launch and presented himself at Bishop's Keep shortly after breakfast, his usual rusty black coat brightened by the unusual addition of a silk scarf gaily striped in the balloon's bright colors.

"Ah," said he to Sir Charles, with all the delight of a schoolboy on holiday, "I see that all is in readiness for your ascent! I expect the sky will clear before it is time to go up."

But Sir Charles was too busy attending to the last details of the inflation to do more than give him a pleasant nod and a brisk hello, so the vicar, not wanting to be in the way, took himself off in search of Kate. He found her with a dour-looking Mrs. Pratt, discussing the details of the dinner that had been planned for that evening.

"Ah, Lady Kathryn," he said happily. "Kate. A lovely day, isn't it? So much excitement to look forward to! Such a bustle in the Park!"

"I suppose," Mrs. Pratt said with a finely honed sarcasm, "that I shudn't expect to 'ave gas in the kitchen when it's time to begin cookin'. I suppose it's all gone into the balloon."

"I doubt that it will be a problem," Kate said. "Once the balloon has gone, the lines will be reconnected and you can use the range without difficulty." She gave the vicar a distracted look. "Oh, Vicar, good morning. How kind of you to come early. Would you mind telling the porter that it is time to open the Park gates?"

The vicar could see that Kate, too, was preoccupied, so he went off to do as he was asked.

There was already a crowd outside the gates, and the minute they were opened, men and women and children dressed in holiday finery streamed in. On Fete Day, no laundry flapped on the village clothes lines, no floors were swept or windows washed, and every family laid its best tablecloth on the table and coverlets on the beds and opened homes and hearts to all the aunts and uncles and cousins who lived within walking distance. It was a day for family reunions and general joy, and the vicar had expected that the balloon launch and motorcar chase could only add to the general excitement.

But this year, the death of Old Jessup seemed to have cast a pall over the celebration. There were many who believed that, one way or another, the old man had been killed by the motorcar, and that the driver—the same man who planned to pilot the balloon—had been egregiously at fault. "Murder," some still whispered, in spite of Dr. Bassett's insistence that Old Jessup had died of natural causes, and regardless of Coroner Hodson's refusal to hold an inquest. And while Young Jessup had been surprisingly quiet for the last week, his friends had plenty to say.

"It's worth yer life to go where them motorcars is," avowed Mr. Grabbner, the miller's helper. "I've tol' me wife that this year we're stayin' 'ome, where we won't be run down an' kilt. We won't step foot near them infernal machines."

"Go to the fete? Not bloody likely," said Godfrey the underbaker. "Wot wi' all those motorcars on the roads, somebody else is bound to be 'urt, an' it ain't goin' to be me er mine."

Such censure notwithstanding, the crowd streaming down the lane was a large one, including many well-dressed gentlemen in snappy vests whom the vicar did not recognize—gentlemen from Colchester, no doubt, and perhaps from Ipswich. For the moment, the balloon was the center of attention. Already it was surrounded by a marveling throng, gazing in wonderment at the silken bubble, so tenuously tethered to the earth. The vicar joined the crowd for a few moments, sharing its excitement and craning his own neck to gaze heavenward at the balloon's immense height, wondering what it would be like to soar up and up, above the clouds.

The repeated *clackety-wheeze* of a motorcar being cranked recalled his attention to the earth, and he left the launch area to stroll in the direction of the motorcars. Like the balloon, they were ringed with wondering spectators, and for a few moments he paused to watch the drivers preparing for the race. Frank Ponsonby and another man were taking turns pulling on the rim of the flywheel to coax the reluctant Benz to life. Wilhelm Albrecht, wearing a blue Motor Car Club jacket and cap, was kneeling beside the Daimler, lighting the flame jets that heated its hot tube igniters. Arthur Dickson was lying under the rear axle of his steam car, trying to light the burner beneath the boiler. And while all this activity was going on, Arnold Bateman leaned against a tree, conspicuously lighting a cigarette and watching the others work with a slight smile. His electric automobile did not require any preliminary warming-up, a fact that he obviously enjoyed.

The vicar stood, taking in these marvels of modern technology and wondering how they would change his quiet parish. What would the village be like when as many as three or four motorcars a day ran up and down the High Street, rattling the glass in the panes and frightening the village dogs? How much would the country road tax have to be raised to rebuild the bridge at the foot of Devil's Hill so that a Daimler or a Benz could cross safely? And as for himself, he wondered indecisively, was he too old to learn how to—

"Good morning, Vicar," said a quiet voice at his elbow.

The vicar turned. "Ah, good morning, Constable Laken," he said, and beamed at the village constable, who was wearing his usual uniform of navy serge. "It *is* a good morning, isn't it? I was just thinking that perhaps I am not too old to learn how to manage one of these extraordinary inventions. What do you think?"

"One is never too old to learn something new," Constable Laken said. He was a short, slender man, with a ruddy face, sandy hair, and penetrating gray eyes that missed almost nothing.

"Why, yes, I see you are right. Dear me, of course I am not too old. And from that point of view, I see that I have an obligation to—that is, I certainly must try my hand at—"

Having thus made up his mind, the vicar brightened. "I hope you are here for pleasure, not duty."

"A bit of both," Laken said. "The loud gentlemen did not wake you last night?"

"That group at The Sun?" the vicar asked. "I heard their voices, just as I was settling in to sleep, but they did not much disturb me. Do I have you to thank for sending them on their way?"

The constable nodded. "There's something in the wind, I'm afraid, sir. You know Tom Whipple, I'm sure."

The vicar frowned. "I know Whipple." He thought, but did not add aloud, that he also knew the man—like his friend Young Jessup—to be a troublemaker. He also did not say, although he was tempted, that there had been something in the wind ever since Old Jessup had died.

"I would appreciate it, sir, if you would get word to me, should you see him here today."

"I shall do it," the vicar promised. He did not ask what Tom Whipple might be up to, for it sounded as if that were the constable's business. *His* job was caring for souls. He smiled at the constable, whom he both respected and liked. "Your Agnes and little Betsy will be here to enjoy the fete, I do not doubt."

"Right, sir," Constable Laken replied cheerfully. "They wouldn't miss it for the world. And I believe that Lady Kathryn has planned a special treat for Betsy."

Agnes's daughter, Laken's stepchild, was a favorite of Kate's, the vicar knew, and he smiled. "Well, then," he said, and raised his hat. "Good day!"

"Good day, sir," said the constable. He became sober again. "And don't forget about Tom Whipple."

As in previous years, the scene was pleasantly tumultuous. Mr. Gresham and his nephew had hauled a roundabout with a hurdy-gurdy from Great Horkesley, where it had done duty at an agricultural fair the week before. Some of the men of the parish had built a pair of swings, and others had erected a cluster of show booths, coconut shies, gingerbread and sweet stalls, and the usual booth for the church jumble sale. The butcher's sons had raised a sturdy greased pole for the leg-o'-mutton climb. For the Flower Show, a large tent and several smaller ones had been erected, and the local gardeners had been bringing their choicest blooms since yesterday. But it was not only flowers—asters and stocks and sweet-smelling crimson roses—on display, but gigantic cabbages and immense cauliflowers, scarlet runner beans and scrubbed vegetable marrows and huge bunches of purple-red grapes and golden melons, as well as glasses of sparkling jelly, pots of jam, and jars of honey. The prizes—ten shillings for a first, seven and six for a second, and five for a third—would be presented by the vicar in the afternoon, after the judges had done their work. And meanwhile, the nervous gardeners could repair to St. Mary's yellow silk marquee, which had been raised under the horse chestnut trees and filled with wooden tables and benches. There they could calm their anxiety with sixpence worth of tea and spiced dough cake served by the Ladies of the Missionary Guild in aid of the poor children of Borneo.

But while the outside observer might be deceived by the pleasant variety of the scene, the vicar was not. Constable Laken was right: there was something in the air, some tension, some apprehension, threaded like a dark lace through the bright morning's activities. As he walked, he noticed small things—two or three men with their heads together, exchanging covert whispers; surreptitious dashings here and there; anxious glances cast toward the motorcars and the balloon. Something was afoot, and Vicar Talbot knew it.

Shortly before nine, the vicar found himself on the east terrace, where the chase participants were convening for a last-minute discussion, the drivers already garbed in motoring coats and helmets, their goggles around their necks. All but one wore worried frowns, the exception being Herr Albrecht, whose supreme self-confidence was unmistakable. At the moment, however, Albrecht seemed to be looking for someone.

"Have you seen Herr Dunstable?" he asked Arnold Bateman in his abrupt, Germanic way. "He is to ride with me, and he has not yet appeared."

"Dunstable?" asked Bateman, with an arch look. "Sorry, I haven't seen the fellow."

"I've been lookin' fer 'im, too," said Sam Holt, frowning. " 'E was supposed to meet me fer a hinterview an hour ago. Ah, there's Sir Charles." He raised his voice. "Sir Charles, 'ave you seen Mr. Dunstable?"

"I have not," Sir Charles said. He and his houseguest Henry Royce had joined the group just as Rolls began handing out Ordinance Survey maps.

Royce settled himself on the parapet. "Dunstable is not here? I thought these were *his* festivities."

Sir Charles sat down on a bench beside the vicar, folding his arms and settling back to watch the proceedings with (the vicar thought) something less than enthusiasm.

"Dunstable is missing?" Ponsonby asked, with a serious look. "Someone had better go and fetch him. He was very anxious to be here. Perhaps something has happened to him."

Arthur Dickson chuckled. "Well, if it has, it can't have happened to a more deserving chap."

Vicar Talbot was right—Charles's enthusiasm for the balloon-motorcar chase had vastly diminished. When Bradford first proposed it, he had eagerly accepted the challenge of producing sufficient gas to inflate the balloon and had looked forward to the prospect of going up with an experienced balloonist—all this without giving much thought to the purpose of the flight.

As the chase neared, though, he found himself anticipating it with a growing uneasiness. For one thing, he agreed with Henry Royce that the vehicles were not engineered for rough travel, and he doubted that they could take the pounding of the country lanes. For another, a chase across unfamiliar terrain would challenge even the most experienced driver's skills, and these drivers were not equally experienced. Albrecht had already won a half-dozen European races. No doubt he would win this one, too, a fact which must be irritatingly obvious to the three inexperienced drivers. And there was the balloon chase itself, an idea that had begun to seem to Charles as fantastical as Jules Verne's fictions. It was absurd to hope that the drivers—who would have to cope not only with the eccentricities of their flimsy vehicles but with narrow, twisting lanes frequented by horse-drawn wagons—could follow the fast-moving balloon closely enough to find its touchdown point. No. As a race, the event was not a fair contest; as a chase, it was a doomed venture.

Bradford Marsden paused beside the bench where Charles was sitting. "I need to speak with you immediately after the meeting, Charles," he said in a low voice. "I'm afraid there's trouble afoot." He was gone before Charles could inquire about the problem.

"So," the vicar said, rubbing his hands with the look of a small boy anticipating the arrival of St. Nicholas. "The winds are favorable for the launch, wouldn't you say? You and Mr. Rolls should have quite a nice flight."

Charles glanced at the Union Jack fluttering from the flagpole on the croquet lawn. The morning mists had cleared somewhat earlier than expected, and a light and variable surface wind blew out of the west. From the look of the gray, fast-moving clouds, it was much stronger aloft. That did not bode well. If the wind were ten knots or better, the balloon would quickly outstrip even the fastest automobile. None of them would be able to locate the landing site.

Beside him, Henry Royce was also glancing up at the clouds. "I am no balloonist," he remarked in his clipped, precise way, "but I should imagine that you and your pilot—what's his name? Rolls?—will have rather a wild ride."

"Oh, yes, a *wild* ride," the vicar said happily. "I wish I could go with you. Where do you think to come down?"

Charles did not answer, because Rolls had raised his hand for attention and was speaking directly to that question. "Judging from the direction of the winds," he said to the drivers, "Sir Charles and I can expect to descend somewhere in the neighborhood of Frinton-on-Sea, fifteen miles to the southwest as the crow flies—somewhat more than that, by road. The winds aloft are a bit chancier, though, and we can't guarantee where we'll put down."

Albrecht seemed surprised. "You cannot tell us where the finish line is?" he demanded. "What kind of a race is this?"

Rolls looked equally surprised. "We have no means of guiding the balloon on such a short course, so we can't say where we will touch down. And strictly speaking, this is not a race but a chase, like hare and hounds. Finding the finish line is one test of your skill."

"Herr Dunstable told me nothing of that," Albrecht said, with a flash of sullen anger. He looked around. "Where is the man? I want to speak with him."

Frank Ponsonby spoke, ignoring Albrecht. "You can surely give us a range of possible landing sites, Rolls."

"The balloon could come down anywhere from Brightlingsea to Harwich," Rolls replied. "We shan't go further, of course." He grinned. "Motorcars cannot yet swim, and Sir Charles and I have no desire to end in the North Sea."

Dickson grunted. "I hope you don't think that's funny."

Lord Bradford stepped forward. "The trick, gentlemen, is to drive generally southwestward, keeping the balloon in sight if you can. If you experience difficulties or find yourself stranded, locate the nearest telegraph office and send a message to Dedham."

Bateman groaned. "Harwich to Brightlingsea! For God's sake, man, we could be motoring for hours along that deserted coast!"

Dickson smiled archly. "Chin up, Arnold. I'm sure you can find a team of horses to tow you when your battery gives out."

Bateman looked dark, but Charles knew that Dickson's insult had truth in it. Unfortunately, the limited charge of the batteries gave the electric car a much smaller range and slower speed than either steam-or petrol-powered cars. The Bateman Electric would never finish the chase.

Dickson pushed out his mouth. "Keep the balloon in sight, you say. That might be easier said than done."

"Perhaps," Rolls said. "We shall try to maintain an altitude that will make it possible for you to see us easily. If we are too low, you will lose us. But if we are too high, we will outdistance you."

"Sounds tricky," Bateman said darkly.

"How long do you suppose your flight will take?" asked Frank Ponsonby.

"We should make ten knots in this wind," Rolls replied, "so we will reach the coast in a little over an hour." He frowned. "One other thing. Some of the village constables may not know that Parliament has raised the speed limit to twelve miles an hour. They may impose the old limit."

"Strictly speaking," Bateman said, scowling, "they would be right. The new law does not take effect until November."

"Strictly speaking, that is so," Rolls conceded, "although constables who are informed of the change will not likely make a case of it. Still, you must beware. And don't forget that some villagers are not enthusiastic proponents of the motorcar." He smiled disarmingly. "Adds to the excitement, doesn't it?"

Dickson, examining the map, did not smile. "When I agreed to drive in this chase, I had no idea of the conditions. I don't like the looks of these lanes. They meander. They are no doubt narrow and dangerous."

Ponsonby chuckled mirthlessly. "A pity for you, Arthur. You should have waited for a race on a flat, smooth straightaway. That heavy boiler hardly fits your steamer for rough terrain."

"My boiler is not so heavy as Bateman's batteries," Dickson retorted angrily. "And as for speed, you will see. At least I won't be giddy with fatigue at the finish, with my teeth jolted out of my skull."

"I wonder whether it would not be better," Bateman said nervously, "to delay a bit. The wind might turn easterly this afternoon. The roads are better in the western part of the county."

"This discussion," Bradford said emphatically, "is of absolutely no purpose. We have already agreed to the conditions of the race. What's more, pairs of men have been dispatched to Brightlingsea, Weeley Heath, and Great Oakley, to recover the balloon should it touch down in those vicinities." He looked at Rolls. "Are we ready for the launch?"

"We are," Rolls said, and raised his hand peremptorily. "Good luck, gentlemen."

111

As the drivers left for their vehicles, Royce, his arms still crossed, leaned toward Charles. "Brash little poppinjay, isn't he?"

Charles grinned. "Rather. But you should become acquainted with him, Royce. He has quite a good mechanical mind, and a great energy. He also seems to have an entrepreneurial spirit. Perhaps the two of you could collaborate on something in the motorcar line."

"I doubt it," Royce said with a dry laugh. "Should I undertake any work in that direction, I shall do it alone. I cannot think what contribution an undisciplined boy could make to any serious engineering enterprise." He frowned. "I am sorry, Sir Charles, to be leaving before you and Rolls are on the ground once again. I had not expected to be summoned back to Manchester this weekend."

"I hope you find your emergency already resolved when you return to your factory," Charles said. "Perhaps next time you are here, I will have implemented your suggestions for improvements, and we will have more time to spend with Lady Kathryn's roses."

He was interrupted by a clamor of loud, hostile voices. Turning, Charles saw a crowd of shouting villagers and farmers some twenty or thirty strong. They had formed ranks four abreast and were marching up the lane, waving sticks and signs that read "No Balloons!" and "No Motor Cars!" Roger Thornton, wearing a caped jacket, a deerstalker on his head, marched at the head of the motley column, flanked on either side by shouting men.

"There they are, damn it," Bradford said furiously. "That's the trouble I wanted to tell you about, Charles. Some of the local people have organized a protest against the chase, and Thornton has joined them. That man beside him is their ringleader, Whipple. Young Jessup is there too."

The fete-goers, suddenly subdued, gave way, and made a wide aisle for the noisy marchers. They seemed to be aiming for the croquet lawn, where the balloon, now tended by the ground crew, tugged at its mooring lines.

The vicar came up to Charles. "We had better send for the constable," he said. "And I shall go and have a talk with the squire. I doubt that he will allow any serious trouble, but—"

Sam Holt rushed up. "There's goin' to be the devil to pay!" he shouted, wild with excitement. "Some of those men are carrying pitchforks. They're after the balloon!"

Rolls grabbed Charles's arm. "There's no time to delay," he said quietly, speaking under the rising din. "To the balloon, Sir Charles, now!"

Kate had come running out onto the terrace, frightened. "What's happening?" she cried. "Who are those men? Charles, what—"

Regardless of the crowd around them, Charles put his hands on her shoulders and kissed her quickly. "I'm off," he said. "Ask Bradford. He'll tell you what is going on."

"Now!" Rolls shouted.

"I'm with you," Charles said, and dashed for the balloon, with Bradford, Royce, and the vicar at his heels. The drivers had scattered in the direction of their motorcars, which were warmed up and ready to go.

A moment or two later, Charles and Rolls were in the gondola, preparing to launch. But the marchers had worked themselves into a frenzy. Shouting and brandishing rakes and pitchforks, they broke ranks and charged the balloon, as Bradford, Royce, and the ground crew struggled to push them back. Roger Thornton strode forward and laid angry hold of the gondola.

"There's no use your launching!" he shouted in an impassioned voice. "We intend to prevent the motorcars from starting. The chase is off, d'ye hear? The chase is off!"

"The chase is off!" the marchers shouted, and sent up a wildly triumphant cheer. "The chase is off!"

The vicar pushed through the crowd, and put his hand on Thornton's shoulder. "Don't be a fool, Roger," he pleaded. "This sort of animosity can only—"

"Are you ready, Sir Charles?" Rolls cried, preparing to cast off.

Royce, holding off an angry attacker, shouted over his shoulder, "If you don't go now, you may not go at all!"

"One more minute," Charles said desperately, reaching for his checklist. "I'm not quite ready."

There was another wild cry. The vicar was shoved aside as the marchers surged angrily forward, rocking the fragile gondola.

"Cast off!" Rolls cried, and the balloon began to rise.

12

"'Then you have discovered the means of guiding a balloon?'
'Not at all, that is a Utopian idea'
'Then you will go—'
'Withersoever Providence wills. . .'"

— JULES VERNE, 1869
Five Weeks in a Balloon

To Charles, the balloon felt like a live thing. The gondola surged under him, and his stomach lurched as it did when his horse cleared a high stone fence. They were rising—no, *shooting* up, in an ascent that was beyond their control, beyond anyone's control. In two beats of the heart—and Charles's heart was beating fast with excitement—they were twenty feet above the milling crowd. The mooring lines writhed like snakes, just out of reach of the grasping hands of the marchers, who were furious to have been cheated out of their victory.

The vicar pulled off his bright-colored scarf and began to wave it. "Goodbye!" he called, his high, thin voice almost lost in the rough hubbub of shouts and jeers.

"Good luck!" Bradford shouted. "Telegraph as soon as you've set down."

But through the din, it was Kate's sweeter voice that rang in Charles's ears, calling with love, "Goodbye, Charles, goodbye, my dear!"

For the moment, there was almost no breeze. The balloon was still rising straight up, as rapidly and effortlessly as if it were a bobbin on a string, pulled upward by a giant somewhere above the clouds. Looking down, Charles saw that the melee, rather than being diminished by the balloon's departure, seemed to be growing. Bradford had picked something up from the ground, a tool of some sort, it seemed to be, and was waving it frantically. Whatever it was, the object renewed the crowd's frenzy, and it surged around Bradford until he was all but swallowed up.

"Can you make out that thing in Marsden's hand?" Rolls asked, leaning over the rim of the gondola. "I trust it wasn't a piece of our equipment."

Charles reached for his field glasses and trained them on the scene below, but the breeze was freshening, wafting them swiftly eastward, and the distance was already too great to make out detail.

"I can't see, I'm afraid," Charles said. He shifted his glasses to the line of motorcars. "It looks as if the drivers will be able to get underway while the marchers are still scuffling, though. There goes Albrecht in Marsden's Daimler, off in a cloud of dust." He frowned. "But he's alone."

"*Still* no Dunstable?" Rolls was dismayed. "Something has happened to the man, Sir Charles, I know it! He is convinced that Albrecht will win, of course, and he has been planning to ride with him ever since the chase was thought of. He would not have missed it, if he had to drag himself on his hands and knees."

"At two hundred feet in the air and rising," Charles said, "there is little we could do to help him."

116

"We shall have enough to do to help ourselves," Rolls said ruefully, picking up a tangle of lines. "But I'll take the joys and risks of the wild blue over a battle with pitchforks, any day, won't you? I say, though, I could cert'nly wish for a more deliberate departure. That lot rather hurried us off."

But Charles, looking wonderingly about him, did not reply. Since his schooldays as a Woolwich military cadet, he had been enthralled by maps, fascinated by their wonderful detail, captivated by their precise location of streams and bridges, roads and villages. Now, the landscape was spread out below him just as he had so often spread a map on a table for study, but in even more exquisite detail than any map could represent it.

To the north and west of the Bishop's Keep woodlands, he could see the village of Dedham, the square gray tower of St. Mary the Virgin rising commandingly in its center. To one side of the church was the bright green of churchyard cemetery, to the other the red tiled roofs of High Street. Mill Lane led to the iron bridge across the silver ribbon of the River Stour, downstream from the locks that raised and lowered the barges out of the mill pond. Beyond the bridge, the river wound its way down to Flatford, through velvety meadows speckled with black-and-white cattle. A few miles to the east and north, the Stour emptied into the silvery flats of Seafield Bay, where Charles could make out the harbor towns of Manningtree and Lawford, and even Mistley, farther to the east. Farther eastward still, the horizon receded into the flat gray-blue of the North Sea. The sense of distance and range he had honed during his brief career as an officer in the Royal Engineers told him that they were two thousand feet above the ground— almost as high as Rolls aimed to go, apparently, for he began to pull on the red-painted ripcord that opened a valve in the top of the balloon, reducing their rate of ascent. They were moving rapidly now, too, as the winds caught the gaily striped balloon and began to sweep it quickly eastward, the gondola swinging beneath like a giant wicker pendulum. With no means of steering, the balloon would go with the wind, and they too, willy-nilly.

Charles recalled himself from the scenic vista. Their departure had been something less than orderly, and he had not been able to go through his prelaunch checklist. His first thought was for his photographic gear—after all, he had joined this expedition in order to take pictures. Moving carefully, for there was no room to spare in the small gondola, he found the canvas bags he had instructed Lawrence to stow, containing two hand cameras (one fitted with a long-focus lens), a box of dark slides, and an exposure meter and its supply of sensitive paper. With the bags was a small packet, and Charles smiled when he opened a corner of it to see sandwiches, biscuits, and an apple. Kate had seen to his lunch.

He took out the camera with the long-focus lens, loaded a changing box, and began to shoot. Having taken a half-dozen photos, he was putting the camera away when his eye fell on a tiny crockery pot, its lid held tight with a wire bail, half-hidden under a canvas bag. Curious, he opened the pot to find a red-colored grease. He worked a small quantity between his thumb and forefinger, then sniffed it and wrinkled his nose. Lard or suet or some such organic lubricant, stirred into a mass of stewed vegetation, colored with something red—blood? Whatever the stuff was, it had a sharp, peculiar odor, quite distinct.

He held the jar up to Rolls. "Some sort of lubricant for your equipment?"

"Never saw it before," Rolls said. He wore a strained look. "I say, Sir Charles, have you seen the grapnel?"

Charles dropped the jar into his camera bag and leaned over the edge of the gondola to look. "Our anchor? It's hanging right here, on the outside of—"

But it wasn't. The five-pronged iron grapnel, on which they depended to arrest the balloon at the end of the flight, was gone.

Rolls hit his forehead with the heel of his hand. "Bloody hell!" he cried. "Could that have been the confounded thing Bradford was waving in the air as we ascended?"

"It might've been," Charles said grimly. If that were the case, then the company on the ground—including Kate— knew of their difficulty. He was sorry for that, because there was nothing anyone down there could do to help them. All Kate could do was worry, and pray. He forced a smile. "I hope at some time or other you've managed a descent without a grapnel."

"To tell the truth, Sir Charles," Rolls said lamely, "I . . . I have never managed a descent at all. Strictly speaking, that is. In point of truth, I mean, sir."

"What?" Charles exclaimed, dumbstruck. "But I thought . . . I mean, you said . . ."

"Awf'ly sorry," Rolls said sheepishly. "I have a vile habit of pretending to more experience than I actually have. Sometimes it's the only way a chap can get on." His boyish grin was embarrassed. "The balloon was loaned to me, d'y'see, and Dunstable was terribly anxious for the publicity and the photographs and all. Marsden said you're a cautious man and wouldn't fly with me if you knew that my two previous flights were made as a passenger, not—I must confess—as a pilot in command. But I can bring us down," he added hastily, "never fear. It is simply a matter of—"

"Only two flights!" Charles cried, indignant. "So you know nothing about ballooning!"

"Oh, I wouldn't say that." Rolls tried to be reassuring. "I know the important things. I mean, I know them, although I may not have *done* them, yet. But don't worry. We'll get down all right, although," he added regretfully, "the descent 'ud be a damned sight more agreeable with that grapnel. I wonder—do you have a suggestion?"

Charles set his jaw. An experienced aeronaut might have gotten them out of this fix, but it wasn't likely that a boy could do it—a brash little poppinjay, as Henry Royce had said, with only two flights under his belt. "We ought to bring the balloon down somewhat," he said, thinking out loud, "and maintain altitude until we get within sight of one of our ground crews. Then we shall have to come down fast. Since we can't anchor, we'll need all the help we can get once we're on the ground."

"Right-o," Rolls said. He reached for the ripcord and vented some of the gas. The balloon dropped swiftly, to an altitude that Charles judged to be about two thousand feet. For what seemed an eternity, they rode in silence, scanning the ground beneath them. Charles spotted the gravel track of the Colchester-Harwich road, and the village of Wix, scarcely more than a collection of cottages and a pub. And then the green and gold of meadows and fields gave way to the gray of the Essex marshes, ruled into sections by the long straight lines of the drains. Turning, he brought up his glasses and scanned the road and lanes behind them, but there was not a sign of a motorcar anywhere. For the cars, as well as the balloon, the chase was a doomed adventure.

Rolls broke the silence. "If I am not mistaken, that is the village of Great Oakley ahead."

"That at least is good news," Charles said. "Lawrence Quibbley was dispatched to Great Oakley. He is a reliable and innovative chap. I should be especially glad of his help." He brought up his field glasses. "At this heading, we will pass directly over the village. If Quibbley is watching, he will see us. But past Great Oakley we shall have to descend at once, Rolls. There is only tideland bog and fen ahead, and large stretches of open water—not the sort of place we should like to put down."

Reaching for the ripcord again, Rolls hesitated. "Bog and fen? Should we go further, then? What is beyond?"

"Beyond?" Charles laughed briefly. "A short way beyond lies the North Sea. Vent the gas and bring us down, Rolls, or you shall find yourself making that crossing you're so keen on." He began to wrap the end of a long mooring line around the middle of a sandbag, tying it firmly. He was working on the second sandbag when he looked up to find Rolls with his hand on the ripcord, staring upward.

"Come on, man, vent the gas and bring us down!" Charles shouted. "We don't have much time!"

"I can't," Rolls replied, and yanked frantically on the cord. "The damn thing is jammed!"

Charles was a calm man, but this news shook him. From everything he had read—including reports of disasters— the landing was the most challenging part of the flight. It would have been difficult enough to land the balloon without the grapnel. But with no means of letting out the gas and bringing the balloon down, it was utterly impossible.

13

"A few weeks ago I read a flourishing account in one of the motor journals written by a female novice, who triumphantly recorded how she had thoroughly mastered the first car she had attempted to drive in the short space of a single half-hour. I confess I entertained sentiments of the profoundest admiration for that lady, and looked enviously upon her as a phenomenon. But a word of caution may not be out of place, especially as such enthusiastic testimonials are apt to prove misleading in the extreme to less highly-endowed mortals. . . . Even when the novice has mastered the steering, and flatters herself she has attained to a wonderful pitch of perfection, she makes a great mistake. She does but stand at the outside portico of motoring knowledge."

—MRS. EDWARD KENNARD
"Motor Driving For Ladies," 1902

ON THE EAST terrace, Kate shaded her eyes, following the balloon as it flew up and up, its gondola dangling under it like a fragile bauble suspended from a chain, and in the gondola the man she loved with all her heart.

"Goodbye, Charles, goodbye," she cried, waving.

Beside her, Patsy Marsden was still taking photographs. "Oh, how I wish we could have gone with them," she sighed. "Think of all they shall see from that height! Imagine the photographs I should get!" She frowned. "But what was all that shouting at the last moment?"

"I don't know," Kate said, turning toward the site of the launch. "I couldn't make out what was going on. It had something to do with that angry group of men who invaded the Park just as—"

"Lady Kathryn! Lady Kathryn!"

Kate turned to see the journalist from *Autocar* running toward her, his coat flapping open, his black eyes popping with excitement. "The balloon," he gasped, as he reached her and skidded to a stop. "The balloon! It went up without its—" He was suddenly seized by a fit of wild coughing. "Without, I mean to say, the device that—" He bent over, red-faced, coughing so hard he could not speak.

Patsy's hand went to her mouth. "Oh, dear," she whispered. "Whatever they've left behind, I hope it's not awf'ly serious. But p'rhaps," she added, seeing Kate's face, "it was only the sandwiches."

Kate did not wait for Sam Holt to recover. Suddenly apprehensive, she picked up her skirts, and forgetting her dignity, ran down the terrace steps, and pushed her way through the crowd of marchers, who seemed to have lost something of their angry energy and were milling about without direction, leaderless.

"Bradford!" she shouted, over the din. "Bradford, where are you?"

"Here, Kate!"

She turned. Bradford and the vicar, grim-faced, were standing at the launch site. With them was Squire Thornton and a thickset man with heavy shoulders, a beetling brow, and stubby red whiskers.

"What's happened?" Kate gasped. "That journalist—he said Charles forgot something."

"It wasn't forgotten," Bradford said angrily, brandishing what looked like a bundle of large iron fishing hooks welded together. "It was snatched from its place and dropped on the ground. By *this* man! Tom Whipple!" And he shoved the grapnel into the red-bearded man's stout stomach. The man doubled over with a loud "Whoomph!" and fell to his knees, grunting, Kate thought, like a stuck pig.

"Lord Bradford," the vicar cried, horrified, seizing his arm and wrestling the hook from him. "Violence will not do. It will not do at all!"

"But his was a violent act!" Bradford exclaimed furiously, pulling away from the vicar. "He has *killed* two men. Without that grapnel, the balloon—" His eyes went to Kate, and he stopped, biting his lip.

Kate forced herself to speak calmly. "Without it, what?"

The vicar affected a smile. "Without it, the descent will be a bit more difficult, my dear," he murmured, in a soothing voice. "But there is nothing to worry about, I assure you. Mr. Rolls is an experienced balloon pilot. He can certainly manage—"

Thornton exploded into a laugh. "Experienced? Why, that young idiot is no more a pilot than I am. He's been up a time or two as a passenger, but as far as piloting a balloon, he has no experience at all." He bent over. "Up, Whipple. Get up, man."

"I didn't do't," Whipple said thickly. He struggled to his knees, clutching his stomach. "I didn't pull that grapnel down. 'Twas someone else!"

"Don't worry," the squire said. "It'll be made right."

Kate only half-heard this exchange, for she had grown icy cold. No pilot? Charles was thousands of feet in the air with a boy who lacked the necessary competence to bring them both down safely?

124

"Rolls has no experience?" the vicar asked, wide-eyed. "On what do you base that assertion, Squire Thornton? Is this hearsay, or—"

Thornton snorted as he pulled Whipple to his feet and supported him with an arm. "It did not require a Sherlock Holmes to investigate young Rolls's background, Vicar. He is a great conniver, but not particularly clever at covering his tracks."

"And you, Roger," Bradford interjected coldly, "were especially moved to uncover them, I suppose. With my sister in mind, eh? I seem to recall that Patsy has preferred Rolls to you of late."

"Indeed, I have had Miss Marsden's welfare at heart in all I have done," Thornton replied stiffly. "But perhaps you would care to tell Lady Kathryn how much *you* knew about Rolls's ballooning experience, and whether you shared that knowledge with Sir Charles."

By this time, there was a considerable crowd gathered around. The lawn was crowded with spectators, and Kate saw Constable Laken elbowing his way through the throng.

The vicar fixed his pale eyes on Bradford. "Is it true that Rolls has no experience, Lord Bradford? And if it is, did you inform Sir Charles about the risk?"

Bradford shifted his feet uncomfortably, avoiding both Kate's and the vicar's eyes. "Well, y'see . . . that is, I—" He coughed. "It was to be a short flight, d'y'know. We did not expect to encounter difficulties." He glared at Whipple. "Or sabotage."

"I di'n't," Whipple whimpered, wiping his nose on his sleeve. "Whoev'r did it, 'twan't me."

"Who can say it was sabotage?" Thornton asked. "Perhaps the grapnel was but carelessly attached."

"Nevertheless," the vicar said, "it would be better— and safer—for the constable to take the man into custody, while we discuss what to do about the—" His eyes went to Kate.

"I want to know," Kate said firmly, "exactly how difficult it will be for Sir Charles and Mr. Rolls to land their balloon without the equipment that has been left behind."

Thornton gave a strangled laugh. "How difficult? In the absence of an experienced pilot, and without that grappling iron to bring themselves down safely, the balloonists are lost."

Kate's stomach was churning and her knees felt rubbery. But she only lifted her chin and gave the three men her most charming, most confident smile.

"Lost, are they?" she inquired in a pleasant tone. "Well, then, gentlemen, I suppose I shall have to go and find them." And with that, she turned on her heel and walked swiftly away.

Kate had driven a motorcar—Bradford's Daimler—only twice before, with Charles at her elbow, instructing her. If she had paused for a moment to reflect on what she was doing, she would not have imagined doing it herself.

But she did not pause, nor did she reflect. Having learned that Charles was in danger, her first and only thought was to go to him—and the quickest means to that end was a motorcar. Unfortunately, the four racing machines had already disappeared down the lane, or Kate might have commandeered one of them, and the driver. Mr. Rolls's Peugeot stood idling nearby, however, its motor having been started as a demonstration. The car was polished within an inch of its life, its wire-spoke wheels and black leather seat gleaming, and the three and three-quarters horsepower engine chugged smoothly, with only an occasional hiccup.

"Pardon me," Kate said, pushing aside the shirt-sleeved man who was extolling the motorcar's virtues to a crowd of marveling spectators. "Mr. Rolls is in need of his motorcar."

The man was horrified. "But this machine is the most powerful in England! It is far too dangerous for you to operate. With all due respect, ma'am, you cannot be allowed to—that is to say, I cannot permit—"

"Step aside, sir," Kate said firmly. Disregarding the man's sputtered protests and the amazed gasps of the crowd, she settled herself on the tufted leather seat, seized the tiller, adjusted the air mixture, and began to ease out the throttle, just as Charles had showed her. She paused, however, when a breathless Patsy Marsden, holding her hat and reticule in one hand and her camera in the other, darted out of the crowd and tumbled onto the seat beside her. She was pursued by an ardent Sam Holt.

"Lady Kathryn!" he cried. "Where are you going?"

"After my husband," she said, adjusting the throttle.

"You shan't have all the fun for yourself, Kate!" Patsy cried. "I'm coming with you."

"But this car *cannot* be operated by a female!" cried the shirt-sleeved man, attempting to lay hold of the tiller. "You will be killed!"

Sam Holt was dancing up and down. "What a story!" he cried. "Beautiful Ladies Commandeer Automobile for Death-Defying Chase!"

"You're sure, Patsy?" Kate asked. "They're right, you know. It is dangerous. I have driven only twice before."

"Dangerous, pooh!" Patsy scoffed. "I'm sure you can do it."

"Very well, then," Kate said, "but you will have to push, if we come to a hill we cannot run up."

Patsy's mouth was determined. "Of course I shall, if I must."

"Then we must be off without delay." Kate engaged the low gear, raising her voice over the earsplitting noise of the motor. "Hold onto your hat, Patsy! Here we go!"

And with that, they rattled at a great speed down the lane, the astonished spectators jumping out of their way, cheering and waving farewell.

Had that motorcar journey been featured in one of Beryl Bardwell's novels, the skeptical reader might have accused the author of painting it in a more desperate light than was really the case. But it was, quite simply, the most harrowing journey of Kate's life. Although she was almost sick with fear for Charles, aloft in a balloon, whipped heaven knew where by the scudding winds, the motorcar so fully occupied her brain and her hands that she hardly had time to think about his desperate plight. Later, when she recalled all that happened, she felt that it was impossible that she and Patsy should have survived.

It was all that she could do to steer the Peugeot and manage the knobs that controlled the car's speed. The brakes—large wooden blocks that rubbed on the tires—were operated with both hand and foot levers, which had to be applied judiciously during the downhill runs. But even with the brakes full on, Kate did not feel as if she had the necessary control over the machine, which accelerated fearsomely as it ran downslope. To make matters worse, the lane was so narrow that had she come upon another vehicle she must necessarily have driven into the ditch, and so full of corkscrew twists that she became dizzy and disoriented, scarcely knowing which way to push the tiller.

The worst moment came near the village of Wix, where they saw a horse-drawn cart approaching. The road was wide enough to pass, but the horse, panicked by the loud, foul-smelling motorcar, bolted across the Peugeot's path, tipping the cart and spilling out two portly passengers— one of whom, Kate saw out of the corner of her eye, was a uniformed constable. Patsy screamed.

With an adroitness born of terror, Kate pushed the tiller hard over and steered across a ditch, dodging between a tree and a stone fence and back onto the road again, bouncing from one side to the other so violently that she feared the Peugeot would roll over. As they careened back into the road, Kate glanced behind her to see the stout constable jumping up and down, waving his hat and shouting, "Halt, in the name of the Crown! Halt!"

"What did he say?" Patsy cried, over the noise of the engine.

"He said, 'Hurry, you'll be late,'" Kate replied, and urged the car forward.

The journey was finally over. As Kate chugged into Great Oakley, where she knew Lawrence Quibbley and her footman Pocket were to have been stationed, she encountered a wizened old man who gaped at the motorcar and its driver in toothless wonderment, then replied, in answer to her query, that Mr. Quibbley and his helper had been and gone.

"It cum down, y'see," he said, in a flat, nasal twang. "They went t'git it."

"The balloon came down?" Patsy cried. The wind had plucked the silk flowers from her hat and she had finally put it on the floor, holding it firmly with one foot and abandoning her coiffure to the elements.

"Aye, the balloon," the old man said. "They went to fetch it. Wot's left o'it," he added knowingly.

Kate's heart seemed almost to stop. Had the balloon crashed?

"Where is it?" Patsy asked. "Tell us where!"

The old man blinked. "Not shure I kin recall jes' wheer," he said.

Patsy reached into her reticule and drew out a coin. "Where?" she demanded.

The old man snatched the coin and bit it. "In Farmer Styles's pasture," he said. "But there ain't no need to drive like the devil's at yer back. They two be deed, along o' Farmer Styles's old brown cow, Bessie. That's wot comes o' flyin'."

"Dead?" Kate gasped.

"Dead?" Patsy echoed weakly.

"Aye, deed." The old man's smile was cheerful, his nod vigorous. "Deed'r'n doornails."

But Charles was not dead, and neither was Farmer Styles's cow, although it had been a very near thing.

He and Rolls had struggled for several minutes with the ripcord, finally freeing the vent valve with a frantic jerk. But this only magnified their peril, for the valve opened partially and refused to be closed, allowing gas to escape with a loud, long *whoosh,* like the roar of a blast furnace. The balloon was suddenly propelled into a pitching descent, the gondola whipping wildly, the balloonists braced and holding on for their lives.

When they reached an altitude that Charles guessed to be about eight hundred feet, they dropped the heavy hempen trailing rope over the side. As the rope's weight was supported by the ground, it acted as discarded ballast, slowing their precipitous fall and bringing their descent at least partially under control. Then Charles, having tied the rope-ends to the gondola, dropped his fettered sandbags. He hoped that they would serve the same function as the missing grappling iron and snag something sturdy enough to anchor the balloon.

What the sandbags first snagged, as Charles discovered later, was Farmer Styles's wood-railed fence, smashing it to splinters. Then they caught in the crotch of an apple tree, serving their purpose with such a stunning efficiency that the gondola was suddenly and fiercely jerked half round and flung to the ground, striking with a violent thump that rattled every tooth in Charles's head. The balloon pitched onto its side, the half-filled bag rolling and heaving like a gigantic whale stranded in a shallow bay.

The envelope fetched violently up against a thorny hedgerow and ruptured. The gondola upended, tumbling Charles and Rolls onto the ground under the nose of a startled brown cow. She, as bewildered as the dazed and unnerved aeronauts, broke into a bawling gallop, full-tilt in the direction of Farmer Styles's barn.

Some moments later, Farmer Styles himself appeared, as astonished as his brown cow at the sight of the bright silk bag draped over his hedge—but not so amazed that he could not immediately demand recompense for his ruined fence and his lame cow. With the farmer was his boy, whom Charles (having somewhat regained his composure) dispatched to Great Oakley with a message for Lawrence Quibbley and his helper, Pocket. Then Charles and Rolls and Farmer Styles, muttering that his fence had been erected just three short years before and did not deserve to be ruined by furriners, began to remove the mesh and coil the lines.

Shortly, Lawrence and Pocket appeared with the wagon, Lawrence looking vastly relieved to see Charles on his feet. "We 'eard you was dead, Sir Charles!" he cried. "The village 'as it that you was killed!"

"Almost dead, Lawrence," Charles said, feeling quite cheerful, now that they were safely on the ground. "As you can see, however, we have escaped."

131

"And a good thing 'tis, sir!" Lawrence replied emphatically. They set about examining the damage that had been done to the balloon, discussing its repair, and folding it. The work went swiftly, and within an hour from the time it had descended so unceremoniously, the balloon and its gondola were loaded on the wagon, ready for return to Bishop's Keep. By prior agreement, however, they were to wait for the arrival of the motorcars—an event which Charles, at least, now believed would never happen.

He was, however, in the wrong. Charles had just paid Farmer Styles what he demanded and was bidding him goodbye when he heard the chugging snort of a motorcar rattling down the lane toward them at a high rate of speed.

"Sounds like a motorcar," Pocket cried. " 'Ear that, Lawrence? Don't it sound like a motorcar?"

"Caw!" Farmer Styles exclaimed, his mouth dropping open. "More furriners!" And he ran toward the road, waving and shouting, "Mind the fence! Mind the fence, now!"

"By Jove, it's the winner of the chase, arrived at last!" Rolls shouted. "Quick, Sir Charles, get your camera. We must have a photograph!" He ran after Farmer Styles.

Lawrence Quibbley glanced toward the road. "Wonder which 'un 'tis."

"Is there any doubt?" Charles remarked dryly, taking his camera out of the canvas bag. "I should have thought that Albrecht was the only possible contender. Dunstable will be quite pleased at the success of his improbable scheme."

But it was not Albrecht who drove onto the muddy field. To Charles's astonishment, it was a disheveled and windblown Kate at the wheel of Charlie Rolls's Peugeot, her yellow dress covered with dust and dirt, her nose and cheeks as red as berries. She was accompanied by an equally windblown and dirty Patsy Marsden, waving the ruin of what had once been a fashionable hat.

The machine skidded to a stop. "Charles!" Kate cried, jumping out and running toward him, her russet hair loose, her petticoats flying. "You're alive! Oh, my love, you're alive!"

"Kate?" Charles whispered, incredulous, as she flung herself into his arms.

"The winner!" shouted Lawrence gleefully, and threw his hat in the air.

14

"'And did none of the four return, not one?'

'Not as expected, certainly. The whole affair was a monstrous great mystery and caused everyone a deal of grief, for it was feared that they were all four lost or dead'

'And were any . . . dead?'"

—BERYL BARDWELL
Missing Pearl

HAD LADY HENRIETTA Marsden been a spectator when the winning motorcar arrived triumphantly in Farmer Styles's field, she would no doubt have been appalled at the sight of her youngest daughter clasped in the fervent embrace of the third (and unpropertied) son of Lord Llangattock. But Lady Henrietta and Lord Christopher were still safely in France (or at least it was supposed that they were), and Miss Marsden and the Honorable Charles Rolls were almost as unrestrainedly enthusiastic in their greetings as were Lady Kathryn and her husband. And why not? Miss Marsden loved Mr. Rolls, or so she told herself, and Mr. Rolls loved Miss Marsden, or so he told her. And in any event, each was very glad to see the other alive, for they had entertained their private doubts over the past several hours whether that might not be the case.

The party remained in Farmer Styles's field for another hour, exchanging tales of their twin journeys, passing the time while they waited—in vain, as it transpired—for the first contestant to arrive. During the interval, Patsy photographed the collapsed balloon and the intrepid balloonists, while Kate related the story of Tom Whipple's sabotage of the balloon.

"So *that's* how it happened!" Charles exclaimed.

"I'm glad I was not to blame," Rolls muttered. "I feared I had been careless when I tied the thing to the side of the gondola." His face grew grim. "The question is, what's to be done with the wretched man? He could have killed us!"

"The constable has Whipple in custody at the moment," Patsy said.

"But is there any evidence against him?" Charles asked. "An eyewitness to the act? If not, he cannot be held for long."

Kate frowned. "No one stepped forward. And Whipple, of course, denied the accusation."

Charles shrugged. "Well, we shall see," he said. "I shall speak to Ned when we return."

When there was still no sign of the contestants and their motorcars by one o'clock, Kate, thinking of her dinner guests and mindful of the situation in the kitchen at home, suggested that she and Patsy go back to Bishop's Keep.

"I'm not anxious to drive Mr. Rolls's motorcar, though," she confessed, thinking that it was just as miraculous that she and Patsy had reached the balloon in one piece as it was that Charles and Mr. Rolls had gotten to the ground safely.

"I suppose we should return, too," Rolls said nervously. "I am concerned about Dunstable." He glanced at Kate. "He did not put in an appearance?"

"I did not see him," Kate said.

So Lawrence and Pocket were instructed to remain until teatime and to telegraph if the other drivers put in an appearance. With Rolls at the wheel and Charles beside him, Kate and Patsy in the rear-facing seat behind, the Peugeot started back to Bishop's Keep, through Wix and Bradfield, to Mistley and thence to Manningtree, Dedham, and home. To Kate, the return, although dirty, noisy, and wearisome, was a considerable degree safer than her own outward-bound journey, and much more agreeable, because Charles was safe and within arm's reach. There remained still a mystery to be solved, though—four mysteries, as it were.

"I still cannot understand," Rolls fretted, "how all *four* of the motorcars should have failed to arrive. Even if they had met trouble or had a breakdown, I should think we would have encountered at least one of them by now."

"They must have taken different ways," Patsy said.

"And wasn't it the point of the chase that each driver should choose his own course?" Kate asked. "The one that would get him to the balloon the fastest?"

"But *you* chose the fastest course," Rolls replied reasonably. "Where the devil are the others?"

The first mystery was solved a little later, on the outskirts of Mistley, where they encountered a disgruntled Arnold Bateman. His Bateman Electric was being towed by a nervous horse while he plodded wearily alongside, his head bowed, his clothing thick with dust. The horse reared and snorted, and Bateman and the animal's owner had to hold it while Rolls eased the Peugeot past. He stopped on the verge, and they all walked back, Patsy carrying her camera.

Bateman did not smile when they greeted him. "Who won?" he grunted.

"The ladies," Rolls said with a rueful laugh, and gestured at Kate. "They commandeered my Peugeot."

Bateman stared uncomprehendingly at Kate. "*You?*"

Kate nodded.

"It must be ruled an unofficial victory, however," Rolls said quickly. "They were not registered as contestants."

"Oh, *come* now," Patsy said in a reproving tone, stepping back to take a photograph.

Bateman's expression had lost some of its grimness and he almost smiled. "Well, at least Dunstable and that deuced German didn't get there first." He looked at Charles. "Speaking of Dunstable, has anyone discovered what happened to the man?"

"I don't know," Charles said, "but I expect we shall hear about it when he turns up."

"*If* he turns up," Bateman said. Kate wondered at his chuckle, which held no mirth.

Rolls cleared his throat. "Oh, I'm sure he will join us for dinner," he said uneasily.

Kate glanced from Bateman to Rolls, wondering whether they knew something of the promoter's disappearance, but she could tell nothing from their faces. "You will be there, I hope, Mr. Bateman," she said.

"I hope so, too," Bateman said. He and the tow horse exchanged malignant glances, and the horse flicked its tail contemptuously. "But I cannot promise."

It was three o'clock by Charles's pocket watch when the Peugeot arrived at Bishop's Keep, where the Harvest Fete was still joyfully underway. The roundabout was turning merrily, the tea-tent was overflowing with thirsty fairgoers, and the motorcars on exhibit were still surrounded by well-dressed gentlemen with their hands in their pockets, putting their heads to one side and the other, pretending to decide on a purchase. The leg-o'-mutton climb was over, and in the temporary pavilion, the band was striking up for the dance, which was always held early so that families with small children could make their way home before dark.

Rolls and Patsy deposited their passengers and drove on to Marsden Manor, Rolls promising to return shortly, Patsy agreeing to come, with Aunt Penelope, for dinner. Charles would have followed Kate upstairs to change out of his muddy clothing, but he was accosted by Sam Holt as he crossed the terrace.

"Sir Charles!" Holt cried excitedly. "Glad to see you back, sir, safe an' sound. Wot car won the chase?" He pulled out a notebook and pencil. "Urgent business o' the press calls me back to London," he added importantly, "but I can't leave without knowin" ow it turned out."

"The Peugeot won," Charles said, looking around. "Have you seen Lord Bradford?"

"The Peugeot!" Holt exclaimed. "You mean, the ladies—"

"Yes," Charles said. "The ladies, indeed. Ah, Bradford!" he said, as he saw his friend hurrying up the broad terrace steps.

"You're safe!" Bradford exclaimed with unmistakable relief. "And Rolls?"

"Safe, too. And the balloon is not too much damaged. It was a near thing, though."

Bradford clapped him on the back. "Well, man, who won the chase? Was it Albrecht?"

"Kate and your sister," Charles said, and laughed at his friend's surprise and evident chagrin. He had spoken proudly, for he was impressed with Kate's mechanical ability, and with her courage, as well. Not many men would have made the attempt to motor such a distance in an unfamiliar machine.

But the news did not please Bradford. "What of the other cars?"

"Bateman's Electric lost power the other side of Mistley and is being towed back. The others—" Charles shrugged. "Who knows?"

"*Three* motorcars are missing?" Holt asked. He pulled out his watch and scowled at it "Confound it all. If I don't leave right now, I'll miss the last up-train."

"Be on your way, then," Bradford said crossly. "I'll telegraph you the results as soon as we have them."

Holt shrugged. "It's been a fool's herrand," he said gloomily. "If I go back, at least I'll get a decent meal."

As the man scurried off, Bradford sighed. "This whole thing *has* been a fool's errand," he said. His face darkened. "I suppose Kate told you about Whipple and his mischief?"

"Yes. I am not sure what can be done about it, though," Charles replied. "No one actually saw the man pull the grapnel down?"

"No one has yet come forward. There was quite a melee, and a great deal of confusion. The constable took Whipple into custody, however. His action calmed them down, and after a while, the crowd dispersed." He looked out over the fete grounds with a worried expression. "I am not sure it was wise, however. I have seen small groups of men with their heads together, muttering. They resent one of their number being held, I am sure."

"I am sure they do," Charles agreed soberly. "And even with a witness, I doubt it could be proved that the man acted with malicious intent. The sabotage might have been an impulse of the moment, and instantly regretted— or it might even have come about by accident. I doubt if Rolls could swear that he properly fastened the line. Since no lasting harm was done, perhaps it would be best to release Whipple."

"I suppose you're right," Bradford muttered, "although you might have a talk with him, to see if he was put up to it. Or ask the constable to—"

Charles raised his head and caught sight of Edward Laken, walking across the gravel apron toward them. "Speak of the devil—hullo, Ned."

"Ah, you've returned!" the constable exclaimed warmly. "And no worse for the experience, from the look of you."

"It was a near thing, though," Charles said. "Without the grapnel, and in the absence of an experienced pilot—" He glanced at Bradford.

Bradford colored. "Sorry, old man," he muttered. "Dunstable said . . . I mean, I certainly did not intend that any harm should come . . ." He faltered.

"You must tell me about it," Charles said, "later." Turning back to the constable, he asked, "Whipple is in your custody?"

"He was." Laken gave him an apologetic look. "I'm sorry I wasn't here to quell this morning's riot, Charles. One of the children fell from the roundabout, and her father and I had to carry her to Dr. Bassett's surgery. The trouble happened while I was gone. I fear that I did not do my duty."

"Nothing of the sort, Ned," Charles said. "I hope the child was not badly hurt."

"No, not badly. As to the Whipple matter, after interviewing the man, I concluded that since there was no witness to his action, he could not be charged with anything more serious than disorderly conduct. Squire Thornton arrived about that time to stand his bail. I explained as much to the squire, and we agreed that we are not likely to get to the bottom of the grapnel business. But that is not the news I came to bring you." He turned to Bradford with the formality he always used in his address to the man, even though they, too, had known one another as boys. "I am sorry to say, Lord Bradford, that one of your motorcar drivers has landed himself in jail."

"Ah," Charles said, raising an eyebrow. "So the second mystery is solved. That leaves only two others."

"I don't know about that," Laken replied. "But I received a telegram from P.C. Bradley of Manningtree some few moments ago." A smile glimmered across his mouth. "He is holding a Mr. Frank Ponsonby, who was apprehended driving his Benz with reckless abandon. His speed was above the new limit of twelve miles an hour—which unfortunately puts it much above the limit in effect until November."

"Ponsonby!" Bradford exclaimed. "He was warned to drive slowly through the villages." He paused. "But why is the man in jail? Why didn't he simply pay his fine and get on with the chase?"

Edward's smile was ironic. "I doubt it was Ponsonby's speed that led to his incarceration. More likely, it was his language—unbefitting a gentleman, according to Bradley, and showing extreme disrespect for Her Majesty's Constabulary. This, after Ponsonby failed to stop for a flock of geese at the foot of the High Street. It seems there were a few feathers ruffled," he added with dry humor. "And some damage to the motorcar."

Charles chuckled, imagining Frank Ponsonby frustrated by a snowstorm of goosedown. "What's to be done?"

"An apology would go a long way toward smoothing things." Edward looked at Bradford. "Perhaps you should drive to Manningtree, Lord Bradford. I would be glad to go with you."

"Not in my Daimler, unfortunately," Bradford said sourly. "Albrecht hasn't turned up with it yet. We'll have to take the gig."

"One motorcar is probably enough for P.C. Bradley in one day, in any event," Laken said. "The Daimler hasn't finished yet? I thought Albrecht was expected to win."

"None of the contestants has finished," Charles said, and told him, not without pride, of Kate's triumph.

"Ah," Laken said, and smiled. "Now that the lady has learned to drive, you shall have to buy her a motorcar."

"Oh, dear heaven," Charles exclaimed. "There's no stopping her already. What would she be like if she had several horsepower at her command?"

Laken laughed, then asked, more soberly, "What of the other motorcars?"

"Bateman's Electric is on its way here behind a horse," Charles replied, "and now that we've located Ponsonby's Benz, we are missing only the Daimler and the Serpollet Steamer."

"And Harry Dunstable," Bradford remarked.

Charles stared at him. "He *still* has not put in an appearance?" Where the devil *was* the man?

Bradford shook his head. "Dunstable is a man of many parts, and not all of them are savory, but he has never played a trick of this sort. I am beginning to think that something has happened to him."

The idea had occurred to Charles, as well.

Kate had planned that night's dinner party for eight o'clock, with the guests expected at seven. It was to be a triumphant affair (seven courses, with three Georgian silver candelabra, flowers from the hothouse, and the best china), during which the intrepid aeronauts, the victorious motorcar drivers, and the organizers of the exhibition were to be toasted in champagne. The situation had altered dramatically, however, on all fronts.

After changing out of her mud-stained dress, Kate went down to the kitchen in search of a cup of tea and a discussion with Cook about dinner. But the kitchen was filled with sulfurous fumes, and Mrs. Pratt, with streaming eyes and a red face, looked as if she herself were ready to explode. Kate braced herself against the blast.

"It's the gas cooker, yer ladyship, mum," Mrs. Pratt rasped hoarsely. " 'Twon't stay lit. Sputters an' burns yellow, 'stead o' blue." Coughing, she waved a towel in front of her face. "An' smells like the divil 'isself, beggin' yer ladyship's pardon."

"Well, shut the thing off, for heaven's sake," Kate exclaimed, suiting the action to the words. "And stop ladyship-ing me and open the doors and windows! The cooker can't be used until we've discovered what's wrong with it. I'll send for Sir Charles."

What was wrong with the gas cooker, apparently, was the gas itself. Appealed to by his anxious wife and hysterical cook, Sir Charles went out to the gas plant and discovered that, after the balloon had been launched, Thompson had stoked the retort from an old batch of soft coal, all that was left of the coal supply. It had proved to be unfit for gas generation.

"I fear," Charles said, when he had explained this to Kate and Mrs. Pratt, "that you will not be able to operate the gas cooker until we have obtained better coal."

"No gas? Then wot's to be done 'bout dinner?" Mrs. Pratt demanded angrily. "Wot's to be done, I ask ye? I kin work miracles, but even loaves an' fishes got to be baked."

"We shall have a cup of tea and a biscuit," Kate said firmly, "and discuss it." Ten minutes later, the kitchen aired, the tea brewed from a kettle on the open fire, and calm more or less restored, they sat over their tea and conferred upon the menu. It was to have included hors d'oeuvres (oysters, prawns, olives, and anchovies), a Consommé de Volaille, Sole Belgravia, Filet in Puff Pastry, Quail in Aspic, Artichoke Bottoms with French Beans, and Vegetable Croquettes, with a molded Bavarian pudding for dessert, and fruit, of course.

"None o'which," Mrs. Pratt said bitterly, "can be made up wi'out a good range." She cast a malevolent glance at the gas cooker. " 'Spesh'ly the puff pastry. That's an art, ye know, yer ladyship. Pastry don't jump into the pan ready-made."

"What about the old coal range?" Kate asked. "Could it be brought back in to replace the gas cooker? I know our coal is not what it should be, but—"

With a dramatic gesture, Mrs. Pratt clasped her hands on her bosom. "Git me old coal stove back agin?" she cried. "Oh, yer ladyship, 't'wud be the dearest wish o' me 'eart! Mayhap 'twill smoke some, but I know 'ow to fix that."

"Can it be done? I wonder," Kate mused.

It could, and it was. The task required several strong men and much grunting and heaving, but in a half-hour the new cooker was gone and the old coal range was restored to its former place, and was already under attack by Harriet and the blacking brush, Mrs. Pratt was bustling around with energy and purpose, and dinner looked as if it might indeed be forthcoming.

"At what time may we expect the first course, do you think?" Kate asked anxiously.

Mrs. Pratt's confidence restored, she glanced at the clock. "Ten, mayhap," she said imperiously. "Considerin' 'ow much there is t'do. The Filet in Puff Pastry, an' all, I mean."

"Then perhaps you can substitute something simpler for the filet," Kate said. "Today has been disastrous for everyone. If dinner is delayed until ten, our guests will either be asleep or in their cups, or both." She stood up, stretching wearily. "I must confer with Mudd about something I want him to do. Then I shall be in my room if I'm wanted."

Mrs. Pratt shifted uncomfortably. "I wonder," she said, "if I cud 'ave a word wi' yer ladyship about—"

Kate sighed. "There is something else to be decided about dinner?"

"No, mum. It 'as to do wi' this mornin', an' the balloon. I was there, do y'see, wi' Bess, watchin' the balloon go up." Her voice grew dark. "I was there, an' I saw Squire Thornton—"

Cook showed signs of rambling, and Kate was very tired. She shook her head decidedly. "Since this does not concern dinner, Mrs. Pratt, let us delay it until later. I have had a long drive today, and I am *very* tired."

Mrs. Pratt mumbled something in a dissatisfied tone, but Kate was determined. After some searching, she found Mudd in the pantry, inspecting the crystal for the dinner that night.

"Ah, Mudd," she said. "I wonder if you would be so good as to help me with a bit of sleuthing."

Mudd looked up quickly. "Sleuthing, mum?"

Kate smiled. She had counted on Mudd once before, to help her in apprehending the villain who had poisoned her two aunts. His assistance had proved invaluable. Now, she needed to use him again—this time, though, in the pursuit of a fictional criminal. Beryl Bardwell's latest fantastical plot demanded that the villain be identified through fingerprints he had left on a crystal goblet, and Kate wanted to see what practical problems would be encountered in performing this procedure.

Fingerprints were a very new tool in the scientific investigation of crime, and as yet almost entirely untested. Mark Twain, of course, had used the idea in an 1883 book called *Life on the Mississippi*, where a bloody thumbprint held the key to the identity of a killer, and again in 1894, in *Pudd'nhead Wilson*. In the same year, Francis Galton had published a book called *Fingerprints*, a copy of which Charles had in his library. It laid out Galton's system for identifying the four basic types of fingerprints and proposed that the police adopt the practice of fingerprinting everyone they questioned. The conservative police did not seem anxious to do this, but that made the process even more useful to Beryl, whose female detective would use it to steal a march on the police.

Kate spent a few minutes showing Mudd what she needed him to do—a very simple thing, really—and then started upstairs, hoping to have some time to herself before she had to face what promised to be a trying evening. As she went up the stairs, however, she was distracted by a loud cheering in the Park, where the dance was coming to its scheduled close in the pavilion. She went to the hallway window and saw a team of Belgian draft horses lumbering heavily up the gravel lane, dragging the Serpollet Steamer behind them, to the delight of the onlookers who had deserted their dancing to cheer the horses. At the tiller of the disabled motorcar, wearing a look of injured dignity, sat Arthur Dickson.

The third motorcar had been found.

15

"'How's old Toad going on?'

"'Oh, from bad to worse,' said the Rat gravely. 'Another smash-up early last week.'

"'How many has he had?' inquired the Badger gloomily.

"'Smashes, or machines?' asked the Rat. 'Ok, well, after all, it's the same thing, with Toad.'"

—Kenneth Grahame
The Wind in the Willows

PATSY AND MISS Penelope Marsden arrived for dinner in the Marsden coach, Patsy demure and lovely in turquoise silk, stout Great-aunt Marsden in fussy olive-green with rows of ruffles around the neck and shoulders.

"So good of you to invite us, my dear Lady Kathryn," Penelope Marsden wheezed, and seated herself with a thump on the sofa, taking up quite a bit of it. She glanced through her spectacles around the room. "And where is that lovely boy this evening? He will be here, won't he? He has absented himself from our evenings at Marsden Manor a good deal lately."

"If you mean Mr. Rolls," Kate said, as Patsy suppressed a smile, "he is with Sir Charles in the library. We are expecting a number of other gentlemen. We three are the only ladies."

The elder Miss Marsden positively beamed, and Kate thought to herself that Lady Henrietta, if she had wanted to keep Patsy safe from the attentions of male admirers, would have done better to have locked her up than to leave her in the care of a shortsighted and spinsterish great-aunt. Kate wondered whether the lady, with her ample bosom, pudgy cheeks, and girlish giggle, had ever had any suitors of her own.

A few moments later, the gentlemen came in to pay their respects, Mudd appeared with the sherry decanter, and even though they were shy several guests, the festivities were begun. The motorcar drivers, however handsome they might be in their evening dress, were a surly, argumentative lot who downed their drink rather too rapidly for any hostess's comfort. Within five minutes Kate had no doubt that the evening would end in disaster, although at that moment, she would have predicted a social fiasco, perhaps augmented by a culinary catastrophe. Neither she nor Charles, nor anyone else of the party, for that matter, could have foreseen exactly what was to come about—although one or two might have guessed.

Frank Ponsonby, newly released from the Manningtree jail through the intercession of Lord Bradford and Constable Laken, wore the same sulky, thwarted look he must have worn during his fateful encounter with the geese. (The Benz had not fared quite as well as Ponsonby, and remained in Manningtree, awaiting repair.) Arthur Dickson, his cravat askew, drank off two sherries quickly and began on a third, obviously trying to erase from his mind the ignominy of being towed back to Bishop's Keep behind a team of horses, the Serpollet having run off the road at Weeley Heath and ruptured its low-hanging condenser on a stump. Arnold Bateman arrived already strongly fortified with liquor. He balanced himself on his toes before the fireplace, rising up and down like a bantam rooster preparing to crow.

"What I want to know," he said, pronouncing each word with elaborate care, "is what has become . . ." He hiccuped. "What has become of our dear friend Harry Dunstable." He made a sound that sounded to Kate like a chortle. "Serve him right if something happened to him, wouldn't you say?"

"Bateman," said Ponsonby, "mind your tongue."

"He drank enough last night to float the Navy," Dickson remarked acidly, "and when our supper party broke off, he ordered another bottle of wine to take off to bed with him. Did anyone check his room at the inn? He's still there sleeping it off, I should think."

"That's odd," Bradford remarked thoughtfully. "I didn't notice that Dunstable drank more than the rest of us."

"Well, he did," Ponsonby growled. "Like the proverbial fish. You were at the other end of the table, Marsden. You probably didn't notice."

Dickson cleared his throat nervously. "It's Albrecht I'm worried about." He pulled his brows together. "The man should have returned by now. There have been no reports of trouble? He hasn't arrived at the landing site, or in that vicinity?"

Rolls shook his head. "If he had put in an appearance there by teatime, the men we left behind would have telegraphed." He turned. "Your telegraph operator *is* reliable, I take it, Sir Charles?"

Great-aunt Marsden answered for him. "Oh, quite reliable, Mr. Rolls, I assure you. We have excellent telegraph service here, you know, quite excellent." Kate smiled to herself, thinking of the punctilious Mr. Rushton, who would offer up his life if he missed so much as a syllable of a telegraph message.

Bateman, who was paying no attention to this exchange, gave a high-pitched giggle. "*You're* worried about Albrecht, Arthur? I don't believe that for a minute, old chap. You were the one who—" He gestured with his glass, spilling sherry on Ponsonby. "Oops," he said, and giggled again. "So clumsy of me, Ponsonby, old fellow."

"Damn it, Bateman," Ponsonby said crossly, dabbing at his sleeve. "Sit down and be quiet. We've had enough of your oafishness."

"You don't suppose they're going to go on like this all night, do you?" Patsy whispered to Kate.

"I certainly hope not," Kate said grimly. She was about to ring the bell for Mudd to inquire when dinner might be served when the door opened and Mudd himself stepped in.

"Ah, Mudd," Kate said with relief. "So dinner is ready at last?"

"Not quite yet, m'lady," Mudd said, "although Mrs. Pratt has sent word that the filet is makin' satisfactory progress. In the meantime—" He raised his voice and clicked his heels together. "Dr. Bassett and Mr. Dunstable."

"Ah," Charles said happily. "I was wondering what had kept the good doctor."

"And it's about time Dunstable showed up, I should say," Bradford growled.

Kate rose to greet the latest arrivals. But she was so startled at the sight of Harry Dunstable that she could think of nothing to say except "Oh, my." Around the room, she heard several gasps, and something like a squeal from Great-aunt Marsden.

Charles stepped forward. "Looks like you've met with a bit of an accident, Dunstable."

Got up in the blue serge jacket of the Motor Car Club, Harry Dunstable may have looked like a Swiss admiral when Kate was first introduced to him. Now, though, he had the color of a badly stored Swiss cheese, his face a mottled yellow, his temple bruised, his right eye blackened, his jaw swollen. The yellow and purple in his face vied with the yellow and green in his embroidered waistcoat, which was draped with a gold watch chain.

"Unfortunately, yes," Dunstable said thickly, speaking through nearly closed lips. "But the doctor says I have suffered no serious harm."

Dr. Bassett nodded. "I happened to be at the livery stable putting up my horse when Mr. Dunstable was . . . uncovered." Kate saw the ghost of a twinkle in his sharp eye. She liked the acerbic, quick-witted Dr. Bassett, who stopped in frequently to discuss the scientific interests that he and Charles shared. "He accompanied me back to my surgery," he added, "and I gave him a good looking-over. He is fit, except for the obvious damage."

"Uncovered?" Rolls asked, his jaw dropping in astonishment. "For God's sake, Dunstable, what has happened to you?"

Dunstable looked sheepish. "I went out for my usual walk last evening after dinner. Two men waylaid on me in the alley and coshed me." He put a hand to his temple.

"Coshed you!" Dickson exclaimed. " 'Pon my word, Dunstable, that's appalling!"

"Pity," Bateman added in a mocking tone.

"Jolly shame," Ponsonby remarked carelessly.

Kate turned. All three men wore looks of concern, but it did not seem to her that there was any genuine compassion in their eyes. On the contrary, she thought she detected a fleeting amusement at the idea that the self-styled "great man" had met such an ignominious fate. But Kate knew very well that Englishmen were accomplished at masking their feelings, and when she looked again, she saw nothing out of the ordinary.

151

"But where have you *been* since last night, Harry?" Bradford demanded harshly. "You were supposed to ride with Albrecht in the Daimler. He had to go off without you."

"Mr. Dunstable," the doctor said, "was discovered under a tarpaulin on the dung heap behind the livery stable. His hands and feet were tightly bound, his mouth gagged. He had been there throughout the night and the day."

"Trussed like a turkey." Dunstable shook his head. "Couldn't move, couldn't shout, could barely breathe for the stench. Begging your pardon, ma'am," he added, bowing in Kate's direction. "I fear this is a topic that's hardly fit for ladies' ears." He turned eagerly to Bradford. "Albrecht won the chase, I s'pose."

Ponsonby coughed. Dickson glowered. Bateman narrowed his eyes.

Bradford cleared his throat. "Er, ah," he said, "nobody won." He coughed. "That is, nobody finished the chase. Reached the balloon, I mean to say."

"That's not true, Bradford," Patsy said brightly. "*We* did. Lady Kathryn and I, that is," she added, turning to Dunstable with a rustle of silken skirts. "When it appeared that the balloon might sail out over the ocean and be lost, you see, we appropriated Mr. Rolls's Peugeot, and Lady Kathryn drove it to—"

"Lost!" Dunstable ejaculated. "But it was a borrowed balloon! The expense will be monstrous!"

"No, no, it wasn't really lost," Kate said. "The grappling iron was left behind and—"

"It was *not* left behind!" Rolls exclaimed hotly. "It was *stolen*! By someone who wished us to be forced to crash-land the balloon."

"Well, stolen, then," Kate said. "Miss Marsden and I feared that Sir Charles and Mr. Rolls might not be able to land safely."

"So we drove out and rescued them," Patsy said with pride. She lifted her chin. "As it turned out, we were the *only* ones to get to the landing site. We have the photographs to prove that we were there," she added. "Or at least, we will have them tomorrow, when I have developed and printed them."

Dunstable stared incomprehendingly. "None of the men completed the chase?"

"Not one," Bateman said, and sighed. "I lost power near Mistley. Dickson ran onto a stump and ripped open the condenser. Ponsonby—" He snickered. "Ponsonby drove into a flock of geese."

"I was detained in Manningtree by an overzealous P.C. who charged me with excessive speed," Ponsonby said with dignity. "The geese were superfluous."

"But what about Albrecht?" Dunstable demanded. He looked around angrily. "The man was supposed to *win*— that's why we arranged this blasted affair. Where the devil is he? Did he quit and go back to Germany? What has happened to the Daimler?"

Bradford gave a helpless shrug. "No one knows."

"Haven't heard a peep from the fellow," Ponsonby added. He frowned. "*Supposed* to win, was he?"

"I shouldn't worry about him," Bateman said cheerily. "If something happened, we should have received word by now. Unless—"

The door opened and Mudd appeared. "Ah, Mudd," Kate said. "Is dinner to be served at last?"

"Dinner is ready, madam," Mudd said. "But there is a boy at the door, 'E has brought a note, requesting the doctor's presence with regard to a professional matter." He held out a silver platter on which lay a slip of torn white paper.

"It is Mrs. Goettemoeller, I suppose," said the doctor with a sigh, reaching for the note. "She is about to deliver her seventh. Another girl, no doubt."

"Her seventh child," murmured Great-aunt Marsden in a shocked voice. She opened her eyes wide. "Fancy that!"

But as Dr. Bassett opened the note and read it, his face changed. "It's from Laken," he said to Charles. "I must go immediately. I am sorry to take you from your guests, but I think it would be a good plan for you to accompany me."

Charles had come to stand beside Kate. "What is it, Bassett?" he asked quietly. "What has happened?"

"Read it for yourself," the doctor said, and handed him the note. He glanced around. "You might as well read it to the others, too. They shall all want to know, I am sure."

Charles unfolded the paper. "'Come to your surgery at once and bring Sir Charles,'" he read aloud, as Kate read over his shoulder. "'There has been a motorcar accident. The driver is alive, but barely. I doubt he can survive long. The motorcar is demolished.'"

Kate pulled in an involuntary breath. Patsy gave a small, half-smothered shriek. The drivers sat for an instant in stunned, staring silence.

And then Dunstable started to his feet. "Albrecht?" he cried. "It is not Albrecht, is it? Tell me it isn't Albrecht!"

"Don't be a fool, Dunstable," Bateman said with immense scorn. "Are there any other motorcars but Marsden's Daimler unaccounted for in the district?"

Dr. Bassett was already at the door. "Forgive me, Lady Kathryn," he said with a quick bow. "We must be off," he added to Charles. "There is not a moment to lose."

"I will go with you," Bradford said, white-faced. "It is my vehicle."

"Yes, yes," Dunstable gabbled. "I must go too. He is my driver."

White-faced, Dickson put down his sherry. "We will all go," he said, sounding almost frightened, and there was a loud babble of agreement.

The doctor raised his voice. "Gentlemen," he said firmly, "my surgery will not accommodate the lot of you, and you can be of no possible assistance in this medical matter. Your hostess has prepared a fine meal. It would be cruelly impolite of you to abandon it."

Charles came to Kate. "You can manage, my dear?" he asked quietly. "Bradford can take my place as host."

"Of course we'll manage," Kate said, with more assurance than she felt, and watched them leave the room.

There was a long silence, broken at last by Great-aunt Marsden's loud exhalation. "Well!" she said. "I must say!"

But whatever she had to say, she did not say it. The silence lengthened. Kate knew that she should rise, take Bradford's arm, and announce that it was time to go to the table, but something—some deep curiosity, some inner conviction that there was something here to learn—held her in her seat, watching the faces in the room.

Dunstable sat, too, as if thunderstruck. "It is beyond belief," he muttered. "Utterly beyond belief. What the stockholders are going to say—" He bit his lip. "It is all very bad. Very bad, indeed."

"Oh, blast the stockholders!" Rolls burst out angrily, his dark eyes glittering. "Is that all you can think of, Dunstable? *We* came here for sport, to test one machine against the others. What did you come for? The publicity only?"

Dunstable looked at him. "Publicity? Yes, that is certainly an angle that should be considered," he said thoughtfully. "The event will attract plenty of press attention, I am sure.

The trick will be to handle it correctly." He looked around. "Has Sam Holt gone back to London? Where the devil is that journalist when I need him?"

"What bloody nonsense, Harry!" Bradford exclaimed, his voice heavy with disgust and revulsion. "The man you paid to come here from Germany to drive for you is dying—dead already, perhaps—and you talk of publicity!"

"And why should his accident be beyond belief?" Dickson asked, rising to reach for the sherry decanter. "It is not Albrecht's first crash, is it? Given the speeds at which we travel, motorcar-racing is a dangerous sport." Nervously, he splashed sherry into his glass, and onto his sleeve.

"Ah, yes," Ponsonby said, with melodramatic flair. "Death waits at every turn. Accidents can happen everywhere." He lifted his glass. "Gentlemen, let us drink to a fallen comrade-in-arms."

"Hear, hear," Bateman murmured, draining his glass. And Dickson added in a strangled voice, "Indeed."

There was a moment's silence. Dunstable raised his head. His eyes were narrowed, and the purplish bruise stood out against the mottled yellow of his face.

"It was no accident," he said melodramatically. He paused, and then repeated, in a harsh, rasping tone, "I'm sure of it. It was no accident! I shall take this to the law!"

Kate frowned. What did the man have in mind? Was he practicing some sort of sensational gesture that would attract public attention? Would he somehow exploit this unfortunate circumstance to sell more shares of worthless stock? Or did he genuinely believe that—

"I'm not sure I understand you, Mr. Dunstable," she said. "Surely you can't think Herr Albrecht would have deliberately endangered his life by crashing Lord

156

Marsden's motorcar." She glanced at Bradford, who seemed remarkably composed, under the circumstances.

"Of course I don't think he did it deliberately," Dunstable said. "It was murder." His voice rose. "It was *murder*, don't you see?" He was looking directly at Bradford.

Bradford colored. "Are you trying to claim that there was something wrong with my car, and that I—"

"Don't even bother to answer him, Bradford," Rolls snapped. "He is behaving like an offensive cad."

"Ah," Ponsonby remarked, his tone archly pleasant. "I fear there is dissension in the ranks of the British Motor Car Syndicate. My, my, gentlemen. Is this a wrangle?"

"The syndicate has nothing to do with this affair, Ponsonby," Rolls said in a dark tone.

"Oh, but it does," Bateman said, and laughed slyly. "You are such a naive boy, Charlie. The syndicate has *everything* to do with it. Why don't you ask your friend Dunstable if he staged Albrecht's crash himself, for the sake of the publicity? Don't forget—*he* was supposed to be in that car, too. If he knew that it was going to crash, is there any wonder he went missing?"

"That is a base canard," Dunstable said hotly. "I spent the entire day in a dung heap. I had nothing to do with—"

"And Albrecht was driving Marsden's car, don't forget," Ponsonby said in a meaningful aside to Bateman. "Could they have come up with this between the two of them?"

Patsy pulled in her breath and Great-aunt Marsden gasped in horror, fanning herself with her lace handkerchief. "Bradford, can this man—I cannot pay him the compliment of calling him a gentleman—be accusing you of . . . of . . . ?" She apparently could not think what Bradford might be accused of, and sputtered into a helpless silence.

Bradford got to his feet and spoke with a firm authority. "I do not believe we are showing ourselves to best advantage here, gentlemen. The evening is, after all, a social occasion. Lady Kathryn and the other ladies would be entirely justified in censuring our behavior."

Kate, too, had begun to feel that things were getting out of hand, although she was reluctant to conclude a conflict which offered such promising revelations. But perhaps the dinner hour would open some new view of the subject.

With a bright smile, she stood and turned toward Bradford. "I understand that our dinner is ready at last, my lord. Shall we dine?"

As they went into the dining room, Kate looked questioningly at Mudd, wondering whether he remembered her instructions about the crystal, and what was to be done with it after dinner. He inclined his head slightly, and she understood. Everything else in the household might run on at sixes and sevens, but Beryl Bardwell's little experiment was proceeding according to plan.

16

"Here's the devil to pay."
—SAMUEL RICHARDSON
Clarissa, 1785

WITHOUT SPEAKING, CHARLES followed Dr. Bassett through the lamp-lit consulting room and into the tiny surgery, more brightly illuminated by hissing gas wall sconces. Albrecht was stretched, gray-faced and motionless, on the examining table, his jacket and shirt pulled open. The room was already crowded: Edward Laken stood stonily at the foot of the table; beside him stood another, younger man, with a pale face and staring eyes and an air of suppressed excitement. A gray-haired, motherly woman with a cloth and a basin was washing Albrecht's bloodied chest. Charles looked once at the gaping wound, winced, and turned his face away. Just above the wound was a massive bruise. He had known it would be ugly, but not as ugly as this. From the look of it, the tiller had impacted the driver's chest and snapped. The shaft had pierced the rib cage.

"Hullo, Ned," the doctor said to Laken, hastily stripping off his coat. He glanced at the other man. "What the devil are *you* doing here, Jessup? Hot water, please, Hester," he said to the woman. "And my surgical instruments." He began to roll up his sleeves.

"Jessup discovered the victim," Laken said evenly, "in the ravine beneath Devil's Bridge."

"The wreckage did not burn?" Charles put in.

"No, surprisingly enough."

"And fortunate," the doctor said, looking down at the man on the table. "Looks like the tiller ran him through."

Laken nodded. "I was summoned, and the two of us brought Albrecht here. I thought Jessup might stay with me until I had the leisure to question him as to the circumstances of his discovery."

" 'Twas Lord Bradford's motor the man was drivin'!" Jessup seemed to be near bursting with an inward excitement. "Same as the one that—" he stopped and swallowed, and his eyes, bright with a kind of triumph, went rapidly from Laken to the doctor, and back to the man on the table.

"Same as the one that didn't kill your father?" Bassett laughed, a harsh, grating laugh. "The devil of a coincidence, wouldn't you say, Laken? The car rumored to have frightened Old Jessup to death is discovered wrecked by Young Jessup. One might almost think there was an invisible hand at work in the affair." He bent over and put his ear to Albrecht's chest and listened intently for a moment. "I doubt that there's anything to be done to save the man," he said, straightening. "But I must try."

As if in response, Albrecht gave a deep, despairing groan, and the doctor turned to put a hand on his shoulder. "Steady there, old chap," he said, in a comforting voice. "I'll be with you in a moment, and we'll see about easing your pain." He looked up. "Take Jessup out of here, will you, Ned? Charles, if you try, you might be able to get something out of our patient. Hester!" He started out of the room. "Hester!"

"How did it happen, Ned?" Charles asked.

"The road leading down to the bridge is steep and treacherous," Laken said. "The vehicle went off the road and into the ravine. I have instructed Thomas Gaskell, the constable from Lawford, to guard the area until daylight, when I intend to go over it carefully. The car is scattered in pieces, all down the ravine." He gave Charles a thin smile. "I have learned from you to be vigilant about the scene of what might be a crime. No one will disturb it."

Charles looked at Jessup, hearing in Laken's words the constable's suspicion that the crash had not been an accident. Jessup averted his eyes, as if he feared something in them might give him away, and began nervously twisting a button on his coat. Charles thought of the new gig he had seen the man driving, and of the rumors that had been flying around the servant hall. But Laken—whom Charles knew to be more competent than most Scotland Yard men—could be counted on to uncover any secrets Jessup might wish to conceal. He could leave the interrogation in his friend's capable hands, although his assistance might be wanted at the crash scene.

"I shall be glad to help in the investigation, Ned," he offered, "with photographs, too, if you like."

Laken nodded. "Shortly after daybreak, then, at Devil's Bridge. I think you know the spot."

"I do," Charles said. Devil's Hill was the steepest in the entire area. He would not have chanced driving a motorcar down its treacherous slope. But then, he knew the area. Albrecht could not have known that the road was so steep.

Laken clapped his hand on Jessup's shoulder. "Come along, then, Jessup. It's time we had a talk." The two men left the room.

Albrecht groaned again, a horrible, bubbling sound, and Charles turned back to the table. He bent over the driver and caught a fleeting phrase.

"No accident," Albrecht said in a guttural whisper. He was racked by a hard cough that shook his entire body. "Brake . . . tampered . . ." He coughed again, and clutched at his chest with one hand. The other came up and Charles grasped it.

"You're saying that the brake failed because it had been tampered with?"

Albrecht's nod, if it was a nod, was barely perceptible. His eyes were closed, his breathing shallow, his lips blue. The only color in his face was the froth of bright red blood and sputum that bubbled from his lips.

"The hill is steep," Charles said, and thought about the braking mechanism, a block of wood faced with leather, designed to rub against the turning tire. "Perhaps the brake simply could not hold the vehicle."

With an enormous effort, Albrecht turned his head from side to side. "Brake slip . . ." he said, and began to cough. "Left brake slippery . . ." He lifted his left hand, and Charles saw that the fingertips bore traces of a greasy substance.

Albrecht shuddered. Grasping Charles's hand, he half-raised himself, opened his eyes wide, and gasped out something unintelligible. Then, with a long, rattling groan, he fell back.

The doctor came hurrying into the room, carrying another lamp. Behind him was his nurse, with a cloth-covered tray. "You will probably want to leave, Charles," he said, putting the lamp on the shelf above the examining table. "This will be a bloody business, and—"

"The bloody business is ended," Charles said, and straightened. He placed Albrecht's hand on his chest and closed the man's eyes with his fingers. "He is dead."

"I'm sorry, my dear," Kate said simply. She rose from the sofa and poured Charles's favorite whisky, neat, as he liked it. As she returned to him, she touched his shoulder, loving the strong set of his jaw and the unruliness of his thick brown hair, and noticing the weariness around his eyes. It was after eleven, and the day had been very long and difficult—more for him than for her. He had endured a dangerous balloon flight which might have ended tragically, and had watched a man die. She had had only to manage Rolls's Peugeot, and dinner, and their guests.

Charles took the glass with a heavy sigh, leaned back in his leather chair and put his feet on the ottoman. "A sad thing," he said, and sipped his whisky. "Gruesome, too. I admire Brax's coolness, Kate. How he can cut into a human body—" He shuddered. "I was not made for a surgeon."

Kate sat on the ottoman and pulled Charles's boots off. "So he autopsied poor Herr Albrecht, then?"

"It seemed the prudential thing to do, especially since the body was already on the examining table. I also sent word to the coroner, mentioning that there might be some concern about the nature of this accident. Harry is to meet us at the scene of the crash after daybreak." He stretched his toes, and Kate took his stockinged feet into her lap. "Given the spot where it happened, there is very little that can be done tonight, except to guard the scene from intruders, of course. Ned has taken care of that."

"And the cause of death?" Kate prompted gently, massaging his instep. This was the evening ritual she loved most: Charles in his chair, she rubbing his shoulders or his feet. Beryl Bardwell (modern woman that she was) might well sniff at the *wifeliness* of it, but Kate found it enormously satisfying—almost as satisfying as when, later, Charles returned the favor.

"The tiller snapped off in the impact and the shaft was thrust through his chest. One lung was punctured and had totally collapsed by the time he was found. It is nothing short of a miracle that he lasted as long as he did—nearly twelve hours." Charles frowned. "He managed to get out

163

a few words, with almost his last breath. He said it was no accident, Kate."

Kate was startled. "Those were Dunstable's words too, Charles! 'No accident,' he said, over and over again." And she told him what had transpired in the drawing room between Dunstable and the others. "I wouldn't have been at all surprised if they hadn't ended by accusing one another of murder," she said earnestly. "There is something going on here, Charles. This is not as straightfoward as it might seem."

"It isn't straightforward at all," Charles replied. "I have not yet seen the crash scene, but Ned suspects foul play. It was Young Jessup who discovered the wreckage, you see. I didn't get an opportunity to talk with Ned because it was urgent that I get what I could from Albrecht. But when I left the surgery, there was a light in the jail. Ned was still interrogating Jessup."

Kate regarded him soberly. Jessup? Yes, she could see that logic. The young man had been loud in his claims, for a time, at least, that Bradford's Daimler was responsible for his father's death—the very same Daimler that now lay in the ravine beneath Devil's Bridge. If foul play were involved, it was logical to think of Jessup first. Perhaps he had only professed to accept the coroner's ruling of death by natural causes and had been waiting to exact revenge in a craftier, more cunning way, by arranging for the motorcar to be involved in an accident, in a spot where a crash was sure to end in serious injury or death for the driver. And that would not be hard to do, Kate thought, reflecting on her own wild ride in the Peugeot. If a pedestrian had stepped into her path, and she had swerved or tried to brake, the motorcar would certainly have tipped over and crashed. The crime would have been nearly perfect, for someone on foot would have left no evidence at the scene.

But as she massaged Charles's heels and began to sort through the myriad images of the evening, Kate could not escape the conviction that Jessup was not the only one who might harbor a guilty secret. To judge from their behavior, her guests—more than one of them—had been hiding something, some individual or shared knowledge. It might not have to do with the wreck of the Daimler, but then again it might.

And Albrecht's death wasn't the only mystery afoot. There was the assault on Dunstable, for instance. According to his report, two men had jumped on him in the alley, hit him over the head, and buried him in the dung heap. Or was that account a clever fabrication, contrived to explain an otherwise inexplicable absence? And there was that mysterious business of the grapnel's removal, which could so easily have resulted in two more deaths. If the balloonists had died, would those fatalities have been thought accidental?

Charles gave her a crooked smile. "And you, my love? How did you superintend that unruly crew through dinner?"

"Swiftly," Kate said with a little laugh, putting her troublesome thoughts aside. "No one seemed to have much of an appetite, so I asked Mudd to see that the plates were removed and the next course brought as quickly as possible. We romped through dinner with very little conversation other than the snapping and snarling among the men. And then the ladies and I adjourned—gratefully, I must say—to take our coffee in the drawing room. That was the moment at which Lady Henrietta put in her startling appearance and—"

"What?" Charles sat bolt upright. "The Marsdens have come back?"

"Oh, yes," Kate said emphatically and laughed again, but with hardly any humor. "I didn't say so straightaway? No, I suppose I was too engrossed in your news, Charles. Yes, the Marsdens are back, both of them, and Lady Henrietta came posthaste to fetch her daughter and her sister-in-law out of the devil's den. She was a bit put out," Kate added. "Patsy and Penelope had brought the coach, so poor Lady Henrietta was reduced to the pony carriage."

Kate smiled wryly as she recalled the scene: Lady Henrietta, red as a turkey, barging imperiously into the drawing room and demanding that her daughter leave immediately; Patsy, pale but far more composed in the face of her mother's wrath than Kate would have thought possible; and Penelope, dithering and blithering through a dozen apologies.

"Lady Henrietta also brought Charlie Rolls's portmanteau," Kate added. "I gather that he is to be evicted from Marsden Manor and denied all association with Patsy. I swear, Charles. If the situation had not been so horrible, it would have been funny, and inspiring. Beryl Bardwell was absolutely enthralled."

Charles scowled at her. "Don't you dare," he said.

Kate sighed, remembering an occasion on which Beryl had used Lady Henrietta in her fiction and had nearly brought herself to grief thereby. "I suppose you're right," she said, and wondered whether she should tell him about Beryl's little experiment with the crystal.

But Charles had something else on his mind. "I wonder what brought the Marsdens back so prematurely from their holiday," he said. "Bradford gave me to understand that they were to remain in France for another few weeks, and then go on to Spain."

"It was a telegram," Kate said. "Someone telegraphed a warning that Patsy was misbehaving, and the intelligence compelled Lady Henrietta to pack and rush home, frothing at the mouth and trailing Lord Christopher behind her."

"A telegram?" Charles looked aghast. "You're joking!"

"Exaggerating, perhaps," Kate said lightly. "But there *was* a telegram, which apparently also mentioned that Bradford had gotten himself into a spot of trouble with his car—the Jessup business, I presume. Lady Henrietta hinted that Lord Christopher would be taking a very strict line with their son." She tilted her head. "Can you guess who sent it?"

"The telegram?" Charles shook his head in bewilderment. "Of course not. Can you?"

"Why, it was Squire Thornton, of course," Kate said decidedly. "I can't imagine anyone else with a stake in Patsy's affairs—nor anyone else who might have been mean-spirited enough to tattle. I certainly hope that Patsy has the spine to stand up to her mother where that marriage is concerned."

"Oh, Kate, Kate," Charles sighed. "The things you see and understand constantly amaze me." He pulled her into the chair with him. "Kiss me, sweet, and take the taste of this wretched day out of my mouth."

The kiss, and those that followed, were distracting, and for a time Kate forgot everything else. But later, lying beside Charles in their big bed, she could not stop turning the day's events over in her mind, and wondering where the truth lay.

Had Dunstable really been hit on the head and dumped in the dung heap? Such a thing would have been simple enough to counterfeit, with assistance—or even alone, if those who discovered him had been too startled to closely examine his bonds and gag. And the fatal motorcar crash: was it an accident, or something else? Was Jessup's discovery of the wreck merely an odd coincidence, or was the man somehow responsible for what had happened? And there was the near-tragedy of the grapnel. Whose hand had pulled it from its place on the gondola? Had it been Whipple, as everyone seemed to think, or someone else?

After what seemed hours, she fell into an uneasy sleep. But even sleep brought no relief, only troubled dreams through which she piloted Rolls's Peugeot down narrow lanes lined with blackthorn hedges, dodging cows and constables. Her arms were weary from wrestling with the tiller, her body ached from the jouncing, bouncing ride.

And then, on the dark edge between dreaming and waking, she found herself at the top of Devil's Hill, overlooking the River Stour. The vista was enrapturing. Dedham Vale lay below, the willow-lined river flowing placidly through emerald meadows that were dotted with fluffy sheep and black-and-white cows, a delicate, romantic landscape from a painting by Constable. But above the valley, as if swept along by a gale, flew the striped balloon, and in the wildly swinging gondola she saw Charles, signaling frantically to her that the grapnel was gone and they were about to attempt a landing.

"Come!" he cried, his voice faint in the distance. "Hurry, you'll be late! Come as fast as you can, and bring the grapnel!"

So Kate, thinking only of Charles's danger, released the brake, speeded up the engine, and started down Devil's Hill. But in her dream, suddenly turned into the most frightening nightmare of her life, she seemed to be driving down an impossible precipice. The fearsome angle of the descent turned her bones to jelly, and her heart began to pound in a rhythm that matched the motorcar's loud chug-chug. She gripped the tiller, braced her feet against the curving floorboard, and slowed the engine speed, hoping it would serve as a brake.

But the motorcar, snorting like a wild rhinoceros, began to gather speed, thundering down the hill until she was flying at the unthinkable speed of twenty miles an hour, the top-heavy vehicle lurching violently, tipping first onto two wheels, then crashing onto four, only to tip to the other side, like a runaway carriage that had broken loose from its horses. She laid her hand on the brake lever but did not push it. At this speed, braking would do no good: the leather-covered wooden blocks that rubbed on the tires would be burned up in an instant. All she could do was hold on, and pray.

This mad, bone-rattling ride went on and on as she plummeted down the hill. But at last she was at the bottom. If she could hold the road, she would shoot across Devil's Bridge and up the hill on the other side of the deep, wooded ravine, where the runaway momentum would be slowed. But just before she reached the wooden bridge, she saw a caped and hooded figure appear as if from nowhere and step into the middle of the road. In its hands was the iron grapnel. The figure turned full toward her and raised the grapnel. In an instant of sheer terror, Kate saw that the figure had no face.

There was only one way to stop. Kate braced her feet, tightened every muscle, and pushed on the hand-brake lever with all her might. The leather-covered block on the right wheel gripped and almost held. The brake on the left did not. The motorcar swung violently to the right, lurched onto the two right-side wheels, and plunged into the ravine. Kate heard the long, shuddering scream rise from her throat as she was flung into the air, and then a deafening crash, and utter silence.

"Kate?" Charles's arms came suddenly around her in the dark, strong and sure, and she gasped with mingled fear and relief. "It's all right, dear," he whispered, smoothing her hair. "You're safe. It was only a dream."

"Yes," she gasped, and clutched him close. "A *horrible* dream." And she told him what she remembered of the nightmare.

"You know," Charles said thoughtfully, "it could have happened in that way—an accident caused when Albrecht was forced to brake too quickly, and went off the road." He chuckled in the dark. "It's too bad your dream personage had no face, Kate. Perhaps you could have told us who removed the grapnel from the gondola."

"Laugh if you like, Charles," Kate said soberly. "But all the same, when you examine the wreckage, you should inspect the brakes. If the left had held as well as the right, I think I could have stopped."

"I shall, of course," Charles replied. "But it was only a dream, Kate. Don't mix the real and the imaginary." He paused, and then said, with a kind of feigned carelessness, "I don't suppose I happened to mention that Albrecht believed that the left brake did not hold?"

"No," Kate said in a small voice. "You did not." And as she lay back against the pillow, her heart still pounding with remembered fear, all she could think of was the runaway motorcar flying down Devil's Hill, and the figure with no face, and the brake that did not hold.

17

"The devil fries fastest in his own grease."
—English Proverb

IN THE ROSE-COVERED gatehouse cottage, Lawrence left his bed and dressed himself in the Sabbath dark, as usual, to save the candle. He was not his usual self, however, having spent a tormented night in anxious tossings, so that the sheets on the bed he shared with Amelia were twisted and drenched in sweat.

Lawrence had heard of the motorcar crash late on the previous evening as he sat by the kitchen fire at Bishop's Keep, waiting for Amelia, who had been helping with her ladyship's dinner party. The news had completely unnerved him, for to Lawrence, there was only one explanation for the Daimler's crashing at Devil's Bridge, at the foot of the two steepest hills in the whole district. He had sat for a full half-hour, watching in his mind's eye as the car flew down one hill, shot across the bridge, and ran partway up the far hill as it lost power and then began to roll backward, out of control. The primitive braking system, which was less effective in reverse, would not have held it, and he could imagine the car rolling backward, gathering speed, the driver desperately trying to brake and steer backward. No, even though Lawrence might have thought of it, *should* have thought of it, the report that the car was demolished and Albrecht dead came as no great surprise.

Lawrence had managed to get through the rest of the evening without the kitchen staff noticing that something was dreadfully amiss. But his apprehension had not escaped Amelia's notice, and once at home, before their own fire, she had compelled him to tell her all.

"Ooh, Lawrence!" she had exclaimed, her eyes gone very wide and her face white as paper. "Wot'll they do to ye, when it's all found out?" She had clasped her hands and held them to her bosom as the tears began to come. "Wot'll become o' us, Lawrence?" she had wailed. "We're as good as dead, like '*im*!"

Lawrence had tried his best to comfort her, holding her in his arms and kissing away the tears. But nothing had availed, and he knew that Amelia's sleep had been as tormented as his own. What *should* he do? What *could* he do? In the sleepless hours, he had thought of a dozen different answers to those unanswerable questions, and had at last decided on one—not a very good one, but the only one that seemed at all workable. Perhaps, as the day went on, another, better answer would come to him.

Lawrence whistled loudly as he dressed, to buoy his spirits and soothe Amelia's, and went to the kitchen to eat the breakfast she had prepared for him: hot oatcakes with a scraping of butter, a boiled egg, kippers, marrow toast, and tea. The food tasted like so much dry hay, but he knew she had cooked it to cheer him. He ate it to please her, who moved like a small wan ghost from stove to table.

He was well into it when there was a knock on the door and to Lawrence's distressed surprise, Sir Charles entered, dressed as for a photographic expedition. He was wearing a brown canvas jacket, well worn, with lumpy pockets which outlined odds and ends of camera gear: a viewfinder, a light meter, an accessory shutter. His tweed breeches were tucked into heavy-soled brown boots, and he wore an old soft felt hat with a mashed crown, pushed to the back of his head.

"Good morning, Amelia," Sir Charles said, and took off his hat. "Good morning, Lawrence. I am sorry to interrupt your breakfasts, but I would like a word, if you don't mind."

"Good mornin', Sir Charles," Amelia whispered, dropping an ungraceful curtsey.

"Mornin', sir," echoed Lawrence uneasily, rising. He gestured to the empty chair. " 'Ave some tea, sir, if ye please, an' an oatcake."

"Sit down," Sir Charles said, as Amelia poured steaming tea into a cup, and placed an oatcake on a plate. "You've heard about the motorcar crash?"

"Last night." Lawrence seated himself, and hardened his voice, taking the tack on which he'd decided. "Ye'll pardon me, Sir Charles, if I say that's wot comes o' lettin' a furriner drive Lord Bradford's motorcar. That's wot I tol' 'is lordship when I saw 'im leavin' the 'ouse last night, 'it's a damn great shame,' I sez to 'im, an 'e sez, 'Yes, Lawrence, it's a shame.'"

"I suppose we should remember that it was a foreigner who built that particular motorcar," Sir Charles said mildly, and added, buttering his cake, "I would like to ask you to come with me to Devil's Bridge, Lawrence. The wreckage must be retrieved and the pieces identified." He paused and added, with what seemed to Lawrence a deep significance, "I believe that you're the man for the job."

Lawrence had raised his kipper-laden fork halfway to his mouth, and there it hung. "The pieces ident'fied?"

"There is some question about the car, it seems." Sir Charles, busy with his food, did not look up, but Lawrence felt his scrutiny.

"Question?" Slowly, carefully, the forkful of kippers descended back to the plate. "Wot sort o' question?"

There was a moment's silence. "It seems," Sir Charles said vaguely, "that the vehicle did not burst into flame." He stirred his tea. "I thought perhaps you might be able to tell me why."

"Me?" Lawrence bent over and shoveled the last of the kippers into his mouth. "Why d'ye ask me, sir?"

Amelia refilled her husband's cup in such a nervous haste that she splashed tea into the saucer. With a desperate attempt at normalcy, she said, " 'E asks 'cause you know more about Lord Marsden's motorcar than anybody." She appealed to Sir Charles, who was finishing his food. "I'nt that jes' like the man, 'idin' 'is light under a bushel?"

Sir Charles gave a dry chuckle. "Indeed, Amelia. Lord Bradford claims that your husband knows every nut and bolt in that vehicle, and I believe him." Lifting his cup, he drained it and stood up. "Thank you for the tea and cake. Lawrence, I shall drive on. I give you leave to absent yourself from Lady Kathryn's household prayers this morning, and when you have finished your breakfast, I should like you to bring the wagon to Devil's Bridge. We shall need it to fetch the wreckage back here to the barn, where you can examine it. And bring a good pair of gloves as well, if you please. I want those pieces handled with as much care as you would use to handle plates in the photography lab."

Lawrence raised his eyes, not wanting to ask because he thought he knew the answer. "An' why, sir, wud ye want that?" In his nervousness, the question was put more forcefully than he had intended.

"Lawrence!" Amelia exclaimed, horrified at his effrontery.

Sir Charles looked him straight in the face, his eyes suddenly gone hard. "Bring the wagon, Lawrence," he said, very low. "And the gloves."

And Lawrence, quaking inside, did as he was bid.

The balmy late-summer weather had turned overnight. The dawn air was chill and the breeze had a cutting edge as Charles arrived at Devil's Bridge, his thoughts troubled by what had just transpired at the Quibbley cottage. That Lawrence had done something to the motorcar he did not doubt, although he could only guess what it had been.

Early as it was, Ned Laken was there before him. The constable had tied his horse and trap at the top of the steep hill, blocking the road, and was standing now at the bottom, surveying the wooded ravine beneath the bridge. With him was Thomas Gaskell, the P.C. from the nearby tiny village of Lawford, who had guarded the area all night.

P.C. Gaskell was a tall, thin scarecrow of a man whose bony wrists extended two inches beyond his cuff and whose trousers ended well up his boots. "Nossir," he was saying to Laken in a squeaky voice, "noffink an' nobody's been 'ere, sir." He rubbed his straw-colored hair, which stuck out over both ears. "Just me an' the owls an' that wreck of a motorcar down there." He gestured toward the Daimler, which had come to rest forty feet below. "Don't trust them 'orseless carriages meself," he added. " 'Tis only the mercy o' Providence as this one didn't burn itself up and fry the poor devil that drove it."

The motorcar was jammed between two large beeches. As far as Charles could see, it had been totally destroyed by the impact, the frame twisted, the two rear wheels at odd angles, and mangled chunks of metal and wood and upholstery scattered among the rocks and trees.

"Jessup reported that he found Albrecht just there," Laken said, pointing toward a large horse chestnut a dozen yards uphill of the wreckage. "In any event, that's where he lay when I arrived."

Charles turned and looked back up the hill, noticing the deep, uneven ruts in the dirt lane—a difficult surface to manage even under the best of conditions. The Daimler must have been flying at more than twenty miles an hour when it reached the foot of the hill, an incredible velocity for so light a vehicle. At that speed, he doubted that Albrecht could have steered safely across the narrow bridge, constructed as it was of uneven planking with gaps between, and hardly passable even for slow-moving horse-drawn vehicles. How had Albrecht managed to keep the Daimler on four wheels as long as he had? And why hadn't the car, loaded as it was with a full tank of fuel, burst into flames when it crashed? There was only one probable answer to that question, and Charles thought he knew what it was.

He looked back into the ravine. "Was Albrecht flung free from the wreckage, or did he crawl?" he asked.

"Crawled, most likely," Laken replied. "He might have been trying to reach the road, where he hoped he would be rescued. Not much of a hope, though," he added thoughtfully. "There is little traffic in this lane, since most wagons must avoid the steep hill."

"Crawlt," agreed Gaskell emphatically. "There's broken bits o' grass an' twig, an' bloody marks where the pore bloke dragged 'isself along by 'is elbows an' knees. Cruel 'ard work, I'd say." He beckoned. "Come an' see fer yerselfs." And picking his way gingerly through the underbrush, he led the way down the hill.

Some moments later, having surveyed the wreckage and the site, Sir Charles found himself in full agreement with P.C. Gaskell. The driver had apparently ridden the vehicle to the bottom of the ravine and had most likely received the fatal injury when the Daimler fetched up against the beech trees. There was blood on the broken tiller shaft, blood on the seat, and blood on a flat rock on the right side of the wreckage. A bloody trail of disturbed leaves and grass could be followed with the eye, up the hill to the spot where Albrecht had been found.

And it took only one quick look to confirm Charles's guess as to why the Daimler had not exploded upon impact—as it certainly should have done, given its engineering design. The engine had a flame-heated hot-tube igniter that was known to present a dreadful fire hazard, and its surface carburetor required a highly volatile petrol which would necessarily have a very low flashpoint. One of the same model had recently crashed and burned near Paris, killing the driver. But when Charles unscrewed the metal cap to peer into the fuel tank, he discovered the reason why this one had not burned. The tank was virtually empty, even though the car had not traveled a great distance. Why?

And to that mystery was quickly added another. When he turned to a close examination of the rear wheels, Charles saw that only one of the leather-covered wood-block brakes—the one on the right, on the driver's side—was in place: the one on the left, the one that might have caused the car to go into the ravine, was missing.

"I'll get my camera and photograph the scene," Charles said, when they stood once again on the road. "Lawrence will be here shortly with a wagon and team to retrieve the motorcar, if Constable Gaskell would be so kind as to assist. Harry Hodson has also agreed to come. And we will need a thorough search of the area," he added, thinking of the missing brake mechanism. "I want to be sure that all of the loose bits of the vehicle have been located, their positions marked and the pieces properly recovered."

"There are skid marks here that you may also wish to photograph," Laken said, and pointed up the road, a dozen yards from the spot where the Daimler had plunged into the ravine.

Charles studied the marks, reconstructing the scene in his mind. The car had come hurtling down the hill, the driver had applied the brake, and then—

He stopped and stared down at the ground, remembering Albrecht's words and Kate's uncannily accurate dream. The right brake had held: in the sandy dirt of the little-used lane, he could see the point at which the right rear wheel had seized, had begun to skid, and then to turn. The left brake had failed, had "slipped," Albrecht had said, and the vehicle had spun to the right.

"I wonder why he pushed on the brake lever so hard," Laken remarked. "Albrecht was an experienced driver, was he not?"

Charles nodded. "I shouldn't have expected him to attempt to brake, unless—"

" 'Less somethink walked out in front of 'im," said Gaskell cheerfully. "A dog er a cat, like."

"Or a person," Charles said. He beckoned to Laken and they turned to trudge up the windy hill to the spot where Lawrence should arrive. "What did you learn from Jessup, Ned?"

"That he spent the day at the fete, in the company of various people, whom he named. I have not yet had an opportunity to confirm his claim that he was present for the balloon ascent. But if it is true, I don't see how he could have interfered with the motorcar's progress. Devil's Bridge is four miles from Bishop's Keep. Albrecht must have crashed only fifteen or twenty minutes after the chase began."

Charles was of the same opinion. "It would also have been difficult for Jessup to predict that Albrecht would use this lane," he added. "The other cars went round Ashton Cross—Albrecht could easily have done the same. I don't see that Jessup—or anyone else, for that matter—could have planned beforehand to interfere with his route."

"But I did learn something of interest from my talk with Jessup," Laken said. "I suppose you have seen the man driving a new gig. And Agnes tells me that Mrs. Jessup has a very fine new bonnet."

"The gig, yes," Charles said. "I wasn't aware of the bonnet." He smiled, making a mental note to tell Kate, who had somehow failed to notice, or at least to mention it to him.

"According to Jessup, the money—thirty pounds—came from Charles Rolls."

"From Rolls?" Charles exclaimed in surprise. "But *he* had nothing to do with the old man's dying. Why should he—?"

He stopped. Thirty pounds was a very large sum for a poor family—a year's wages, and something more. Was there more to Old Jessup's apoplexy than they had known or thought?

"Indeed," Laken said thoughtfully. "Why should he? I must say, however, that I am not entirely convinced that Jessup was telling the truth. There was something about his behavior that—"

This puzzled Charles even more. "But what could the man gain from a lie? And if the money did not come from Rolls, where did he get it?" From Bradford Marsden, perhaps? It was his Daimler that Rolls had been driving on the night of the old man's death.

"I don't know," Laken confessed. "The business is deuced puzzling." He shook his head. "But I could get nothing out of the man except his continued reiteration that the money came from Rolls's purse."

Lawrence was waiting with the wagon at the top of the hill, hunched against the chilly wind, his coat collar pulled up around his ears. As Charles came toward him, he climbed down and held out an envelope sealed with a flat blob of red wax.

"From Lord Bradford, sir," he said. " 'Twas left at Bishop's Keep fer ye." Not meeting Charles's eyes, he gestured nervously toward the bridge. "Shud I take the wagon an' 'orses down there an' get started?" Then he stopped, and his mouth fell open. "Lor' bless me, it crashed on *this* side o' the bridge!"

Hearing this, Charles gave him a quick look. "Did you think otherwise?"

"Why, er," Lawrence stammered. He sucked in a deep breath. "I s'pose I thought—that is . . ." He stopped, and stood without speaking.

"I see," Charles said. He began to open the envelope. "I'll show you what must be done in a moment, Lawrence. I want to photograph the scene first, before you begin." He scanned the letter, then read it again, more carefully, frowning.

Marsden Manor
Sunday, September 27, 1896

My dear Charles:

As you know by now, my father and mother returned last night. My father and I have had a fearful row, and I am returning to London. It is my understanding that the Daimler is wrecked beyond repair. I leave it to you to decide what is to be done with the remains. And since the motorcar is gone, I no longer require Lawrence's services. I should be most grateful if you could help him secure another place.

On the matter of that sum I owe you, be sure that I shall pay as quickly as may be. For the next few days, you may reach me at my club. Goodbye, old fellow! Do look me up when you come to London.

Yours faithfully & etc.
Bradford Marsden

Eyebrows raised quizzically, Laken had been watching Charles as he read. "What is it?" he asked.

Charles folded the letter. "Bradford has removed to London," he said evenly.

"Ah," Laken remarked.

"To London!" Lawrence exclaimed, almost involuntarily. "But wot 'bout me?" He stiffened smartly, remembering his place. "Pardon, sir."

"I think we need not concern ourselves with that at the moment, Lawrence," Charles said. He turned to Laken. "If the others—Dunstable, Bateman, and that crew— are still at the inn, it might be a good idea to keep them there."

"Most decidedly a good idea." Laken took out his pocket watch. "They are likely still at their breakfasts. If I hurry, I can reach the inn before they depart." He looked at Charles. "You believe, then, that there is evidence of foul play to be found here?"

"There may have been foul play," Charles said. "Whether we will find the evidence of it remains to be seen. But by all means, Ned, go to the inn."

Five minutes later, Charles and Lawrence, in the company of P.C. Gaskell, stood at the side of the road, overlooking the scene of the crash.

"Blazes," Lawrence muttered. "There's not much left o' the pore thing."

"Can it be rebuilt, do you think?" Charles asked. Without waiting for an answer, he knelt to open his leather camera case.

"May'ap, with work." Lawrence shook his head. " 'Tis sad as seein' a fine 'orse lamed."

P.C. Gaskell shook his head emphatically. "Ye kin repair a motorcar when the wheel comes off. A 'orse loses 'is leg, ye've got t'shoot the beast." He cast a look at Charles, who was getting out his camera. "If ye don't mind me askin', Sir Charles, wot's that for?"

"I am taking photographs which may aid in the investigation of the crime—if a crime is indeed what we have here."

P.C. Gaskell regarded the camera with a skeptical look. He must have heard by now, as had even the most remote provincial policeman, that Scotland Yard photographed every criminal who came through the metropolitan jails. He may also have read in *The Times* that the French *Sûreté* was beginning to experiment with crime scene photography. But it was not very likely that P.C. Gaskell of the tiny hamlet of Lawford, in the borough of Colchester, County of Essex, had ever witnessed an actual photographic documenting of a crime scene—an event that would not become common police practice for several decades.

Charles felt that the constable's skepticism was quite understandable and hence explained, in some detail, his plan for recording the scene. He was using, as he often did for outdoor photography, a Lancaster Rover, a hand camera with a seesaw shutter, adjustable diaphragms, and a viewfinder. It held twelve unexposed plates that, at the touch of a lever, fell one after the other into position. With another lever, the exposed plate was shifted to a chamber at the back of the camera. He had also brought a larger, tripod-mounted camera—a favorite in his collection—that had been made in Paris in 1890. Its fine Eurygraphe Extra-Rapid Number Three lens made it ideal for work that required careful exposures where focus was critical. He would use the hand camera to make an overview of the scene, and the tripod-mounted camera to capture the details.

P.C. Gaskell did not yawn, but he was scarcely impressed. "Let's 'ope as it's not a waste o' time," he remarked.

Lawrence gave the man a hard look and turned to Charles, who was still kneeling beside his gear. "D'ye need a 'and with that work, Sir Charles?"

But Charles did not hear the question. He had opened the canvas bag that had gone up with him in the balloon the day before and found the tiny crockery pot he had placed there—the pot of red-colored grease, with the sharp, peculiar odor, quite distinct.

18

"Why are women like telegrams? Because they are so often in advance of the mails in intelligence."
—*Punch*, 1878

WHEN HOUSEHOLD PRAYERS had been said, Kate climbed into the pony cart and clucked to Macaroni, the little gray pony that Charles had bought for her. She would have preferred to have ridden her bicycle, but that would not do at all, for she was on her way to Sunday services—after she had visited her friend Agnes Laken, who lived in the nearby village of Gallows Green. In the large wicker basket at her feet were a napkin-wrapped parcel of scones, two jars of Mrs. Pratt's red currant marmalade, and a fine cheese. It was still early morning and there was quite some time before the service would begin. She and Agnes planned to have a bit of breakfast and a comfortable visit together.

Some time before, Agnes Laken (then Agnes Oliver) had suffered a dreadful tragedy. Her husband, Arthur Oliver, had been murdered and her daughter Betsy abducted, and it had only been through the combined efforts of Charles and Kate (at that time unmarried) that the perpetrators of these crimes had been apprehended and brought to justice. After a suitable period of mourning, Agnes had married Charles's friend Ned Laken, and the friendship between Kate and Agnes had flourished. Kate looked forward eagerly to the mornings they spent together in the Laken cottage where Agnes was awaiting the birth of Ned's child, due early in the next year.

The hamlet of Gallows Green lay on the slope of a green hill above the River Stour. Its twenty or so cottages, the inn, a grocery, and a smithy were arranged on four sides of the rectangular green. One of the cottages was the Laken cottage, whitewashed, with a thatched roof, red brick chimney, and diamond-paned windows with green shutters. The dooryard was bright with autumn asters and late-blooming daisies, and a pot of bright red geraniums stood beside the door. Jemima Puddle-Duck was there too, preening her white feathers under a fragrant rosemary bush. The white duck received Kate's stroking with equanimity, for the two were old friends, Jemima being Betsy's pet duck.

The pretty, brown-haired Agnes greeted Kate with pleasure, and the two women settled themselves in front of the kitchen fire with a china pot of tea and a plate of scones and red currant marmalade, the cheese having been set aside for Ned's tea. Kate enjoyed Agnes's small kitchen, where a red-and-blue braided rug warmed the stone floor, a casement window let in the sun, and an ancient clock marked the hour with a musical chime.

The conversation immediately turned to the events of the day and evening before, and Kate told Agnes all that she had not already heard from Ned—about the angry exchange in her drawing room the night before and Lady Marsden's unexpected after-dinner arrival in the pony cart. Then Agnes told Kate one or two things that *she* did not yet know: that Ned had interviewed Jessup until late the night before and felt that he was innocent of any complicity in the motorcar crash. Jessup had confessed, however, that his gig and his mother's bonnet—in fact, the grand sum of thirty pounds—had come from the Honorable Charles Rolls.

"Rolls!" Kate exclaimed. "That's absurd! Why should he do such a thing?" She frowned. "I don't believe it. Something is not right here, Agnes."

"Ned questioned the claim as well," Agnes said, buttering another scone. "But where else could the Jessups come by such a sum? They are poor as Job. Mr. Rolls must have given it out of the kindness of his heart, to assuage the Jessups' grief."

Kate did not think that such a thing would occur to Charles Rolls, especially since the payment of money to the dead man's family would be judged by those who heard of it to be an admission of guilt. Rolls was certainly clever enough to think of that.

"I believe," she replied thoughtfully, "that I shall try to learn where the money came from."

"If you do, you shall be ahead of Ned," Agnes said. "He was puzzling his brain over the same question this morning. How do you think to discover it?"

"Why, from Mrs. Jessup herself," Kate said. "Where else?" She stirred a lump of sugar into her tea. "I understand from Cook that the lady is staying for a few days in the village with her cousin, Miss Crosby. After services, I believe I shall call there to pay my condolences to the widow."

"Your way to Dedham will take you past Devil's Bridge," Agnes remarked. "Ned went there early this morning."

"And Charles went there to take photographs," Kate said, glancing at the clock. "He must have gone by this time too. I suppose there will be precious little for me to see."

As it turned out, however, there was a great deal to see.

When Kate arrived at Devil's Bridge, the coroner had just taken his leave and ridden off. Lawrence and P.C. Gaskell were using the team to drag the wreckage of the Daimler up out of the ravine, while Charles, on his hands and knees, was scouring the area where the motorcar had rested. Kate looked around, remembering her dream and feeling a little frisson of recognition. The two situations were amazingly similar—the dusty lane, the hill, the bridge. Closing her mind to the recollection of the faceless figure of her dream, and glad for her stout boots and sensible skirt, she climbed down the steep hill to the place where the wreck had been.

"I thought you had gone to the Sunday service," Charles said, getting to his feet.

"I'm on my way. I stopped for breakfast with Agnes." She glanced around. "Whatever are you looking for?"

"The left brake shoe is missing," Charles replied. "A wooden block about six inches long and three wide, covered in leather. The other crucial parts have been located, but that one has yet to turn up." He rubbed his hand through his brown hair, anxious. "It is the most important of all. It *must* be found."

"Then why not enlist Lawrence in the task? He is familiar with every part of the car—he would know what to look for."

"Because," Charles said in a low voice, "I have not yet cleared him of suspicion."

"But you can't think *Lawrence* had anything to do with the crash!" Kate exclaimed. "Why would he—?"

Then she fell silent. Why would Lawrence tamper with the Daimler? The answer was quite simple, really: he had meant to destroy the motorcar so that he and Amelia should not have to accompany it to London.

"Oh, I hope it is not true," she said after a moment.

"Yes," Charles said. "I have kept a close eye on him all morning, and asked P.C. Gaskell to do the same. I am quite sure that neither of them have found the missing brake."

Kate turned to look up the hill, her attention caught by the trail of broken grasses that led up to a large horse chestnut tree. Following her glance, Charles said, "Albrecht crawled up to that tree. Jessup found him there."

Kate shivered, thinking once more of her dream, and of the dying man's agony. What had been in his mind as he dragged himself up that hill on his knees and elbows? Had he feared death? Had he hoped for rescue? Musing, she walked slowly up the hill and stood for a moment beside the tree, imagining how the handsome, arrogant young German had lain there, his life and strength and self-confidence ebbing away, leaving only the ragged breath, the unendurable pain, the light dying into dark.

As she stood, her eye suddenly caught a rectangular object, half-buried in a mound of brown leaves. Without touching it, she bent over for a closer look. It was a narrow wooden block, six inches long or so, faced with leather. The leather covering seemed to be impregnated with a greasy red substance. The back was splintered, as if the block had been forcibly struck from its securing mechanism.

"Charles!" she called, and waved.

A moment later, Charles confirmed that she had indeed discovered the missing brake shoe, "It must have broken off in the impact and Albrecht found it," he said. "Then he carried it with him up the hill to this spot." He picked up the wooden block and sniffed it.

"But why?" Kate asked wonderingly. "It would have cost him some effort, when the poor man had precious little to spare. Why did he do it?"

"Because it proved his theory of the cause of the crash," Charles said, "and he wanted to be sure that it was found." He held out the block to her. "Do you recognize this odor, Kate?"

She sniffed it as well, and pulled back. "Phew!" she exclaimed. "What *is* it?"

"I don't know," he admitted. "But whatever it is, it may be the same substance I saw on Albrecht's fingers last night."

"On his fingers?" She frowned, studying the leather-covered block in Charles's hand. "But the brake is greasy, Charles! Is *that* what caused the crash?"

"Very likely," Charles replied. "The right brake caught and held, the left brake slipped, and the motorcar spun out of control. But let me show you something else." And he took her to where his canvas bag lay, pulled out the small crockery pot, its lid fastened on with a metal bail, and opened it "Smell," he commanded.

"It's the same stuff!" she said when she had sniffed it. She looked at the jar, frowning. "Charles, that pot. I recognize it! It is one of the set of three little mustard pots Eleanor sent us from France some weeks ago." She turned it over and pointed to the tiny word *Dijon* stamped on the bottom. "You see? But that awful substance inside is certainly not mustard."

"Are you sure of that, Kate?" Charles's voice was tense. "That this pot came from our kitchen, I mean."

Kate, suddenly sick at heart, knew what he was thinking: that Amelia could have taken the mustard pot from the Bishop's Keep kitchen to the Quibbley cottage, where Lawrence found it and filled it with the grease that ended up on the Daimler brake.

"Well, I'm not absolutely sure, I suppose," she said hesitantly, even though she *felt* sure enough. "I shall have to see whether Mrs. Pratt can produce all three pots. Where did you get it?"

"I found it hidden in the gondola yesterday, under a pile of ropes."

"In the gondola?" Kate looked at him, perplexed. "I don't understand."

But the moment the words were out of her mouth, she thought she *did* understand, after all. Lawrence had had full charge of the balloon on several occasions in the last few days. If he had wanted to cache something where he could readily retrieve it, he might have thought the gondola to be a handy hiding place.

"Oh, dear," she said sadly.

Charles met her eyes. "Yes," he said. "Oh, dear."

After the service that morning, Kate walked across the green churchyard to Miss Crosby's house. Kate had been raised a Roman Catholic, but the nearest priest was several miles away, across the River Stour at East Bergholt, and she regularly attended services at St. Mary the Virgin, on the High Street, in Dedham. The walls of the old church, which dated from 1492, were built of gray stone from Caen, while the imposing tower was faced with the local knapped flint. In the tower hung the bells, five of which had been cast before 1552, as Vicar Talbot was fond of boasting. But because of Warden Russell's fears of damage to the tower, the bells had only been chimed for the past few years, not rung—a sad loss to the village, the parishioners lamented. A solicitation (not the first, according to parish history) was underway to repair the tower.

The small gray cottage belonged to the village school, which kept it for the use of the teacher. She was Miss Estelle Crosby, sister to the apothecary and cousin to the Widow Jessup. Kate's knock was answered by the girl of all work, and she was ushered into the small, chilly front parlor. A coal fire was lit in the fireplace and Mrs. Jessup sat close beside it, her lap covered with a shawl, her slippered feet on the fender. Mrs. Jessup jumped to her feet, dropping the shawl, and ran away to fetch her cousin, who had also just returned from services.

The two ladies, quite flustered, accepted Kate's apologies for calling on Sunday and hurriedly produced an embroidered cloth, a pot of tea and three cups, and a chipped china plate filled with sticky buns. Miss Crosby, clearly sensible of the honor of her ladyship's visit, remarked more than once how good it was of Lady Kathryn to call on her and her poor, bereaved cousin, and the widow herself several times repeated how grateful she was for her ladyship's magnanimous offer of the loan of a pony cart, although of course her poor son, Tom—fatherless now, and brokenhearted—was now possessed of a gig, so that she would not be required to trespass on her ladyship's extraordinary kindness. They had already heard of the wreck of Lord Marsden's motorcar on the previous day, and were anxious to know if her ladyship had any news of the tragedy. But Kate pled innocent to any knowledge of the crash, and turned their attention back to themselves by mentioning how satisfied she was to find them in such fine health, which gratified them both.

"Another bit of bun, if it please your ladyship?" asked Miss Crosby, offering the china plate so that her hand hid the chipped edge.

"Oh, do," urged the Widow Jessup, and removed the striped knit tea cozy to peer into the pot. "An' 'ave another cup o' tea, as well, my lady. It's Sunday, and there's a-plenty."

Kate obliged, and the three ladies were quite companionable for a few moments, sipping their tea and munching their sticky buns and speaking cozily of village matters. Miss Crosby, who seemed to know everything that was going on in the village, regaled them with a report of Mrs. Goettemoeller's seventh child, born that very morning—a boy at last, after six girls, and as fine and lusty a boy as was ever seen, black-haired and sweetly plump as a baby pig. Of Rachel Elam's dahlias winning the first prize at the fete the day before (when everyone knew that Mrs. Gotobed's were by far the nicer), and Tom Whipple's arrest on disorderly conduct charges, and of Squire Thornton's generous payment of his bail.

And then Kate remarked that she had noticed Mrs. Jessup's quite lovely bonnet as that lady had walked on the High Street the week before, and begged, if it were not too great a trial for the widow, to be allowed to see it.

Once the bonnet was on the table before them, in all its splendor of black crepe and black velvet ribbon, it was quite natural of Kate to praise the widow's fine taste in millinery and to inquire where such a fine bonnet might be purchased, and to listen for the widow's next remark, which quite naturally revealed what she had come to hear.

"O' course," Widow Jessup sighed, reverently wrapping the bonnet in tissue, preliminary to replacing it in the cardboard bonnet box, "I could niver in a 'undred years 'ave afforded such an extravagance if it 'adn't bin fer the squire, bless 'is soul."

"Nor Tom 'is fine gig," observed the widow's cousin.

"Nor Tom 'is gig," agreed the widow.

"Nor Whipple his bail," said Kate, thoughtfully.

"Oh, aye," said the widow. "The squire's bin a tower o' strength, 'e 'as, an' gen'rous b'yond tellin'." She colored, and added hastily, "But I shouldn't say so. 'E 'as asked Tom an' me pertic'larly *not* to."

Disregarding the last remark, Kate said warmly, "I am *so* glad to know that it was the squire who has helped you. I had heard it said round the village that it was Mr. Rolls."

The widow reddened. "Well . . ." she said slowly.

"Mis-ter Rolls!" sniffed her indignant cousin. "I'd like to know why 'e 'ud want to 'elp. Mis-ter Rolls, indeed!"

"Now, Stella," the widow said, and nervously turned her bonnet in her hand. "Remember wot the squire sez. We must 'old no grudges." She looked at Kate. "The squire sez t'wud be good if 'twere believed as Mr. Rolls 'elped us out. Not to lie, o'course. But wot's past is past, as Jessup 'isself allus sez, an' people wud be more willin' to fergive if they thought the gen'leman were willin' t'pay."

Miss Crosby sighed heavily. "Yer a real Christian soul, Tildy." She appealed to Kate. "Ain't she, my lady? A real Christian soul—as is the squire, bless 'is 'eart. Didn't 'e go an' stand bail fer poor Whipple, too? Ye don't 'ear of Mis-ter Rolls standin' bail for nobody, I don't suppose." Her smile was distinctly uncharitable.

After a few moments, Kate repeated her praise of the bonnet and added a few words in favor of the sticky buns. Taking her leave, she departed into the crisp and refreshing outdoor air.

But while the invigorating chill did much to clear Kate's head, it did little to lift her spirits. She had got the intelligence she came for, but it left her with more questions. Why had Squire Thornton involved himself in this affair, which was truly none of his business? What had he to do with the Jessups, or with Whipple, or with any of it? It was all very confusing.

But the sadness that most heavily burdened Kate as she rode along had nothing to do with Squire Thornton. Her concern and distress lay much closer to home, in the rose-covered cottage at the foot of the lane. She could believe that Lawrence Quibbley had intended to disable the Daimler, although she felt sure he had not intended to kill the driver. But dead was dead— or at least, so a jury would most likely reckon. Poor Lawrence—what would become of him? And what would happen to Amelia—sweet, loving Amelia—if her husband were arrested and brought to the dock for the death of Wilhelm Albrecht? How would she bear it? What would she do?

Kate clucked to the gray pony, hurrying him homeward, wondering whether there was any way that she could help.

19

"The number of owners and drivers of motorcars who are not gentlemen, would seem to be unduly large. There is no turning a cad into a gentleman, but there is such a thing as making even cads fear the law."

—*The Times*, September 1901

"Y**OU CAN'T BE** serious, man!" exclaimed Arthur Dickson. He rose from his chair at the inn's breakfast table and glowered at the constable. "You expect us to stay *here*, in this wretched inn? Until what o'clock?"

"Until," Laken said quietly, "the inquiry is complete." He studied Dickson, thinking that the man looked as if he had scarcely slept. His eyes were shadowed, his pale face lined, and when he sat back down and lifted his teacup, his hands trembled visibly. "I cannot promise you what time it will be concluded, Mr. Dickson. That depends upon Sir Charles's progress in his investigation of the motorcar, and upon the outcome of my interviews with you and these other gentlemen." He thought of Squire Thornton and the absent Bradford Marsden, who might also be able to throw some light on the shadowed subject. "And one or two others," he added.

Arnold Bateman threw down his fork. "This is what comes," he said, with a dark look at Harry Dunstable, "of crying murder."

Dunstable raised his chin, indignant. "I did not *cry* murder," he said loftily. "I merely stated my belief that Albrecht's death was no accident. That is all." With a hand that was almost as unsteady as Dickson's, he poured himself a cup of coffee from the pot in the center of the table. "And if the constable wishes to question me, I shall be glad to offer what information I possess that may bear on the matter. I hope it is helpful." Laken observed that the latter remarks carried an undisguised significance, and were accompanied by a sly glance around the table.

Ponsonby rose to the bait. "And what sort of information would that be?" he demanded gruffly. "If you intend to aim any irresponsible allegations at me, Dunstable, you had better remember that you are in a most vulnerable position. One word from me and the British Motor Car Syndicate is ruined." His voice began to rise. "Ruined, do you hear? I will see that every one of your notes is recalled for immediate payment. I will—"

"*Harrumph!*" Bateman cleared his throat loudly and cast a meaningful glance in Laken's direction. Ponsonby colored and fell silent.

Dunstable sipped his coffee. "I doubt that you will recall any notes, Ponsonby," he said, drawling out the words offensively. "If that happens, I may find it necessary to speak publicly about Mrs. Vickers's sad end—a sensational story, I fear, and hardly to your credit."

"Don't be afraid of him, Ponsonby." Dickson's words were acid. "No one will believe him."

"And who would believe you, Arthur?" asked Dunstable with a poisonous laugh. "Your perjury in the matter of those patents makes it impossible for anyone to trust your word." He glanced at Bateman. "And you, Arnold. Arthur injured you once, in that little *contretemps* at the Crystal Palace, and you let him off. How much did he pay you? Are you going to lie for him again?"

The silence was fruitful. Laken allowed it to ripen for a moment before he turned to Charles Rolls, who was seated at the end of the table. "I assume that you will have no objection to speaking with me, Mr. Rolls."

"Not in the slightest," Charlie Rolls said, with a careless air. "I have no secrets. In any event, I had intended to remain here for a day or two, since there is some repair that must be made to the balloon before it can fly again. I heartily agree that we should see this business to its conclusion before we leave," he added, "whoever is to blame." And he cast a glance around the table, allowing it to linger on the three drivers.

"But it was an *accident*," Ponsonby objected. He turned to Laken, speaking desperately. "I have business in London, Constable. You can't possibly mean to keep me—"

"Indeed I do," Laken said with authority, feeling that it was time to exert control over the situation. "I mean to keep *all* of you until this affair is concluded. Mr. Dunstable, I shall begin my interviews with you, if you please, in this room." He looked at the others, who seemed to be in varying stages of confusion, according to their temperament: Rolls the coolest, Ponsonby the most agitated. "I shall appreciate your waiting in your apartments, gentlemen—without consultation among you."

"Apartment, hah!" Ponsonby ejaculated. "It's no more than a broom closet."

"But you have a broom closet to yourself, Frank," Bateman said with a laugh. "The rest of us are sharing a broom closet."

"And a bed," Rolls said with disgust. He sighed. "The sooner you begin, Constable, the sooner this business will be concluded. Go to it, *do*."

And so Laken began a disagreeable task which he expected would take most of the morning and yield very little of substantive information.

Lawrence was also carrying out a disagreeable task. Under the supervision of Sir Charles and with the help of P.C. Gaskell, he had hauled the wrecked Daimler from the ravine beneath Devil's Bridge, carted it to the gatehouse cottage, and unloaded it in the drafty, dirt-floored barn which served as his mechanic's shop. Now, Sir Charles had charged him with reassembling as much of it as he could—which was not going to be much at all, he thought, surveying the shattered wreckage.

"Pardon me, sir," he said to Sir Charles, "but ye don't expect this car to be driven again, do ye?"

"No." Sir Charles gave Lawrence a glance in which he could read coldness and enmity. "I believe that the vehicle has been tampered with, Quibbley, and I would like your confirmation of my suspicions. I shall observe you as you do your work and raise queries from time to time."

These chilly words pierced Lawrence to the very heart. As the morning had worn on and no questions had been put about his part in the demise of the Daimler and its unfortunate driver, he had begun to breathe somewhat easier. But he could not forget the hard look that Sir Charles had aimed at him across the breakfast table that morning, and he knew he was being watched as he loaded the wreckage into the wagon. And that cold tone just now, edged with suspicion, where before had been trust and confidence— it robbed Lawrence of every hope of escaping undetected and made him quite sure that Sir Charles had found him out. And if that were the case, was it not better to confess what he had done before he could be accused of it, and throw himself on the mercy of the court?

"Sir Charles," he said, taking his hands out of his pockets and standing straight, a man who has made up his mind to be honest, even though he speaks a bitter and shaming thing. "I must tell ye the Lord's truth, sir. *I* tampered wi' that car, an' I'm desprit'ly sorry fer it."

And in the next moment, he had confessed all. How Lord Bradford had insisted that Lawrence accompany him to London to look after the motorcar. How deeply distressed Amelia had been by the idea of exchanging her beloved rose-covered cottage for low, smoky rooms, and how he had begun to seek some means of preventing their departure. How he had believed that if the Daimler were somehow disgraced in the balloon chase, Lord Bradford might think better of the London plan. And how he had cast about in his mind for ways to effect this disgrace, and determined at last on the scheme of siphoning out all but a small portion of the car's petrol. When he was done, he stopped.

The silence lengthened. After a moment, Sir Charles said, "Well?"

"Well, sir?"

"Is that *all*?" Sir Charles said.

Lawrence wanted to ask whether that were not enough, but the question seemed an effrontery. "Yes," he said, and hung his head. "The breakdown cudn't point to me as a pore mechanic, y' see. It had t'be somethin' as wudn't connect to me at all, if ye see wot I mean, sir. That's why I concluded on the petrol. Albrecht insisted on fuelin' the car hisself, so I cudn't be blamed if it came up short. An' I had the oppertun'ty, d'ye see, when I had t'stay up all the night to look after the balloon an' the gas plant."

There was a moment's silence, and then Sir Charles spoke, very gravely. "And you did not tamper with the brake?"

Lawrence looked up, surprised. "The brake, sir?"

"Yes, the brake, Lawrence. The *left* brake."

"Oh, no, sir," Lawrence said emphatically, shaking his head. "I didn't *touch* the brake, 'cept to tighten the bolts as 'old it to the lever mechanism, sir. All I did was siphon out the petrol. O' course, when I 'eard about the crash, I thought sure—" He stopped and swallowed.

"You thought that the motorcar had stopped partway up the hill on the far side of the bridge, and run backwards down the hill. Is that right?"

Lawrence felt himself among the lowest of men. "I did, sir," he said at last. "All last night, I felt a mortal fear as I'd caused the wreck an' killed 'im, sir. It was a pure misery, sir, not but wot I deserved it fer wot I done."

"I'm sure it was a misery, Lawrence," Sir Charles said gently, and Lawrence heard the understanding in his voice. There was another silence, and then Sir Charles walked to the rear of the vehicle. "Well, then, let us get started. Let's see—where is the left rear fender?"

Lawrence sprang to attention, feeling a great relief. " 'Ere, sir," he said eagerly, and lifted the fender from a pile of loose wreckage. It was a curved piece of light metal four inches wide by eighteen inches long, designed to deflect mud thrown up by the turning wheels. It had been torn from the Daimler's body upon impact, and Lawrence had pulled it from the thorny coppice where it had been flung. " 'Tis all over dents, sir," he said with regret, thinking how, freshly polished, both fenders had gleamed.

"Put it on the floor here and let's have a look," Sir Charles said, taking a magnifying lens out of one of his capacious pockets. He began to examine the top surface of the fender, then turned it over to inspect the underside, which was coated with a fine, flourlike gray dust. After several moments, he stopped, moved the lens, and turned the fender toward the light for a better view.

"If ye'll pardon me, sir," Lawrence said, "wot are we lookin' for?"

"We are looking for some means of identifying the person who might have tampered with the brake, Lawrence," Sir Charles replied. He took out a small leather case, opened it, and extracted a glass microscope slide. With a pearl-handled penknife, he scraped a dab of a greasy substance from the underside of the fender and deposited it onto the slide, then topped the smear with a circular glass cover.

"What sort of grease," he asked, holding the slide to the light, "might this be, Lawrence? Something you regularly use on the vehicle, perhaps?"

Lawrence looked up at it. With the light shining through, he could see that the substance, whatever it was, was decidedly red and contained minuscule bits of something—grass, perhaps, or leaves.

"Don't b'lieve so, sir," he said doubtfully. "The grease I use on the wheel bearin's is yellow, like, an' 'asn't got 'ny leaves in it, I can show it to ye, if that would 'elp."

"Yes, that *would* help, later," Sir Charles said, bending over the fender again. After a moment, he said, "There's something else I want you to see," and handed Lawrence the lens.

Lawrence looked at the underside of the fender. He saw a long smear of reddish grease, dusted over, and a smudged and dusty fingerprint, with a pattern of ovals and whorls resembling one that Sir Charles had once shown him, enlarged, in a photograph. On that occasion, Sir Charles had said that the print, which had been left by the tip of a man's finger, could be used to distinguish that particular man from any other individual in the entire world. Lawrence was unclear as to the details of the process, but that Sir Charles understood and could practice it, he had no doubt.

"Ah," Lawrence said, straightening up. He wanted to say more, but could think of nothing to add.

Sir Charles took out another leather case from a different pocket—a fingerprint kit, it proved to be, containing a small inking pad and several small white cards. "Let's see *your* fingers, Lawrence."

Instinctively, Lawrence put his hands behind his back, momentarily disconcerted. What if the print were his? What if he had inadvertently placed a fingertip in that smear of grease while he was polishing the upper side of the fender, or tightening the brake? If it *were* his print, would it incriminate him?

But Sir Charles was standing before him, the fingerprint kit in his hand, and there was nothing for it but to assent. So Lawrence wiped his fingers with a clean cloth, then allowed Sir Charles to roll each one first upon the inking pad and then upon the card. Then Sir Charles spent several interminable moments comparing the impressions thus obtained with the print on the fender. After a while, he glanced up.

"No, Lawrence," he said, "I do not think the print is yours."

Lawrence gulped. "You ain't sure, sir?"

"Unfortunately, the print on the fender is smudged. I believe I can ascertain enough points of comparison to rule you out as its maker, however."

"Well, sir," Lawrence said, with some relief, although he could wish that the comparison had been more definitive.

Sir Charles put Lawrence's fingerprint card into an envelope and the envelope into his pocket. "So, Lawrence," he said sternly, "you emptied the petrol tank. I suppose that explains why the vehicle did not explode when it hit the trees."

"I s'pose, sir." Lawrence could feel the weight of Sir Charles's disapproval. "By the time the Daimler got to Devil's Hill, it wud've bin nearly out o' fuel, like. Not much left to explode, sir."

"Then it was providential indeed that you removed the petrol, Lawrence."

"Excuse me, sir?" Lawrence blinked, thinking he had not heard aright. "Prov'dential, sir?"

"Exactly so. If the fuel tank had been full of petrol, as it should have been at that point in the chase, the open flame of the hot-tube igniter would certainly have caused the wreck to explode into flames. The driver, poor fellow, would not have survived to offer a clue to the cause of the crash, and the vehicle, together with any evidence of brake-tampering, would have been destroyed."

"Well, sir," said Lawrence with circuitous logic, "it cud not 'o bin me 'oo mucked up the brake, fer I knew that the tank was empty."

Sir Charles's mouth relaxed into a rare smile. "I may not praise you publicly for what you did, Lawrence, but I will tell you privately that I am damned glad of it." He clapped Lawrence on the shoulder. "Damned glad of it, indeed."

Lawrence felt himself almost overwhelmed. "Yessir." He gulped. "Thank ye, sir."

"Right," Sir Charles said, putting his fingerprint kit into another pocket. "Now, all we have to do is find the match of that print under the fender and the law shall have its man."

But the look on Sir Charles's face gave away his apprehensions. Finding the man would not be quite so simple as that. And Lawrence suddenly realized that if the man behind this crime were not discovered and brought to justice, he himself might remain forever under suspicion, not in Sir Charles's eyes, perhaps, but in the eyes of others—and of the law.

20

"When the cook and the steward fall out, we hear who stole the butter."

—Dutch Proverb

"'ERE'S THE LIST, 'Arriet," Sarah Pratt said, giving the daily garden order to the kitchen maid. "An' mind ye don't let Thompson gi' ye any backchat. This is wot's wanted, no more an' no less, an' if 'e's got any problem wi' it, ye kin tell 'im to kindly come an' speak wi' me."

"Yes, Missus Pratt," Harriet said demurely. She went off with a spring in her step, for today was Sunday, and she was to have a half-holiday that afternoon. Lady Kathryn preferred light meals for the household on the Sabbath, so the order was not large, only a basket of French beans and a bunch of New Zealand spinach for the upstairs dinner, and two collards and a basket of broad beans for the servants' hall. When Harriet had collected the vegetables from Thompson, she would carry them in baskets suspended from a yoke across her shoulders into the vegetable pantry, where she would place the beans and greens into their appropriate slats and replenish the

205

wooden bowls of water that kept them fresh until it was time to prepare them.

When the girl had gone, Sarah poured herself a cup of tea and sat down with it at the scrubbed pine table. Tranquillity had been restored to her kitchen with the return of her cherished iron range, and she was comforted by the fragrant pot of soup stock that simmered congenially on the back of the vast stove and the three pigeon pies bubbling in the oven and the trough of dough put down before the fire to rise.

But peace had not been restored to Sarah's spirit. She was in possession of two rather important mysteries—at least she thought that they might be important, no, that they *must* be important—and she was much troubled as to what to do with them. At household prayers that Sabbath morning, she had offered up a special petition for help in resolving these matters, and now she sat at the table with her tea and waited for help to come to her.

One of these mysteries involved her friend Bess Gurton. On the way home from her sister's birthday supper on Friday night, Sarah had encountered Bess, wrapped like a Pharaoh's mummy in a black shawl and skulking around Lord Marsden's motorcar like a common thief. Questioned, Bess had stammered out that she'd come to see the balloon before it flew away the next morning and had stopped to peek at the motorcar to see whether it was every bit as dangerous as she had remembered. "I meant to put me 'ead in at the kitchen door," she had added, "but the light was out an' I thought ye'd already taken yerself off to bed."

Sarah had not believed a word of this voluble stream of protestations. She and Bess had both grown up along Black Brook, playing together in the strip of garden that separated their two cottages, shooing the hens off their nests in the little shed at the foot of the garden to steal their eggs, and spending hours on their stomachs lying under the bushes at the mill, watching the fat corn sacks being hauled up by a pulley from the great yellow four-horse wagons.

But as they grew older, Bess had gone her own independent and willful way, neither marrying nor going into service but supporting herself by her own wits and gaining a reputation in the village for all sorts of sinister nonsense. Witchery nonsense, that is, like that practiced by Bess's Grandmother Gurton, who was reputed by some of Dedham's older inhabitants to have been adept in the black arts. If those old folks spied Gammer Gurton lingering too close to a cow or a sheep that had happened the next day to fall ill or injure a hoof upon a stone, they knew exactly who and what to blame.

And Sarah, while she was not *very* superstitious, firmly believed that Bess Gurton had been up to something wicked on Friday night—something that had to do with the balloon and Lord Marsden's motorcar, and perhaps with the pig's blood that Bess had begged of her several weeks back. At the time of the request, Sarah had surmised that Bess might be planning to employ the blood in some sort of charm or bit of magic, and wondered whether it was right to give it to her. But Sarah did not really believe that Bess could do any damage with her spells, and Bess was a friend. In the end, Sarah had reluctantly obliged her.

Now, however, in light of what had happened to both the balloon *and* Lord Bradford's motorcar, Sarah thought she should not have been so quick to assist Bess in her mischief, whatever it was. Sarah was not *very* superstitious, indeed, but one had to keep an open mind on such matters, and it was still whispered among the village oldsters that Bess's grandmother had been seen, now and again, to *fly*. Bess might not be to blame for what had happened to the balloon and the motorcar, but then again she might. And some might even argue that Sarah herself was to blame, for giving Bess what she asked for.

But Bess was not the only friend with whom Sarah had had a falling out. The other was Squire Thornton—not a friend, exactly, but someone of whom Sarah had thought highly. She had grown up on one of the outlying farms of Thornton Grange, and her mother and father had been tenants of Squire Thornton's father, and his own tenants until their deaths some few years before. The present squire, while not by nature a generous man, had allowed the old people to stay in their cottage for a month or two without the payment of rent, and Sarah had been grateful. What she had seen him do at the time of the balloon launch had therefore filled her with great shame.

She was even more shamed, and angered, as well, when she reflected that someone else had gotten the blame for the squire's actions. Tom Whipple, who had courted Sarah when she was still a girl, before she had lengthened her skirts and put her hair up, who had sworn to love her forever even though she refused him and married Pratt instead, worse luck. Whipple, who, though headstrong and impetuous, was a just man, and true as steel. Whipple had been blamed and Sarah knew for certain fact he was not at fault, for she knew who *was*. Should she tell? *Who* should she tell? And how could she tell it without the squire hearing that she was the one who had revealed his deception?

Sarah was turning these matters over in her mind when Lady Kathryn opened the courtyard door and came into the kitchen, bringing with her the chill, fresh air. Ladies, Sarah had been taught, *never* used the courtyard door, but dismounted from their carriages and came through their fine front entrances. But her ladyship (an American, and Irish) stood on no ceremony where doors were concerned, leaving every door in the house standing ajar so that air might circulate from room to room, and using whichever door she pleased, even the courtyard door that led from the garden and stables into the kitchen, and the green baize door that divided the house into upper and lower. Miss Ardleigh—Lady Kathryn, as she was now, following her marriage to Sir Charles—had been headstrong and individual since her arrival at Bishop's Keep, and no amount of remonstrance was likely to change her.

To tell the truth, Sarah Pratt admired her ladyship's progressive, not to say radical, ways, her American practicality and lack of pretense—and her stories. For Sarah was fully aware that her ladyship regularly occupied herself as an authoress, and that she concealed her work under the name of Beryl Bardwell, whose numerous detective stories featured fascinating, fearless women and whose reputation was virtually certain to someday equal that of Conan Doyle and his precious Sherlock Holmes.

"Good morning, Mrs. Pratt," Lady Kathryn said, taking off her woolen hat and dropping it on the table. In the way of hats and garments, too, her ladyship differed greatly from other fine ladies, preferring a modest hat without frills, or a woolen cloche, and insisting (even for Sunday services) on sensible boots and rational dress that allowed her greater freedom of movement, like the shorter, narrower skirt of the brown suit she was wearing.

"Good mornin', yer ladyship," Sarah said.

Lady Kathryn cast a look in the direction of the kitchen range. "I am glad to see that things are back to normal once more, Mrs. Pratt. If you like, I shall speak to Sir Charles about leaving your iron range where it is and installing the gas cooker somewhere else. In the pantry, perhaps?"

Sarah beamed. "The pantry will do very well, ma'am," she said gratefully. "Thank ye, yer ladyship."

And then, like a flash, it came to Sarah that the help she had hoped and prayed for might be standing before her, in the very flesh, as it were. For who was Lady Kathryn but Beryl Bardwell, the solver of insoluble mysteries? And who better than Beryl Bardwell, the female Conan Doyle, to give her the answers she was seeking?

"I wonder, ma'am," she said, "if ye've time to give me a word or two o' advice."

Kate's drive from the village back to Bishop's Keep had taken her through a very pretty lane, where the frosty air presaged an early autumn. The coming weeks were the time of year Kate loved best, when the woods garbed themselves in a kind of contradictory magnificence, at once splendidly gaudy and quietly somber. The birch and oak would soon be wearing bright yellow, while the beech and larch on the hill would blaze a deep copper and orange. The edges of fields would be frilled with the sweet pink of campion and the more modest flush of willow-herb, and the brash magenta of loosestrife might still enliven the brookside. Charles would take her through the woods and show her the wonders of English fungi—some the size of the tiniest pearl buttons and some bigger than a basin, and magnificently colored white, black, cream, purple, yellow, scarlet. And the prickly chestnuts would come showering down around them, their cream-colored cups opening to show the chestnuts like shiny dark pearls inside.

While Kate was thus happily anticipating the coming autumn, she had also been turning over in her mind the information she had gleaned that morning. Having concluded that she could do little to help Lawrence—that was up to Charles, who seemed to have the investigation fully in hand—she turned her attention to Squire Thornton, who figured mysteriously large in the course of the last few weeks' events.

The new gig and splendid bonnet were Thornton's gifts, and he had insisted that the Jessups give the credit for them to Charles Rolls—thereby making it seem to any who heard of it that Rolls had assumed responsibility for Old Jessup's death. The squire had also stood bail for Whipple, who was thought to have pulled the grapnel from the gondola. Knowing him to be a hard man, Kate did not for a moment believe that the squire had acted out of the generosity of his heart where either the Jessups or Tom Whipple were concerned. Why, then, *had* he acted? Why had he been so eager to part with his money?

Kate was still mulling over these questions when she arrived at Bishop's Keep. She had handed Macaroni's reins to Pocket and entered the house the most convenient way, encountering Cook in the kitchen. A few moments later, she found herself seated at the kitchen table with a cup of tea, listening with some surprise as Mrs. Pratt poured forth her mysteries. The first, which had something to do with pig's blood and witchcraft and a friend of Mrs. Pratt's who had been seen lurking about on a dark night, was rather too incoherent to be easily teased out. The second, however, brought her at once to attention.

"Squire Thornton?" she exclaimed. "You saw *Squire Thornton* pull the grapnel out of the gondola?"

"That I did, yer ladyship," Mrs. Pratt said stoutly. "I'd jes' come down through the garden from talkin' wi' Thompson about the artichokes fer the dinner, ma'am. 'E'd sent word as 'e 'ad only 'alf a dozen, an' that wudn't be nearly enough. Ye'll remember as we serve only the bottoms on the plate, an' 'ud 'ave to 'ave three dozen, at least. When Thompson sent me the bad news, I 'ad t' go down to the garden to see wot cud be put in the place o' the missin' bottoms." She frowned in remembered annoyance. "But Thompson, 'e—"

"I believe I understand why you were out and about that morning, Mrs. Pratt," Kate put in hurriedly. "Why don't you just tell me what you saw."

"Wot I saw," Mrs. Pratt said with some energy, "was the squire marchin' up to the balloon, shoutin' an' wavin 'is arms. Sir Charles an' that other man—"

"Mr. Rolls?"

"Sir Charles an' Mr. Rolls was busy tryin' to get ready to go, an' there was a deal o' shoutin' and shovin', so the squire jes' reached out 'is 'and an' pulled that big fish'ook right off the basket an' dropped it on the ground. Afterwards, pore Whipple got the blame, an' the constable took 'im off to jail." She shook her head sorrowfully. "God knows wot's become o' 'im."

"Nothing has become of him," Kate said. "The constable determined that there was not enough evidence to charge him with the offense. He *was* charged with disorderly conduct, however, and Squire Thornton stood his bail."

" 'Twas no more 'n 'e should do," said Mrs. Pratt indignantly, "allowin' pore Whipple to be taken off to jail fer something 'e did 'isself." She was quiet for a moment. "But I'm that glad to 'ear it, I am," she added in a softer tone. "It settles me mind, wi' regard to the squire. I reckon 'e'll give Whipple somewot to make it good."

"I suppose he will," Kate said, wondering what she should do with this new bit of information. Of itself, of course, the intelligence had little significance, but taken together with the rest of what had been learned that morning, it seemed important—*very* important, in fact. If the squire had sabotaged the balloon, very nearly resulting in the deaths of both Charles and the Honorable Mr. Rolls, was it possible that he had also tampered with the brake on Bradford's motorcar, resulting in Albrecht's death? That question reminded her of another, and she hastened to ask it.

"Mrs. Pratt, do you recall those three small crockery pots of mustard that were sent to us from France? I should like to see them, if you don't mind."

Mrs. Pratt stared at her, her eyes narrowing. "The mustard pots? All three?"

"Yes. Is there some problem?"

Mrs. Pratt bit her lip nervously. " 'Ow about two, yer ladyship? Will they do?"

"Where is the third?"

"The third? Well, ye see, yer ladyship . . . that is, I—" She stopped, looked up at the clock, and cried, "Oh, laws, but it's time to start the luncheon!" Jumping up from the table, she went to the range, picked up a wooden spoon, and began to stir the soup, with rather more violence than was necessary.

Kate rose too, and went to stand beside her. "Mrs. Pratt," she said gently, "did our Amelia borrow the third mustard pot?"

"Amelia!" Mrs. Pratt exclaimed, turning around. "Oh, no, yer ladyship!"

"If Amelia didn't take it, who did?" Kate asked gently. "Mrs. Pratt, the missing mustard pot, by itself, is of no importance to me. I am seeking only to get to the bottom of a very troublesome matter, and the pot may help to do so. Tell me, do, please. Who has the mustard pot?"

Mrs. Pratt hung her head. "I give it to Bess fer 'er birthday, full o' quince jam. 'Twas the night she got tumbled into the ditch by Lord Marsden's motorcar, when she come to fetch the pig's blood."

"Bess?" Kate asked, confused. "Pig's blood?" So then she had to hear the story of Bess all over again from beginning to end, or at least to the point on Friday night at which Mrs. Pratt had observed her lurking near Lord Marsden's motorcar. This time, Kate understood far more than she had before—enough to persuade her that she needed to speak to Bess Gurton immediately.

"This Bess," she said. "Where may I find her?"

"Find 'er?" Mrs. Pratt asked wonderingly. "Why on earth wud yer ladyship want to—"

"So that I may *speak* with her, of course," Kate said, impatient. "It's urgent that I learn what she was doing here on Friday night."

Mrs. Pratt reflected. "Well," she said at last, "ye must take the lane to the village, but ye don't go quite that far, jes' to Ashton Cross and one lane beyond, then turn to the right an' go as far as the lane which ends at Black Brook, an' after that—"

"Get your shawl, Mrs. Pratt," Kate said, taking the spoon from her.

"Me shawl, ma'am?"

"And your bonnet. I shall never find that cottage by myself. And anyway, Mistress Gurton is more likely to be willing to speak to me if you are present, and encourage her. Now, come along."

"But wot about luncheon?" Mrs. Pratt cried, hanging back.

"Luncheon can wait," Kate said firmly, and marched her cook to the door. "This business is more important than a bit of cold joint and a pudding!"

21

"A curse is like a stone flung up to the heavens, and maist like to return on the head that sent it."

—SIR WALTER SCOTT
Old Mortality, 1816

BESS GURTON HAD had more shocks and surprises fall on her head in the past few weeks than ever before in her life, but the greatest shock of all came on Sunday morning, when she learned from her friend Sally Munby that Lord Marsden's motorcar had been destroyed in a crash on the preceding day.

" 'Tis the Lord's doin'," Sally had pronounced piously over the low hedge that separated their back gardens.

"Or the devil's," Sally's daughter Martha remarked from the doorway, as she spread the dish towel to dry on the rosemary bush. "They say the devil takes 'is due, an' o' course it 'appened at Devil's Bridge. I 'eard that the man 'oo was drivin' 'ad both 'is legs cut off at the knees. 'E died a 'orrible death." She paused, savoring this information, then added, in a harder tone, "But 'e was a furriner."

" 'Tis the Lord's doin'," Sally repeated. "I say, let this be a lesson to those 'oo go bargin' down the roads, murderin' innercent old men."

But Bess, when she had recovered her breath, knew otherwise. The wreck of Lord Marsden's motorcar was neither the Lord's doing nor the devil's, but *hers*, and the thought was distinctly unnerving. She hurried inside and shut the door and sat herself down before the fire. Her first thoughts were almost triumphant, as she recalled her ignominious leap into the muddy ditch, and the subsequent curses she had laid on the offending motorcar. That would teach them to treat Bess Gurton uncivilly, and to withhold from her the respect she deserved!

But as she continued to reflect, Bess's thoughts took on the color of remorse. Some poor man had got his legs cut off at the knees because of her, and died a horrible death. What was her dignity in comparison to a man's life, even though he was a foreigner? Who was she to take on such a fearsome responsibility? *Vengeance is mine, saith the Lord.* But she had exacted the Lord's vengeance—and the devil's due, too, come to that, and she thought fearfully that it might even be said in some quarters that she had done the devil's work for him.

This new thought banished the last shred of Bess's triumph and made her shiver to the very roots of her soul. Would the devil be offended at the way she had raised herself above herself? Or would he, seeing how effectively she worked, now come to her to ask her to do other jobs for him? Both ideas filled her with alarm. But what could she do? The deed was done and a man was dead, and there was no undoing either.

The clock on the shelf clanged the noon hour, but Bess, lost in thought, failed to notice. Finally, at half-past, she rose from her chair, made a pot of tea, boiled an egg, and toasted a bit of bread. But when she sat down to it, she found that she could scarcely eat, and after a while she pushed it away.

Bess was clearing this unfinished repast from the table when a knock sounded at the door. She opened it to discover, on her very doorstep, her friend Sarah Pratt, bonneted and shawled, and, standing with her, Lady Kathryn, in a smart brown wool suit and brown boots, with a woolen hat pulled over her ears and a very serious look on her pretty face.

"Lor'," was all she could say, before making a clumsy curtsey.

"Well, Bess," Sarah demanded, for all the world as if she were accustomed to her friends dropping curtseys before her. "Ain't ye goin' to ask 'er ladyship to come in?"

Bess recovered enough to offer the invitation, which was accepted with alacrity. Introductions were brief and hurried, and then the kettle was refilled and placed on the fender, and the three took seats around the table, Sarah on a broken stool, her ladyship on Bess's chair, and Bess herself on an upturned wooden box.

"Lady Kathryn," Sarah said sternly, " 'as summat to ask ye, Bess, summat important. Ye must tell the 'ole truth, so 'elp ye God."

That stung like a stone. "I don't want anybody to teach me 'ow to tell truth, Sarah Pratt," Bess said with asperity. "I wudn't tell a lie if you was to give me a gold sov'rin."

"I am very glad for that, Bess," Lady Kathryn said, in a grave but kindly tone, "for much depends on the truth you tell us. I understand that you came to Bishop's Keep a fortnight ago to obtain—" And she proceeded to recapitulate the tale she had been told (she said) by Bess's friend Sarah. Her *former* friend, that is, Bess thought, with a hard look at Sarah.

"Now, then, Bess," Lady Kathryn said, having finished the story, "is all that true?"

"Well," Bess said guardedly, "it's the truth that I came fer the pig's blood an' took the quince jam in a lit'le stoneware pot, which Sarah said was my birthday gift, along o' a cake." She stopped, thinking how to tell truly what was required of her without telling *all*. "An' it's true that I came to see the balloon—"

"In the dark o' the night?" Sarah demanded.

"There was a moon," Bess said defensively. "I cud see the balloon perfec'ly well."

"And did you stop by the motorcars?" Lady Kathryn asked.

Bess nodded slowly.

"And did you touch Lord Marsden's car?"

"Well," Bess replied, "not to say *touched*." She raised her head and looked Lady Kathryn squarely in the eye. "I didn't touch the motorcar, yer ladyship. As God is me witness."

Lady Kathryn looked back at her, equally squarely. "You are telling me that you did not tamper with it in any way?"

That presented Bess with a great difficulty, and she was silent for a moment. "Well . . ." she said, and stopped.

"Let us not quibble, Bess," Lady Kathryn said firmly. "Tell me, please, exactly what you did."

Bess saw that she was not going to evade her ladyship's questions. She hung her head and waited for the stone to fall. "I cursed it."

Lady Kathryn stared at her. "You . . . cursed it?"

And then the simple story came out. She had first cursed the motorcar in anger the night she was forced to fling herself into the ditch. She had cursed it again on the night she had visited the balloon, not in anger, but with a cold resolution. "I'm not sorry the motorcar's gone," she said at the end, with a touch of defiance. "But I didn't mean fer the furriner t' die. Fer that, I'm sorry."

Lady Kathryn frowned. "There's more to this than a simple curse. What was in the mustard pot that you dropped into the gondola?"

Bess felt her breath catch in her throat. How did her ladyship know about *that*?

When Bess did not immediately respond, her ladyship went on, "I must tell you, Bess, that we have the mustard pot, and that we have established a clear connection between the pot and the wrecked motorcar. Now, the truth!"

"A connection?" Bess asked, frowning. "Wot connection?"

But Lady Kathryn only shook her head, and Bess saw that there was nothing for it except to tell the truth. Again, her telling was short and the story simple, and when she was finished, she could see that her ladyship and Sarah were utterly amazed.

"Ye wanted to *fly*?" Sarah asked incredulously. "*That's* why ye wanted the pig's blood?"

"The receipt was in Gammer's book," Bess said, "so I knew the ointment t'wud work."

"The ointment," Lady Kathryn said. "Just what did you put in it?"

Bess scratched her head. "Pig's blood," she said, "an' goose grease an' honey, and some herbs, water hemlock and chicory, like, an' a few others." She frowned, trying to remember what herbs she had added at her own inspiration. "Oh, an' raw plovers' eggs, an' a pinch of chimney soot."

"Sounds like a witch's brew t' me," Sarah said darkly.

"It sounds to me," Lady Kathryn said, without batting an eyelash, "as if it might work very well. I should perhaps like to try it myself, Bess, if you don't mind."

Bess was startled, but inexpressibly pleased that Lady Kathryn herself should want to sample her ointment.

There was one drawback, however. "It smells," she said, mindful of the faint scent of Lady Kathryn's floral toilet water. "Smells rather 'orrid, as a matter of fact."

"Pshaw," Lady Kathryn said. "Smell is no deterrent. Not if you really want to fly."

Bess understood that she had at last met a woman after her own heart. "That's 'ow I sees it," she said, dropping a triumphant glance on Sarah. " 'Ow I sees it ex-actly."

"Once the ointment was made," her ladyship asked thoughtfully, "what did you do with it?"

"I put it in the jam pot, an' in another little jar I had."

"An' then you dropped the pot into the gondola?"

"I thought as if the ointment flew up in the balloon," Bess said, "it might work all the better."

"A logical assumption," Lady Kathryn said. "Have you had an opportunity to test it? The ointment, I mean."

Bess shook her head. "I meant to git it out o' the gondola, but when I 'eard about the crash an' the pore furriner—" She swallowed, weighed down once again by the guilt of what she had done. "I'd be much obliged to 'ave it, if it's all the same to you, yer ladyship," she said humbly.

Lady Kathryn thought for a moment. "You dropped the pot into the gondola, and then you went to the motorcar. Were you carrying your other jar of ointment with you?"

"I was," Bess said, "but I lost it. I had it in me pocket, an' it fell out."

"Where?"

Bess could only lift her shoulders and shake her head. She had no idea where she had dropped the jar—in fact, Sarah Pratt had so startled her with her loud question out of the dark that she had not missed it until she was well and safely down the lane.

Lady Kathryn leaned forward. "And you're certain that you did not touch the motorcar?"

"No, yer ladyship," Bess said, with emphasis. "On me 'onor."

"Well, then," her ladyship said briskly, "I think we have learned what we came to learn." She stood and held out her hand. "Thank you for your candor and helpfulness, Bess." She paused reflectively. "Tell me, this desire of yours, this wish to fly—is it of long standing?"

"Of long standin'?" Bess cried. "I've wanted to fly since I was a girl an' saw Gammer Gurton goin' over the 'edge on 'er—" She stopped, and felt the color mount in her cheeks. She was coming to trust her ladyship, but it wouldn't do to tell all that she had seen. "Since I was a girl," she finished lamely.

"Well, then," Lady Kathryn said, putting her hat on her head without respect to the way it flattened her curls, "perhaps something can be arranged."

"Something . . . ?" Bess asked wonderingly.

"Something in the flying line. If so, I shall send for you. Come, Sarah." Lady Kathryn put on her gloves and went to the door, stood for a moment with her hand on the latch, thinking, then turned again.

"Bess," she said, "on second thought, I believe it might be a good idea if you were to come with me to Bishop's Keep. Sir Charles will want to know precisely what is in that ointment, and I doubt if he will believe *me*."

Bess's eyes widened. "Oh, no, me lady," she whispered. "I could niver—"

"But you *must*." Lady Kathryn spoke with a firm assurance. "You must indeed, Bess, for a man's guilt may be discovered by what you say—and your own innocence established."

Bess was taken aback. "Me . . . innocence?"

"Indeed. It appears that someone found the jar of ointment you dropped, and rubbed it onto the brake of

221

Lord Marsden's car. The car was wrecked as a result, and the man killed."

It took a moment for this to sink in. "Yer ladyship is sayin'," Bess said finally, "that it wasn't me *curses* that wrecked the car an' killed that pore furriner?"

Sarah snickered, and Lady Kathryn frowned at her. "No, Bess," she said gently, "it was not your curses. Now, will you come?"

So Bess Gurton, her heart suddenly relieved of its load of guilt, climbed up beside Sarah Pratt in the pony cart and waved goodbye to a dumbfounded Sally Munby, who watched through her cottage window as Bess drove off with her ladyship.

22

"Where will it ever end? The next we know, a man may be condemned by the voice of his own blood."
—EDWARD LAKEN

CHARLES CAME INTO the library looking for Kate. When he did not find her there, he rang loudly for Mudd.

"Where," he asked, "will I find Lady Kathryn? I should like to speak to Cook, as well, if you please." He glanced at the gold clock on the mantel. "And what time will we have lunch?"

"Luncheon, I fear, sir, is delayed. It seems as 'er ladyship and Mrs. Pratt 'ave gone off together, sir, leaving no instructions as to the kitchen. Miss Marsden *is* 'ere, 'owever," he added. "She is at work in your darkroom, with your permission, she said. If you should like me to interrupt her—"

"That is not necessary," Charles said. "Let her work. But you say Lady Kathryn and Cook have gone off together? Where have they gone?"

"I can't say, sir. They was in a 'urry. 'Er ladyship took the pony cart."

223

Before she left Devil's Bridge that morning, Kate had told Charles about her conversation with Agnes and her plan to speak to the Widow Jessup. He had encouraged her, having learned from experience that his wife had ways of discovering information that he could not—a woman's touch, approach to, entirely wanting in his investigation. He also guessed that Kate had stopped in the kitchen to ask Cook about the crockery pot of red grease, although he could not hazard a guess where she and Mrs. Pratt had gone. As to luncheon, however, he knew how to fend for himself.

"Well, then, Mudd," he said, "I trust we might find a bit of bread and cheese in the larder, and perhaps a slice or two of cold meat, and some drink. See what you can discover that might do for myself and Constable Laken, please, and bring it here shortly. I am expecting the constable at any—" He heard the crunch of wheels on gravel. "Ah, there he is now."

When the constable came into the library, Charles observed that his friend wore a disgruntled look. "Your interviews at the inn did not go well?" he asked.

"Go well?" Laken asked with some sarcasm, dropping into a chair. "Say, rather, Charles, that they went too well. Every man Jack of that crew has a motive to murder every *other* man. It is hard to say which of them hates the most vehemently. And to a man, they all hate Dunstable, who seems to have done them each a vile injury." He wrinkled his nose as if he were smelling a bad odor. "If what they tell me reflects the reality of London life in these days, I am heartily glad to be elsewhere. It's a wonder that the dock isn't overflowing with murderers, and the morgue with victims."

Charles sighed. "They are. But before you begin, I had best tell you what I have learned about the cause of the accident." It took only a minute or two to describe what had been done to the brake, to show Laken the pot of grease that had been used, and to mention the fingerprint.

"Such luck," Laken said, with a touch of humorous sarcasm. "Dactyloscopy to the rescue, eh?"

Charles sighed. Unfortunately, the Home Office held the same skeptical attitude toward the use of fingerprints. In fact, the Troup Committee, which had been charged in '93 to study the problem of criminal identification, had last year come down against dactyloscopy and in favor of anthropometry: the complicated system of physical measurements of the length and circumference of the head, length of arms, of fingers, of feet, and so on, that had been developed over the past two decades by Alphonse Bertillon in Paris. *Bertillonage* seemed to have conquered Europe, its practices being introduced into the police systems of Portugal, Denmark, and Holland, and most recently, in the German Empire. Meanwhile, dactyloscopy, which Charles regarded as a much more reliable tool of identification, was viewed as an interesting but impractical scientific curiosity. Only Francis Galton, the old friend of his father's who had brought fingerprinting to Charles's attention in 1888, was continuing to collect fingerprints. He asked all visitors to his laboratory in the South Kensington Museum to leave their fingerprints and had photographic enlargements made of the most interesting, studying the patterns of lines and whorls until he had finally created a system for classifying the similarities and differences. But even though Galton's system of identification was (to Charles's mind, at least) far more manageable than Bertillon's, it had not found nearly such wide acceptance.

"I doubt if dactyloscopy can come to the rescue in this instance," Charles said with some regret. "The print is smudged and incomplete, and may prove only partially useful. And of course, we should have to match it against a known print. That's why it is important to narrow down the field of suspects." He paused. "And what of your morning's work, Ned? What were you able to learn?"

Laken took out a small notebook and began to flip through the pages. "I might as well begin with Rolls, although I saw him last. He seems to me to have the least motive to harm Dunstable or Albrecht or destroy Marsden's motorcar, and in fact, to have a substantial stake in Albrecht's winning the chase. He is also the most congenial of the lot, although I found him (if you don't mind my stating an opinion) to be rather a wild young man. He has a taste for loose women—at least, if Frank Ponsonby is to be believed. Ponsonby appears to know all about him."

"Ah," Charles said gravely, thinking of Patsy Marsden.

"But it is likely not true," Laken said. "If Rolls *were* given to the wrong sort of woman, Bradford would surely not have brought him to Marsden Manor. Or if he had, he would have forbidden his sister to have any relationship with the man."

"Don't be too sure," Charles said, remembering Patsy's obvious infatuation and making a mental note to ask Kate's opinion as to what to do with Ponsonby's tittle-tattle. "What about Ponsonby, then?"

"An insolent bastard." Laken spoke with unaccustomed feeling. "You know, don't you, that he's a bill-broker, in addition to importing the Benz?" Charles nodded shortly, and he went on. "The man also deals in rumor and hearsay and takes great delight in passing along whatever ugly bits of information he may possess. I am sure that he doesn't scruple to use it, too, to obtain what he wants from his victims."

"Blackmail?" Charles asked.

"Blackmail," Laken agreed. "Especially where encumbrances and liens are concerned. That, at least, is the accusation of Arnold Bateman, who also told me that Ponsonby and Dunstable were caught up in a sordid bit of business with a married cousin of Ponsonby's—a certain Aurora Vickers, who killed herself after Dunstable dropped her. Unfortunately, she committed the fatal act in Ponsonby's own bathtub, thereby leading to certain rumors that—" he shook his head. "It is too wretched to repeat. But the story certainly suggests that Ponsonby hates Dunstable with a very great passion. I don't believe he would hesitate to disgrace him, or even to do him in."

"By sabotaging the motorcar in which he should have ridden," Charles mused, "which might do for either contingency."

"Exactly so." Laken looked down at his notebook. "And then there is Dickson."

"Ah, yes, Arthur Dickson," Charles said. Poor Dickson, who had made his fortune, and his reputation, in steam locomotives, and was as devout a steam man as there was in all England. If Dickson had his way, they would all be driving steam cars within another decade—perhaps not a bad outcome, all things considered. In Charles's view, steam was the most imminently practical motive power. It was a proven technology, and therefore did not face the uncertainties and complications of the as-yet poorly tested internal combustion engine.

"As I understand it from Rolls," Laken said, "Dickson is in serious trouble. He has been accused by a competitor of having stolen a patent and now must defend himself. Not an easy task, I am given to understand, since he has recently suffered a substantial reversal of fortune. For which," he added, "the man blames Dunstable."

"Dunstable!" Charles said, in some surprise.

"I am still looking into that one," Laken replied. "Bateman claims, however, that Dickson's feelings toward Dunstable are quite bitter."

"And what of Bateman himself?"

"Not much there, I'm afraid. He appears to have no special grudge against Dunstable or Albrecht. He and

Dickson tangled in some sort of fracas at the Crystal Palace Exhibition, but—"

"I know about that one," Charles said, "a minor accident. I hardly think it is relevant here. I did hear something once about Bateman and Dunstable and the Peters Pneumatic Tire Company, however. Marsden might know the details."

Charles looked up as Mudd came into the room, bearing a heavily laden tray. "Ah, luncheon! Put it down in front of the window, please, Mudd." To Laken, he added, "It appears that Kate has made off with our cook, so I cannot guarantee a fine lunch." He gestured to the tray, on which was arranged sliced cold meat, sardines, bread, lettuce, radishes, sliced tomatoes, pickles, mustard, and horseradish, as well as a cheesecake and several jam puffs. "But from the look of it," he added, "I believe it is adequate."

"Adequate, indeed," Laken said, rising to join his friend at the table where Mudd had deposited the tray. He took a plate and began to help himself to the sliced cold meat. "Of course, the very absence of motive intrigues me, where Bateman is concerned."

"Ah, yes," Charles said, making up his own plate. "The others appear to have too much motive, so Bateman is distinguished by having too little." He reached for the carafe. "Wine? Or here is beer, if you like."

"Beer would suit me," Laken replied, as they sat down with their lunches on their laps. After a moment, Charles said, with his mouth full, "And of course, there's Dunstable himself."

Laken made a disgusted noise. "You know, I hardly know whether to credit that cock-and-bull story about the man's being beaten and chucked in the dung heap. It is all too convenient, if you ask me—takes him out of suspicion."

"You think he might have made it up? But he *was* found in the dung heap, was he not?"

"Oh, that's right enough. Discovered under a tarpaulin, with his hands tied behind him and a wadded-up kerchief thrust into his mouth. But the man is a charlatan, through and through. I did not myself observe the knots in the rope, nor the gag—and it would have been entirely possible for him to have crawled into that dung heap unobserved at any time during the day."

"And his injuries?"

"I've seen far worse self-inflicted wounds." Laken chewed reflectively. "And, of course, there is also the possibility that he hired a couple of village lads to tap him lightly on the head with something that would leave a mark, if he were not confident of managing it himself."

"But to what end?" Charles asked. "And with what motive?"

"I've been thinking about that. The man is known to be a publicity hound. Perhaps he meant to disable Marsden's Daimler, then cry foul, expecting that the newspaperman who was here yesterday would blow the whole thing up and that he would gain attention and sympathy thereby. Of course," Laken added, "he would not have counted on Albrecht's going into a ravine and impaling himself on the tiller." Laken took up a pickle.

"There is also the matter of opportunity," Charles said. "I suppose you looked into that."

"For what little good it did me," Laken said wryly. "Assuming that the stuff was smeared on the brake some time after the Daimler was left in the Park on Friday night and the start of the chase on Saturday morning, any of the drivers, and Dunstable as well, had the opportunity. Not to mention the villagers and the workers who were setting up the fete."

"Or handling the balloon," Charles said.

"Indeed," Laken replied. "What, by the way, exactly *is* the substance that was smeared on the brake?"

"I have absolutely no idea," Charles admitted. "But I certainly intend to spend some time this afternoon in the laboratory, attempting to analyze it. If I can determine the type of lubricant, perhaps we can trace it to its manufacturer, and hence to one of our suspects."

"But that is likely to take some time," Laken objected. "Those fellows will not consent to remain for much longer, and it will be difficult to hold them if they should choose to go." He looked up at the clock. "It is already nearly two."

"I know," Charles said. He put aside his plate. "We had better get busy. While I am working in the laboratory, perhaps you can return to the inn and obtain the men's fingerprints."

"Their fingerprints?" Laken frowned. "On what grounds?"

"On suspicion of—"

"I'm afraid that won't do, Charles," Laken said, shaking his head. "It won't do at all. These men may not be gentlemen, in Society's definition of the word, but they have a high standing in London commerce and are sure to have powerful friends. Anyway, this fingerprinting is a nasty business. You can hardly expect such men to willingly smear their hands with tar and press them upon—"

"Printer's ink," Charles amended. "It is readily removed."

"That may be, but this is England. A man is innocent until a jury of his peers pronounces him guilty."

Charles stared at his stubborn friend, the frustration mounting. "But how are we to discover the guilty man *without* this evidence, Ned? And don't forget that Scotland Yard is taking the fingerprints—"

"—of convicted felons who have already forfeited their freedom, not of free men who have not yet been charged with a crime."

"But what then do you do with the fingerprints that are left at the scene of a crime?" Charles asked. "Is it an invasion of a man's privacy to take those prints, for possible use against him?"

Laken frowned. "At the scene of a crime? I think we may suppose that those prints are those of a criminal and—"

"If you concede as much, then, you must also concede that prints that are left *anywhere* may be taken, for possible use in the solution of a crime. Am I correct?"

"Anywhere?" Laken looked doubtful. "Well, I suppose—"

"Very well, then," Charles said. "I propose that you go to the inn and see if you can find some objects that have been handled by our suspects, so that we may take those fingerprints. You yourself said, don't forget, that any of these men may have committed this crime."

"And don't *you* forget, Charles: while you and some of your scientific friends may hold dactyloscopy in high regard, no court has ever used such evidence to convict a man."

"But that is only a matter of time," Charles objected. "When the method of classification is perfected—"

"Perhaps. But even then, there will be difficulties. While judges may be prepared to deal handily with such technical information, juries will scarcely know what to do with it. And privacy is one of the most sacred of our rights. To compel a man's own hands to bear witness against him . . ." Laken shook his head, intently serious. "Where will it ever end, Charles? The next we know, a man may be condemned by the voice of his own blood."

Charles shook his head. "If you refuse to obtain the suspects' fingerprints so I can compare them to the one on the fender, I fail to see how we can—"

He stopped as the door opened. Kate came in, looking extraordinarily pretty in a brown wool suit and close-fitting wool hat, askew on her windblown hair. She was followed by a small, round, nervous-looking woman wrapped head-to-toe in an old blue shawl.

"Hullo, Charles," Kate said brightly, and, seeing Laken, added, "You too, Ned."

"We've eaten lunch without you, I'm afraid," Laken said apologetically.

"Oh, good," Kate said, taking off her leather driving gloves. She smiled. "I've been to the village, where I found someone who may be able to clear up part of our mystery." She took the reluctant woman's hand and led her forward. "Gentlemen, this is Mistress Gurton, who has always had a great desire to fly."

23

"If ever there was a case of clearer evidence than this . . . this case is that case."

—WILLIAM ARABIN, 1773–1841

KATE WAS GRATIFIED at the courteous, the *rapt*, attention that the two men paid to Bess Gurton's story, as that woman told it from beginning to end, hesitant and fearful at first but gaining confidence as she went.

"Pig's blood!" exclaimed Charles, when she had finished. "What confounded good luck that you thought to include pig's blood in your ointment, Mistress Gurton. You may have given us the key to solving this mystery."

"I fail to see," Laken said, "the particular significance of pig's blood as evidence in this case."

"The significance, Ned? Simply put, it lies in the fact that the platelets contained in swine blood are distinguished by their large size. When we use a microscope to compare the grease I removed from the Daimler's fender with the ointment in the mustard pot, we shall no doubt discover in both samples the same large corpuscles."

"Corpuscles," Kate said in an ironic aside to Laken. "Why in heaven's name didn't *I* think of that?"

Bess's eyes were wide. "Cork-puskles? But 'ow did corks git into the blood, me lady?"

Charles, however, was continuing. "The soot particles will be abundantly obvious. The vegetative tissue should also display similar cellular structure in both samples. Had we a mind to it, we could confirm the identification by comparing that tissue to fresh leaf samples from the same herbs."

Kate sighed, thinking that whatever the question, Charles would have a scientific answer. She did not mean to be disrespectful to her husband, but in her judgment, scientific evidence did not always take them closer to the truth. Sometimes truth was a matter of human spirit, not intellect.

"Can we not simply take Mistress Gurton's word for what is in the ointment, Charles?" she asked.

"But that would not yield the information we are seeking," Charles said, growing even more excited. "You see, if a *third* trace of this same distinctive substance were to be located—on the clothing, say, of one of the suspects— we would have incontrovertible evidence of the man's involvement."

"And if he attempted to deny it," Kate said, seeing that in this instance, science might well be of service, "the man could be confronted with the proof and might be surprised into revealing his guilt?"

"Exactly so." Charles was pacing up and down, his hands behind his back. "The case should be much stronger than one built solely on dactyloscopic evidence."

Bess bent toward Kate. "Dac-te-scoop-a-which, ma'am?"

"Fingerprints," Kate whispered. "The marks on the tips of your fingers."

Bess turned her hands over and began intently to examine her fingers.

"Yes, yes, indeed," Charles said, striding on. "Our single piece of physical evidence is a smudged fingerprint—which, as you say, Ned, a jury would find hard to swallow." (At this, Bess put her hands in the pockets of her woolen skirt.) "Were we to find traces of the substance—"

"I suppose," Laken said dryly, "that you want me to return to the inn and examine the clothing which the men were wearing yesterday."

"And their pocket handkerchiefs," Kate put in. "I know that if I were to discover Mistress Gurton's ointment on my hands, I should want to remove it as quickly as possible. A pocket handkerchief might well provide evidence."

"I think it a very good idea to have a look at the clothing," Charles said, and added, "if it does not strain your ethical principles, Ned."

"But if I had soiled my clothing in that way," Laken objected, "I should give it immediately to the laundress to be cleaned."

"Cleaned?" Bess asked. "An' 'oo should be doin' the wash of a Sunday, I'd like to know? Sart'nly not our Peg. She's on 'er knees at chapel all the Sabbath."

"Mistress Gurton is right, Ned," Kate said. "It is not likely that the clothing has been washed. Your search may prove more fruitful than you expect."

The constable nodded. "I shall do it."

"And while you are at it, you might look for the jar," Kate said. At Charles's quizzical expression, she added, "Well, of course. If I had picked up Mistress Gurton's jar of ointment and used some of it, I should certainly put the jar into my pocket. I shouldn't want to leave it lying about as evidence, should I?"

"Very well, then," Laken said, "I shall look for the jar too. As for fingerprints, however—" He paused and gave Charles a dark look.

"Yes, yes, I know," Charles said impatiently. "But if you should happen upon an object that bears a clear fingerprint, perhaps you could remove it and—"

"I shall not." Laken's voice was firm. Nodding to Bess and bowing to Kate, he left the room.

Bess turned to Kate. "Wot," she asked in a whisper, "about fingerprints?"

So Kate, making as quick a job of it as she could, gave Bess the details as Beryl Bardwell understood them. "With luck," she concluded, "the fingerprint will identify the person who found your ointment and applied it to the motorcar's brake."

There was a moment's silence. Then Bess, with a long sigh, said, "Would ye need to take mine?"

"Yours!" Charles exclaimed. "I should be very *pleased* to take yours—for purposes of elimination, of course."

"Sir Charles means," Kate interpreted, "that he can then show that *you* are not the guilty person."

" 'Lim'nation," Bess said heavily. "I thought as much." She screwed her eyes tight shut, turned her head to one side, and held out her hands. " 'Ere they be, then, yer ladyship. Take 'em. I only ask—" She seemed to choke. "I only ask that ye leave me one er two on each 'and, if ye please. I makes me livin' wi' baskets, like, an'—"

"Oh, dear, no!" Kate exclaimed. "Your fingers won't be cut off, Bess! They will merely be inked, and their impressions taken."

Bess's eyes opened and her countenance cleared. "Oh," she said, quite relieved. "Well, then, ye kin 'ave all ten o' em, if ye like, yer ladyship, an' welcome."

When the simple procedure was over, Kate thanked Bess warmly. "Please stop by the kitchen and give my compliments to Mrs. Pratt. Perhaps you and she might stop together for a cup of tea."

At Bess's frown, Kate said, "I know you are upset with her for speaking to me. But I think you will have to agree that things have turned out for the best."

"That's true enough, yer ladyship," admitted Bess, "although Sarah do let 'er tongue run on a bit long."

When Bess had gone, Kate turned to her husband. "What *was* that business about Ned and the fingerprints?" she asked curiously. "And why did you make that odd remark about ethics?"

"Ned has a particular antipathy to taking the fingerprints of a person who has not yet been accused of a crime," Charles replied, with some irony. "He argues that it is an invasion of privacy."

"But a crime cannot be solved without evidence," Kate objected. "Is not the detective obligated to use every available piece of evidence he is able to discover? Or *she*," she corrected herself, thinking of the latest adventure of Beryl Bardwell's female detective.

"It is a vexed question," Charles said. "Suppose that science should somehow permit us to see into your mind, Kate, and determine whether you are telling the truth or a lie. Should the scientist be permitted to intrude on your privacy—even if you are suspected of murder?"

"But if I am guilty—"

"Just so. But what if you are entirely innocent? And who is to know until the scientist completes his probe of your thoughts, thereby violating your privacy? And what if the scientist's instruments are in error, or his conclusions wrong? Who should be the final arbitrator of such methods?"

"A jury, perhaps?" Kate offered tentatively.

"A jury?" Charles chuckled without mirth. "Would you care to put *your* life into the hands of twelve jurors who may be good men and true, but may also be incapable of weighing such delicate evidence?"

Kate searched for an answer, but realized, uncomfortably, that she could find none.

"Ned, and many others, for that matter," Charles went on, "question the propriety of obtaining and using evidence such as a man's fingerprints on the grounds that to do so is an invasion of privacy. The issue is one that is likely to see much debate over the next few years, and I myself have not determined where I stand on such matters." He paused. "But I am particularly distressed in this case, for there *is* a fingerprint on that fender, and without Ned's help, I see no easy way of matching it against the fingerprints of the suspects."

Kate stared at him for a moment, comprehension beginning to dawn. "And the suspects are—"

"The three surviving drivers, of course, as well as Harry Dunstable, Charles Rolls, and Roger Thornton. And, for the sake of completeness, I suppose I should include Bradford Marsden."

"*Not* Bradford!"

"Why not? He has as much reason to hate Harry Dunstable as the next man, perhaps more. No, if only to eliminate him, I should obtain his prints, as I have already obtained those of Lawrence and Mistress Gurton. But I cannot do that easily, for he has gone off to London."

"To London?"

"Yes. He has quarreled with Lord Christopher—or rather, Lord Christopher has quarreled with him. I cannot get his fingerprints at the moment. But, oh that I had the rest!"

Kate looked at him steadily. "Perhaps you shall," she said. "But first, I need to speak to you about Squire Thornton. Mrs. Pratt told me this morning that she saw him pull the grapnel from the gondola. *He*, not the unfortunate Mr. Whipple, is the man who sabotaged the balloon."

Charles stared at her, incredulous.

"And it was Squire Thornton," Kate continued, "who gave the Jessups that thirty pounds—and who had it noised about that the money came from Charles Rolls."

"But why should Thornton do *that*?" Charles asked.

"I am only guessing, of course," Kate replied, "but I think perhaps he wanted to make it appear that Rolls was responsible for Old Jessup's death. You remember, of course, that he was driving Bradford's motorcar that night. And it is Rolls who threatens to snatch Patsy from him—at least as Squire Thornton sees it."

"But no one believes that Rolls killed the man. The coroner did not even have enough evidence to—"

"Lord Christopher and Lady Henrietta might believe it," Kate said, "if Squire Thornton told them it were true, and if the victim's family gave it about that Rolls had compensated them."

"You're saying that Thornton constructed this elaborate charade in order to cast a contender for Patsy's affections into disfavor with her parents?"

"Men have practiced stranger ruses against their rivals," Kate said with a little shrug. "It is the same motive, I believe, that led him to pull the grapnel from the gondola. The act was impulsive, no doubt, and entirely in character—he simply seized the chance that opportunity presented to him."

"You believe, then, that he intended to cause Rolls's death."

"Or simply to cause difficulty," Kate replied, "and keep his rival from becoming a hero." She frowned. "I also think it is entirely possible that he is the man who sabotaged Bradford's Daimler. I am sure that he had as much opportunity as anyone, and it is certainly in keeping with his other act of sabatoge. He might have found the jar of ointment where Bess Gurton dropped it, applied it to the brake, and gone on about his business."

"And why should he?"

"To even the score with Bradford, perhaps. After all, it was Bradford who brought Rolls here. Or he might have wanted to cause trouble for the chase. You saw how he opposed the whole affair. Or perhaps it was a mixture of motives, and given the opportunity—"

Charles's brow was furrowed. "I see all that you say, Kate, and grant you its plausibility. But if Thornton should deny Mrs. Pratt's accusation, how many do you think would take her word against his?"

"Not many, I fear," Kate said gloomily. "If only we had some other evidence—another eyewitness, perhaps, who could corroborate Cook's testimony."

"I think perhaps we do," said a woman's voice.

Kate turned, startled. The speaker was Patsy Marsden. Her face was pale and very serious, and in her hand she held a photograph.

24

"A Lady an explorer? a traveller in skirts?
The notion's just a trifle too seraphic:
Let them stay home and mind the babies, or hem our
   ragged skirts
But they mustn't, can't, and shan't be geographic."
                              —*Punch*, 1893

I T TOOK ONLY a moment's examination for Charles and
Kate to determine that Patsy's photograph, taken
from the vantage point of the east terrace, had caught
the squire red-handed, in the act of jerking the grapnel
from its mooring at the side of the gondola. But it
took some moments more to decide what to do with
the photograph, and still more for Kate to explain the
evidence *she* had gathered, without at all anticipating
its actual use, at the ill-fated dinner party the night
before—evidence which at this moment rested on a shelf
in Mudd's pantry.

In the end, after much debate, it was Kate and Patsy who
put on their cloaks and set off to visit Roger Thornton.
Charles was not entirely happy with this arrangement

and expressed his dissatisfaction with some force. But as Kate quite reasonably pointed out, he had far too much to do with the fingerprint evidence to spend time chasing about after errant squires, and Patsy was really a far more suitable agent. Patsy herself had a very strong motive to undertake the assignment, and was quite persuasive on her own behalf.

"I *want* to do it," she said earnestly. "I will smile prettily, and toss my head, and the squire will be flattered into believing that I am the very sweetest and most compliant sort of young lady. He might say no to you, but he will not be able to resist *my* invitation."

"There really can be no danger, Charles," Kate said. "There are servants at hand, of course, and Patsy shall tell the squire that I am waiting in the carriage. And all she has to do is show him the photographs that she took of the balloon launch—"

"Not the one of his dropping the grapnel, though," Charles said grimly. "That, we shall save for later."

"But the others will do quite well," Kate said. "You see how glossily enameled they are."

So their plan was formed. Charles dispatched the gardener's boy to the Marlborough Head with this message for Constable Laken.

Bishop's Keep, September 27

My dear Ned—

I may after all be able to use that fingerprint to good effect. Please inform Ponsonby, Dickson, Bateman, Dunstable, and Rolls that they are expected to join us here at seven this evening. Light refreshments and entertainment will be provided (I am thinking of a magic lantern show, with lantern slides of the balloon and the chase and so forth). I feel quite safe in saying that Thornton will also be in attendance. I trust that your own researches are progressing. Let me hear what you have found.

Yours faithfully,
Charles Sheridan

Kate consulted briefly with Mrs. Pratt on the menu; then she and Patsy climbed into the closed carriage and were driven by Pocket to Thornton Grange. Once there, Kate remained in the carriage like a very grand lady, waiting nervously and wondering whether, after all, it had been a good idea to send Patsy on this errand.

But there was no reason for nervousness. Patsy returned with a satisfied smile. "The squire sends his compliments to Lady Kathryn, and is pleased to join her and Sir Charles at seven this evening."

"And the photographs?"

She displayed the large envelope she had taken with her. "He took them with some apprehension, carried them to the window, and examined each one carefully, turning them over to read the legend I had written on the reverse. I'm sure he was worried that I might have captured his despicable act on film. But when he saw nothing incriminating, the man was all smiles. He returned the photographs to me with a very pretty compliment as to my artistic prowess. I am sure they have his fingerprints all over them."

Kate smiled. "I hope your performance was not too successful, Patsy. You may have encouraged him to believe that you will accept him as a suitor."

"When the time comes," Patsy said grimly, "I will very quickly disabuse him of that notion." Her voice changed and she held out her hand. "I must seek a favor of you, Kate—quite a large favor, I am afraid."

"You know that anything I may do for you, I shall," Kate said. "What is it, Patsy?"

She did not answer for a moment, and when she did, she spoke first of her brother. "Bradford and Papa quarreled last night. Papa says that Bradford is disgracing the Marsden name with his motorcars and the like, and has vowed to stop his allowance."

"That is a regular threat," Kate said. "According to Bradford, at any rate."

"This time, I think, Papa is quite serious—and so is Bradford. *He* vows to have nothing more to do with Papa's money, and says that, from this moment forward, he will earn his own."

"Commendable," Kate said dryly. "I understand that he has gone to London."

"By the early train this morning. I expect to follow him in a fortnight or so. In the meantime—and this is the favor I must ask of you—I would like to stay at Bishop's Keep." She raised her head, and Kate saw the determination written on her face. "I can no longer remain with my mother and father. I am going away."

Kate was silent for a moment, thinking of the implications of this. "Has Mr. Rolls asked you to marry him?"

"No, he has not," Patsy said fiercely. "If he had, I should have refused him."

"Ah," Kate said, more happily, and relaxed. So this was not a matter of disappointed love, or a broken heart. She had not thought so, but she was glad to be sure.

"Indeed," Patsy said, with the same intensity, "this does not concern Charles Rolls, although Mama is sure that he is the root of my disaffection. She has ordered him out of the house to protect my virtue. My *public* virtue, that is," she added bitterly. "I have assured Mama over and over again that nothing untoward has occurred between us, and never will. But she thinks more about the appearance of things than the truth of them. I do believe I could be a private strumpet of the wildest sort, and if word of it did not get out, I should be quite safe in Mama's eyes."

"I see," Kate said gravely—and she did see the pain in Patsy's eyes, and the hurt in her voice, and understood the girl's heartache. "If you should leave, where do you mean to go? What will you do?"

Patsy looked out the window. "I don't know," she confessed with a sigh. "The truth is that I don't really understand myself, or have more than the vaguest of ideas what I really want. All I know is that I must get away from Mama and Papa—and from England, too." Her voice took on a fierce intensity. "Living here is like living in a hothouse, Kate. I am rooted in soil that is too rich, and pampered and petted as if I were some sort of delicate, exotic plant. I am closed in from the weather, from the cold and from storms. I scarcely know what real life is like, except that it cannot be like *this*."

"I understand, Patsy," Kate said quietly. She loved Bishop's Keep and was grateful to the generous aunt who had made it possible for her to have a life here. And of course, she was deeply in love with Charles, and for the most part, her heart was content. But happy as she was, there was another part of her that longed to be gone, to be moving through the world, unencumbered and alone, as she once had been, and free to choose where she should go and what she should do without consulting anyone.

Patsy turned eagerly to her. "Oh, Kate, how I envy you! Growing up in New York, with a policeman for an uncle. Making your own way as a governess, and as an authoress, a *famous* authoress—" She stopped, suddenly conscience-stricken. "Oh, *pshaw*. Now I've let the cat out of the bag. What a dunce I am!"

Kate stared at her for a long moment. "How did you know?" she asked finally.

"*Everyone* knows," Patsy replied, abashed. "Your servants may be very loyal, but one simply can't keep secrets from them. I suppose one of them said something out of turn just as I have done. It is a fascinating story, and the news is all over the village—all over the county, I daresay. Even those who do not read detective fictions read Beryl Bardwell's, for they know them to be *yours*. And to be worth reading, of course," she added hastily. "Your stories are very much admired."

Kate sighed, resigned. "I might have known," she said, "that I could not keep Beryl Bardwell's secret forever." Then, a little disconcerted, she thought of Charles's mother and brother, and his own future position, and added, "I do hope, however, that the report does not travel far. There are certain people—"

"Certain people?" Patsy prompted after a moment.

But Kate had thought better of the confidence, for it was not likely that the news would go as far as Somersworth. Anyway, she could not fret about what Charles's mother might think; there was nothing at all she could do about it. "My occupation and what people think of it is neither here nor there, Patsy. We were talking of *you*, and what you are to do in the world. You seriously intend to leave your parents' home?"

"I do," Patsy said with great earnestness. "I don't know everything I want—but I *do* want to see the world. And perhaps that will teach me to know what I want."

"But you could see the world with your mother, or your sister."

"But I could *not*, Kate," Patsy said, almost indignant. "Mama and Eleanor frequent only those places where other English people go, and stay in hotels with their English friends, and go to balls with other visiting English people. If I went with them, I should not see the world as it *is*, but only as a pale reflection of England." She shook her head emphatically. "No. To see the world truly, I must not expect it to suit me, or to meet the expectations I have already formed. I must go out *into* it, like a child who does not know what she shall find."

"Like Mary Kingsley," Kate suggested with a smile, thinking of a woman whose writings she had recently read, "paddling her canoe through the swamps of West Africa, dodging the crocodiles—and then sitting down in her tent with a candle to write about it."

"Exactly, Kate! Only *I* shall take the crocodile's photograph, not merely write about him. And I shall photograph giraffes and rhinoceri and elephants and tigers, and send the pictures to you." She thought for a moment, then added, in a breathless rush, "No! Rather, you shall come with me on one of my expeditions, after I have gotten entirely used to seeing the world alone, and we shall motor across Europe, and ride camels across the Gobi, and climb the Swiss Alps. I shall take pictures of everything, and you shall write about where we have been, and we shall see ever so many strange sights, and be thought the very strangest sight of all! We shall be a pair of those 'globe trotteresses' that *Punch* is always poking fun at. What do you say, Kate?"

"I say bravo!" Kate smiled. "And when we return, we shall travel all around, lecturing to enormous crowds about our exploits and giving magic lantern shows of your photographs."

Patsy reached for her hand. "Promise me, Kate," she said solemnly.

"I promise," Kate said, and squeezed her young friend's hand, thinking that Patsy would do, after all. She would do very well indeed. "But before then," she added, "we have tonight's lantern show to arrange."

"Yes," Patsy said, and lost some of her eagerness. "But I must first go back to Marsden Manor to bid Mama goodbye and pack my dressing cases." She managed a smile. "A fearless explorer must certainly have something decent to wear."

"But surely you can postpone your departure for a few days, Patsy—not that I don't want you to come to Bishop's Keep, of course. But your mother has just returned from abroad and—"

"Which makes it exactly the right time for me to do it," Patsy said decidedly. "If I were to remain with her longer, I might come to fear her again—so much that I should not be able to leave." She shook her head. "No, Kate, now is the time to begin. A fearless explorer I shall be, fearless and reckless. And I have *you* to thank for showing me how!"

25

Develop\dĭ-vĕl'-əp
1) To set forth or make clear by degrees or in detail (expound)
2) To make visible or manifest that which is latent
3) To subject exposed photographic material to chemicals in order to produce a visible image
4) To evolve the possibilities of; to promote the growth of; to make available or usable.

CHARLES'S LABORATORY AND adjoining darkroom were located in the servants' area of Bishop's Keep, in what had once been a game larder. Since the room was below ground level and often cold, he had installed a gas fire to warm it, and gas lighting above his worktables. The laboratory was one that any scientist could have claimed with pride, equipped as it was with glass-fronted oaken cabinets filled with chemicals and glassware, solid worktables, a gas burner and sink with both hot and cold water, chemical balance, and other scientific equipment. On one table was his Lancaster achromatic microscope. It was fitted with rack and fine screw adjustments and a condensing lens on a universal joint. Now that his electrical plant was in operation, he planned to install electrical wiring, as well. He could then make use of the newly acquired Crookes tube and a Tesla coil from which he hoped to cobble together a homemade X-ray apparatus built to the specifications in Professor Roentgen's recently published paper.

The smaller, windowless darkroom was adjacent to the laboratory. It was outfitted with worktables, a sink with an ample water supply, porcelain developing tanks, washing and drying racks, an Eastman clock, a Knox enameler, shelves filled with photographic chemicals, printing papers, and supplies, as well as a paraffin-burning ruby safelight (soon to be replaced by electric safelights), and a line for drying prints. There was also a Koresco reducing and enlarging camera, and another purchased from Fallowfield in Charing Cross Road, designed exclusively to produce lantern slides, for which Charles had paid four pounds five shillings. This camera had won a silver medal at the Hackney Exhibition, and was one of his happiest purchases, in spite of the cost.

Charles himself was seated on a stool at a laboratory table, intently studying a number of items on the table before him. At his elbow was an enlarged print of the fingerprint he had found on the Daimler's fender. Occasionally, he shifted from an examination of one of the objects to the enlargement, and then back again.

He looked up when he heard a tap on the door. Lawrence came into the room, still wearing the muddy corduroy trousers and brown jerkin he had worn that morning, when they hauled the motorcar out of the ravine.

"Ah, Lawrence," Charles said. "Did you find anything more of interest in your examination of the motorcar?"

"Not a thing, Sir Charles," Lawrence said. "Pocket sez I'm to 'elp ye in the darkroom?"

"I would like you to make a dozen or so lantern slides," Charles said. "They must be ready by seven without fail. The negatives have already been developed—you'll find them in the rack. I won't need the limelight, so you can use it with the enlarging camera, and the Central Oxygen Works has sent down a fresh cylinder of hydrogen gas, if that proves necessary."

"Thank ye, sir." Lawrence shifted uncomfortably. "Before I begin, sir, there's somethin' I needs to tell ye about. Somethin' dev'lish."

Charles, wearing a pair of thin white gloves, had picked up his magnifying lens and returned to his examination. "Something devilish?" he asked absently. "What is it?"

"The gentl'man 'oo was dug out of the dung heap, sir," Lawrence said grimly. "I know 'oo put 'im there."

"You don't say!" Startled, Charles put down his lens. "Well, then, who *did* put him there, Lawrence?"

"Dick Quilp, Sir Charles. An' 'e was 'elped by Fred Codlin."

"And who," Charles asked, in mild astonishment, "are Dick Quilp and Fred Codlin?"

"Dick is Amelia's cousin, I'm ashamed to say," Lawrence replied with a long face. " 'E works in Mr, Hogarth's mill, sackin' grain. Fred Codlin is the boy 'oo sweeps the crossin's on the 'Igh Street. Each was paid two shillin's to cosh the gentl'man an' bury 'im in the dung heap. Leastwise, that's wot Amelia's cousin Jemmy told 'is mother, 'oo told Amelia when she went to chapel this morning."

Charles stared at him, marveling, once again, at the way information was passed around the village. "And did

Amelia's cousin tell his mother *who* paid these fellows two shillings for such a task?"

At that moment the door opened, and Constable Laken put his head in. "Mudd said you were here, Charles. Are you fit to be interrupted?"

"Come in, Ned. You are just in time to hear the last of Lawrence's story. He is about to tell us who hired Dick Quilp and Fred Codlin to lam Dunstable on the head and bury him in the dung heap."

Laken came into the room and put down a brown-paper parcel on the table. "Quilp and Codlin," he snorted. "I shall haul them in for assault. But who was it who hired them?"

" 'Twere two men. Jemmy says 'e don't know their names," Lawrence replied, "but 'e's seen their motorcars. One o' 'em drives the 'lectric. The other drives the Benz."

"Bateman and Ponsonby!" Laken exclaimed. "Well, now!"

"Good work, thank you, Lawrence," Charles said, feeling no great surprise. Listening to the pair and watching their interactions with Dunstable the night before, he had rather suspected them. "The darkroom is yours," he added. "If you have any questions, of course, I'll be right here."

When Lawrence had gone into the darkroom and closed the door, he turned to Laken. "Bateman and Ponsonby, eh?"

"I suppose this clears Dunstable," Laken said crossly. "And Bateman and Ponsonby as well."

"You have no liking for Dunstable?"

"He is a vulgar rogue, if you ask me."

"That may be. But as to clearing Bateman and Ponsonby, I don't think it does. There is nothing to say that they could not arrange Dunstable's lamming *and* sabotage the car in the bargain."

"Perhaps." He began to unwrap his parcel. "I did not find the jar of grease you were looking for, but I made off with a pair of tweed trousers." He pointed. "The right leg, below the pocket, bears a streak of red grease with a certain, quite distinctive odor. The clothing belongs to—"

"Stop." Charles held up his hand. "Don't tell me, Ned, until I have been able to look at the material under the microscope. In any event, I have something to show *you*." He gestured at the nine wine goblets arranged on the table before him. He had dusted each with talcum powder, revealing several clear fingerprints on each glass.

"Where did you get those goblets?" Laken asked in some surprise.

"Mudd took them from the dinner table last night, labeled them with the names of those who drank from them, and placed them in his pantry. A most fortuitous bit of business, wouldn't you say?" Charles gave a short, dry cough. "It relieves me of the need to bully you to obtain the suspects' prints, while it provides us with sufficient evidence to make the comparison. These glasses represent all of our suspects except Roger Thornton—and I have hopes of obtaining his prints by a different method."

Laken was now in a state of utter stupefaction. "I confess, I am staggered," he said, still staring at the goblets. "Why in heaven's name should Mudd undertake to perform such an amazingly peculiar task? He could not have known—"

"It was Kate's idea."

"Kate?" Laken took his eyes off the objects of his amazement and raised them to Charles. "But how . . . and why—"

Charles smiled with some discomfort. "I suppose I should have told you this before now, Ned, but I did not see any reason to burden you with the knowledge. My wife, it seems, has a secret identity. She is—"

"I know who she is," Laken said tersely. "She is Beryl Bardwell, the female Conan Doyle. She writes those ridiculously popular fictions in which some lady detective or another is always making the police look like fools."

Charles raised both eyebrows. "You know about Beryl Bardwell and Kate, then? *How* did you know?"

"Come now, Charles. Everyone in the village and all about knows of Kate's scribblings. Once the servants discovered it, there was no keeping it secret. I myself have often wished to ask her to present the police as more intelligent and progressive, but—" Laken shrugged. "I did not like to tell her that her secret was known to one and all." An ironic smile came and went at the corners of his mouth. "I was also half-afraid that I was the model for her dim-witted policemen."

"Everyone in the village, eh?" Charles remarked thoughtfully, wondering how soon the news would travel to Somersworth, where it would no doubt send his mother into a hysterical fit. But everything about his wife seemed to affect his mother in that way, from Kate's Irish heritage to her American upbringing—why should this be any worse or better?

There was a pause, and when Laken spoke, there was an edge to his voice. "I am curious to know what led Lady Kathryn to collect these goblets last night, before there was any suspicion of a crime. She could not have suspected that the fingerprints on them might be put to use today— or could she?"

"She was conducting an experiment," Charles replied, with a certain pride. "The solution to Beryl Bardwell's current mystery hinges on fingerprints, you see. Kate has read Galton's work on the subject, but she has never actually studied prints. She collected the goblets with some rather unformed idea of examining the fingerprints on them in order to see what problems her detective might face."

"Most remarkable."

"Indeed," Charles returned. "It was a piece of unbelievable good luck that she also thought to ask Mudd to label the glasses as he took them from the table."

"Lord preserve us," Laken muttered.

"I believe He has," Charles replied, almost smugly. "You must admit that Kate's idea was most fortuitous." He smiled a little. "I sincerely hope that she has not offended your ethical sensibilities, Ned—as an intelligent and progressive policeman, that is, who is concerned to preserve the privacy of the citizenry."

Laken looked embarrassed. "Perhaps I overstated the case earlier this afternoon. I do not believe that my conclusions are as settled as I may have made them appear."

"I am glad for that," Charles said thankfully. "I was beginning to fear—" he was interrupted by a knock, and then the door opened.

"Excuse me, gentlemen," Kate said. "I hope I am not interrupting you." She held out an envelope. "I have brought the photographs that Patsy gave Squire Thornton to look over. She reports that he handled each of them. I dare say you will discover the evidence you need."

Charles took the envelope and, opening it carefully, laid out several photographs on the table. "Yes," he said, "there are a number of quite clear prints."

"From Squire Thornton?" Laken shook his head, bemused. "We seem to have a surfeit of evidence."

"I doubt it," Charles said. "And I must remind you of the point you quite properly raised earlier, Ned. This fingerprint evidence—I am not at all sure that it can be presented to a jury, or that its import could be understood and weighed fairly." He sighed, remembering the difficulty his friend Tom Stevens had experienced in the trial of George Lamson fifteen years before, when he had presented some sophisticated toxicological evidence to the jury. The poor jurors, several of whom could not read, had not understood a word of it. "But we are far from having a case to present to a jury," he added. "First, we must examine—"

"*You* must examine it, I fear," Kate said. "There is a certain young gentleman in the drawing room, who wishes to speak to me on a matter of the heart. At least, that's what I presume his errand to be, since he asked to see me privately."

Charles raised both eyebrows. "Indeed? And who is the young gentleman?"

"Mr. Rolls," Kate said, and saying nothing else, turned and left the room.

Laken looked very cross. "I told that boy to stay at the inn."

"I imagine he came to see to the repairs on the balloon," Charles said. His magnifying lens in hand, he bent over the photographs and began scrutinizing the fingerprints on their glossy surfaces. For a moment he said nothing more. Then, as he shifted to an examination of one of the goblets, he added, "He is not the sort of young man to take orders, even from a constable."

Laken spoke cautiously. "Did you tell Kate anything about—"

"Rolls's malfeasance? No. I took it to be rumor. In any event, it is none of my business. Marsden must look after his sister, and would not take kindly to another man's interference."

And with that, Charles handed his friend a magnifying lens and pointed with his pencil at something.

"Take a close look at this fingerprint, Ned, and then at the one in this photographic enlargement, which I took from a photo of the fender of Marsden's Daimler." He pointed to the enlargement on the table. "Tell me what you see."

There was silence for the next few moments, as Laken bent over first one fingerprint, and then the other.

"By Jove," he said at last, and a grin broke across his boyish face. "I believe we have found a match!"

26

"In a nutshell, you have the whole matter."
—WILLIAM M. THACKERAY
The Second Funeral of Napoleon

"You WANTED TO speak to me, Mr. Rolls?" Kate asked, sitting on the sofa in the drawing room.

The Honorable Charles Rolls—his trousers and boots muddied, his collar loose, his hair damp and hastily combed—looked very young, Kate thought. And very vulnerable. She smiled at him. "Please, take a chair. Or come and sit beside me."

" 'Pon my word, I—I'm not fit to make a call," he muttered uncomfortably. "I hope you will forgive me." His jaw and cheeks were suffused with a red blush. "I have been repairing the balloon this afternoon. I should have gone back to the Marlborough to change, but that would have taken more time. And I would certainly not have presumed, except—"

"Except that you have something of importance to say to me," Kate said. "Please, Mr. Rolls, sit down and say it, without delay. You will make my neck very tired if you force me to keep looking up at you."

Reluctantly, Rolls sat down on the sofa beside her, being careful not to touch her skirt. "I . . . I feel I might talk to you, if you don't mind my saying so. You are Patsy's friend. And you're an American, after all, and in my experience—not that I am all that experienced, of course, or have known that many women intimately, so to speak." He coughed. "But I have observed . . . I mean to say that I—I have remarked on several occasions that American women seem to understand certain matters better than English women. Matters of the—of the, well, tenderer sort." He cleared his throat again and added, with a heartfelt desperation that Kate found quite touching, "May I come straight to the point, Lady Kathryn?"

"If you don't," Kate said, "I shall never forgive you. Have you come to speak about Miss Marsden?"

The young man's dark eyes opened wide. "Why, yes," he said. "However did you know?"

Kate chuckled. "I did not notice that you made any secret of your attentions to the young lady. You seemed to speak to her a great deal more freely than you are now speaking to me."

"Come to that, I don't suppose I did make any secret of it," Rolls said, rather abashedly. "But the thing is . . . that is, you see—" He shook his head. "The devil take it, I hardly know what to say. The plain truth is, Lady Kathryn, I have been something of a cad. And as a result, Patsy has gotten into serious difficulties with Lady Henrietta and Lord Christopher, and I can't for the life of me think of how to get her out without—" He stopped, and the red rose from his cheeks to his forehead.

"Without offering for her hand, I suppose you mean. And you do not wish to offer for her hand."

"It isn't so much that I don't wish . . . I mean, Patsy is a perfectly lovely girl, but . . . to be beastly honest, I am

259

just not cut out for— and I don't suppose her mother and father would—" He took out a white handkerchief, mopped his face, and gave up the effort to explain. "In a nutshell, yes, Lady Kathryn. To be perfectly honest, that's it, in a nutshell. I do not wish to offer for her hand. I suppose," he added in a self-accusatory tone, "I must look a perfect fool, and worse. I'm a lot too cheeky and rash. Imprudent, too."

Unhelpfully, Kate said nothing.

"Well, I shouldn't blame you for believing that of me," he said after a moment, with a look of abject misery, half of which Kate thought was feigned—but only half. "I suppose you know that I've been chucked out of the house over there. Her mother told me, in so many words, to pack my cases and leave and never again darken their doorway."

"Miss Marsden has told me as much," Kate acknowledged.

"I say!" He ducked his head. "I don't suppose I have to assure you that I—that we, I should say, Patsy and I— we have done nothing wrong. Not a thing in the world, by George, beyond an innocent kiss or two in the rose garden." And he struck his fist on the knee of his muddied trousers. "That girl is every inch a lady, no matter how she tosses her head and flirts." His color became brighter. "That is, I mean—"

"I know what you mean, Mr. Rolls," Kate said gravely, "and you do not have to assure me of Miss Marsden's virtuous character. I know that nothing more than a bit of mild flirtation has taken place." He started to speak, but she held up her hand. "Hear me out, won't you? At the risk of preaching a sermon, I must add that sometimes even a small flirtation can create a very *large* expectation."

He chewed on his lip. "I don't believe . . . you can't mean . . ." He raised his eyes, and they were full of consternation.

"But I thought she was *safe*! Like me, I mean. Just out for a bit of fun and all that. You don't think I've hurt her, do you? I say, I wouldn't—oh, not for the *world*! Patsy's a reg'lar *peach* of a girl!"

Kate began to take pity on this very young man. "In this case, Mr. Rolls, I think you are right, Miss Marsden is quite 'safe,' as you put it. You may have played with her heart, but I don't believe you injured it. In another instance, however, with a less confident and assured young lady, such an amusement might have a very different result."

He started to speak, but she laid her hand on his, silencing him. "I don't presume to tell you how to behave, Mr. Rolls. But a girl may be out in Society, and have gone to dozens of balls and entertained a half-dozen offers for her hand, and still not be 'safe,' as you mean the word." She paused, and added, with a smile, "I hope you will consider what I say. I am not speaking of morality, at least not as the word is commonly used. I am speaking of hearts."

"Oh, I shall consider it," he said earnestly. "I am considering it at this very moment. Then she is all right? But Bradford has told me that she plans to leave! I can't really believe it, but . . ." he stopped and shook his head. "There was a filthy family row, you know, over the motorcars and the balloon and me and . . . they were *all* in on it, and Bradford has already cut and run for London. I would have gone with him, if I hadn't had to deal with the balloon, which must be repaired before the owner sees it again."

"Yes," Kate said, "I believe she does mean to leave."

"But . . . where will she go? How will she live?" He swallowed, and the apprehension came back into his voice. "You are *sure* that she does not expect me to—"

261

"She does not expect anything of you, Mr. Rolls. Please do not flatter yourself that her leaving Marsden Manor has the slightest thing to do with you, except insofar—and this is my own interpretation—that she admires your freedom and wishes to have some of it for herself." She smiled. "I also think, Mr. Rolls, that you need have no special concern for her welfare. Miss Marsden is perfectly competent to choose her own direction and purpose. She has a spirit that is every bit as lively and adventurous as your own, you know."

"Oh, yes, I know. I do indeed." A reminiscent smile flickered across his face. "It was her spirit that attracted me to her in the first place."

"Well, then. Perhaps you will not be surprised when you hear, some day, that Miss Marsden has photographed the Alps from a balloon, or motored across Russia with her camera, alone."

"Motored across—" his eyes were like saucers. "You're joking, Lady Kathryn! That kind of adventure would be far too dangerous for a woman!"

"And why should men enjoy all the danger, and monopolize every adventure?" Kate inquired sweetly. "No, I think you must not be surprised when you open a magazine or a book and encounter Miss Marsden's photographs of the African crocodiles, or the Bengalese tigers. Or, for that matter, the naked cannibals of New Guinea, about to roast their dinner. And that is it, Mr. Rolls, in a nutshell."

And she rose and swept out of the room, leaving the Honorable Charles Rolls with his mouth hanging open.

27

"Behold, I shew you a mystery."
—I CORINTHIANS 15:51

LIGHT REFRESHMENTS, LADY Kathryn had ordered, and
Sarah Pratt had been hard at it all afternoon with only
a few moments out for tea and a biscuit with Bess, who
seemed to have forgotten her animosity, although she had
made a remark about tongues that ran on a bit too long.

In truth, Sarah was glad that her friend had been
exonerated of all—well, *nearly* all—misdeeds. It had
been wrong of Bess to conceal the jar of ointment in the
gondola, and *very* wrong to lay a curse upon the motorcar,
although of course there could be nothing at all to the
curse, so perhaps that did not even count. But whatever
Bess's faults, she seemed to have redeemed herself by
revealing the secrets of her ointment (although why
Lady Kathryn and Sir Charles should take an interest in
such a foolish business, Sarah did not for the life of her
understand). And having told Lady Kathryn about the
squire's removal of the grapnel, she certainly felt easier in
her spirit. Whipple could not be blamed for what he had

not done, and perhaps Sir Charles could make the squire own up to it.

In the event, Sarah was happily at work, sailing back and forth from the stolid, predictable iron range to the skittish gas cooker, snapping orders to the kitchen maids and feeling that she was once again mistress of all she surveyed. Lady Sheridan's light refreshments were to include a sliced cold joint; a cold turbot, placed white side up and garnished with caviar and green mayonnaise; an ornamental salmagundi salad that showed off its colorful layers in a straight-sided crystal bowl; small sandwiches, cut into shapes and prettily decorated; a molded strawberry jelly; several hot and cold savories; and fruit. It was the first meal in weeks that Sarah felt confident of producing without mishap—and all because her iron range had been restored to her, and peace and harmony to the kitchen.

Entertainment, Sir Charles had announced for the evening, and put Lawrence in charge of the preparations. Lawrence had spent most of the afternoon in the darkroom, preparing lantern slides from various negatives, some of which had been taken by Miss Marsden, others by Sir Charles. The preparation of the slides was made much simpler by the enlarging camera that Sir Charles had recently purchased.

Lawrence enjoyed his darkroom work, especially now that he was relieved of the guilty burden that had so oppressed him this morning. Knowing that the Daimler had not crashed because he had siphoned out most of the petrol but because someone else had smeared grease on the brake, he could turn his mind to other matters, to the present work, although he had become so adept at it that it hardly required any special attention. And to the future—his and Amelia's future—for which he must now construct some plan.

With the Daimler wrecked and Lord Bradford gone off to London, it did not seem so likely that Lawrence would be summoned thence. But that was not the end of it. His greatest hope had been the prospect of being employed by Sir Charles at Bishop's Keep. But if that could not be, he would have to find work elsewhere. How far would he have to go? What would he have to do? If he had to travel as far as Colchester—fifteen miles away—to find employment, it would mean a choice between Amelia's going along and giving up her situation and the cottage, or his living for the week in Colchester and seeing her only on Sundays and holidays.

But Lawrence did not have to puzzle over these problems for too many hours. He finished mounting the slides and took them out for Sir Charles to inspect. Constable Laken had gone, and they were alone.

"Thank you, Lawrence," Sir Charles said. "I have taken several more photographs—here are the dark slides for you to develop and make into lantern slides. When you are finished, we can turn our attention to preparations for the evening."

"Ah, Sir Charles," Lawrence said hesitantly, "if ye 'ave a moment, I 'ave summat to ask ye, sir."

Sir Charles looked up from the lantern slides he was examining. "What is it?"

" 'Tis about work, sir." Lawrence was not accustomed to speaking humbly, but he did his best. "It seems that Lord Bradford will not be needin' my services, now that the motorcar is no more. I've been hopin' . . . that is, Amelia an' I, we—" he stopped, cleared his throat, and blurted it out. "Truth be told, Sir Charles, I 'ud rather work fer ye. An' Amelia an' I 'ud far rather stay at Bishop's Keep than go to London. I know I kin be useful wi' the gas plant an' the 'lectric an' the photographin' and such," he added hurriedly, feeling that he was placing too much stress on what he and Amelia wanted, rather than on what they had to offer. "An' o' course, Amelia is 'elpful to 'er ladyship. If ye kin see yer way clear to allowin' us to stay, sir, we'd be most grateful, an' work *very* 'ard."

Sir Charles put down the slides and regarded him thoughtfully for a moment. "I have been thinking of purchasing a motorcar for Lady Kathryn."

"I cud take care o' it fer 'er, sir!" Lawrence burst out eagerly. "Ye'd niver 'ave to worry about 'er safety, with me takin' care of it. An' I cud keep the gas plant an' the 'lectric an'—"

"Yes, I daresay you could do all those things, and quite handily, too. And in fact, Lord Bradford has already asked my help in finding you another place. If you prefer to work here, I think we have discovered a happy solution."

Lawrence felt himself beaming from ear to ear, and so full of ecstasy that he could scarcely contain himself. "Oh, sir, thank ye, sir! Amelia will be overjoyed. An' I—"

"I daresay the arrangement will be to all our advantages," Sir Charles said. "Now, back to work. Let's finish up with the slides, and then we shall set up tonight's entertainment. Oh, and by the by, ask Mudd to step in here, will you? I have written notes that must go immediately to the coroner and to the doctor."

Mrs. Pratt's light refreshments (which were set out on the dining table and eaten standing, in the latest London fashion) were received with surly cheer but consumed, Kate observed, with a more ready relish. The conversation, however, rather lagged—Ponsonby, Bateman, and Dickson occasionally speaking to one another but never to Dunstable, Dunstable (resplendent in an embroidered purple vest) speaking to none but Charles, and Rolls failing miserably in his few attempts at wit. Charles himself seemed engrossed in his thoughts, and ate and drank hurriedly and then disappeared. The only guests who seemed to enjoy an amiable conversation were Vicar Talbot, Coroner Hodson, Dr. Bassett, and Squire Thornton—and of course, Patsy and Kate, the two ladies. Thornton, who had been watching Patsy with an avid eye, made several attempts to speak to her, but each time she avoided him.

Promptly at eight, after a murmured message from Mudd, Kate clapped her hands. "Sir Charles promised an evening of photographic entertainment," she said. "It is ready, if you would care to adjourn to the drawing room."

"Lantern slides?" Bateman muttered to Ponsonby. "They had better not be photographs of somebody's trip to the Holy Land, or I tell you, I shall leave."

"It will take more than an evening's amusement to wash out the taste of the weekend's woes," Ponsonby agreed. He cast a nervous eye in the direction of Harry Hodson. "But I fail to see why that fellow is here—the coroner, isn't he?"

Kate spoke lightly, as if she had caught just the last question. "Harry Hodson? He is a dear old friend, and a great admirer of Sir Charles's photographic work."

"Indeed," Hodson said, coming up. "I am most eager to see what our wizard has been up to with his camera lately, Lady Kathryn. I have always enjoyed his revelations of photographic mysteries."

"A documentation of the weekend's events, I am told," the vicar said. "The balloon ride and the chase."

"And including," the doctor added, joining them, "some lantern slides of the Daimler's wreckage. Most appalling, I am told. Not for the faint of heart." He frowned a little at Kate. "Perhaps not for the ladies, either."

Kate gave a smiling shrug. "Ah, well," Bateman said, with more interest, and even Ponsonby looked curious.

In the drawing room, Kate saw that Lawrence had set up the lantern screen with several rows of chairs facing it. Charles stood at the rear of the chairs, his projecting lantern on a small table, a box of slides beside it. The lantern was of the double-lens type, consisting of two optical tubes arranged one above the other. It enabled the projectionist to dissolve one photographic image into another, superimpose two images, or cast two images upon the screen simultaneously, one above the other.

"What *is* he going to do?" Patsy whispered curiously, as she and Kate took seats in the back row.

"I really can't say," Kate said. "He was too busy this evening to confide all the details to me. But if things go as he wishes, I suspect that the entertainment may well tend more to high drama than to light amusement."

When the guests were settled in their chairs, Kate relaxed, curious to see how Charles would handle the presentation. She had no doubts about his skill, of course, but he would be dealing with men of volatile tempers. She was glad that the coroner and the doctor were there, and the constable not far away.

Charles signaled to Mudd to turn out all but one of the lights, and spoke. "The weekend has been a memorable one, gentlemen. I thought you might enjoy seeing pictures of its more interesting moments. The first few shots I will show you were taken in the Park yesterday morning by Miss Patsy Marsden, an excellent photographer." He threw a slide onto the screen. "Mr. Bateman, I believe."

"That's me, all right," Bateman said, grinning at the picture of him standing beside a tree, smoking a cigarette and watching as the other drivers labored to start their cars. "See how easy it is to start an electric? Push of the button is all it takes. No crawling, no cranking."

"But don't forget where it ended," Ponsonby said, with a snicker. "At the end of a tow rope." A ripple of laughter went through the group.

Charles inserted several slides, one after the other, of the waiting motorcars, the fete activities as they got underway, and the balloon, surrounded by curious spectators, ready to go up.

"Ah," Rolls exclaimed with satisfaction, "isn't she beautiful! A work of art."

"And here is one of our departure," Charles said with a little laugh, "under duress, as it were. We are being pursued by natives armed with pitchforks." He put up a slide of himself and Rolls scrambling into the balloon, while the ground crew held the mooring ropes. "And another. Thornton, I believe this is a picture of you."

The slide was met by a momentary silence. Then, as the stunned audience took in the significance of the scene, gasps and murmurs were heard.

"Why . . . why, it *is* you, Roger," the coroner exclaimed in gruff amazement, "pulling the grapnel free! Why in heaven's name would you do a thing like that?"

"Bless me, Harry, you're right," the doctor said, loudly incredulous. He nudged Thornton, who was sitting between them. "You sly dog, Roger. So *that's* why you stood poor Whipple's bail. You didn't want to see the poor man suffer for something you did."

The coroner leaned forward to speak to the doctor across Thornton. "Well, I don't suppose I'm surprised, Bassett. I'm told that Mrs. Jessup has finally revealed that it was our squire here, and not Mr. Rolls, who paid the Jessups that mysterious thirty pounds."

The doctor became suffused with astonishment. "Roger? I am utterly astounded. Why in the world—"

Thornton jumped to his feet. "I had nothing to do with it!" he shouted. "Not any of it!" He pointed at the screen. "That picture is a fake!"

"It is not," Patsy replied with dignity. "I took the photograph with my Frena and developed it myself. And that *is* you, Squire Thornton. The camera caught you red-handed." Her eyes narrowed and her voice became steely. "Telegrams may lie, sir, but not photographs."

The squire turned and looked at Kate and Patsy. He was about to speak, but their words seemed to have robbed him of the power. He started to stumble over the doctor's feet as if making to leave, but the coroner took one arm and the doctor the other and pushed him back into his chair.

"I think, Roger," the coroner said sternly, "that you had better stay."

"Indeed," said the doctor. "I'm sure there is more to be revealed."

"On a happier note," Charles said, putting up the next slide, "here are the winners of the chase. The informal winners, of course."

This slide, of Kate and Patsy posed in Rolls's Peugeot, laughing and waving at the camera, was greeted by the three drivers with grunts and discontented shufflings.

"Congratulations, ladies," said the vicar. "I must confess to a great admiration for anyone who could manhandle one of those machines through our terrible lanes."

"Sheer luck that they got that far," Dickson muttered.

"Oh, I don't know," said Charles mildly, putting up another slide of the two ladies, this one posed with Rolls and Farmer Styles in front of the deflated balloon. "There was quite a bit of skill involved, not to mention strength and good judgment."

"*I'd* say," said Rolls. "Three and three-quarters horsepower, you know. Frankly, I'm amazed that a woman could manage it. Lady Kathryn, you have my greatest respect."

Kate was about to respond to this, but Charles had gone on to the next slide. "And here is the car that came closest to finishing," he said, and put up a picture of a dejected Bateman, his disabled electric, and the tow horse, its lips pulled back from its teeth in a malevolent horselaugh.

"Ha!" laughed Ponsonby. "Bateman, what a fool you look!"

"This picture demonstrates," Dunstable said pompously, "precisely why electricity cannot be taken seriously as an automotive fuel. Petrol is the only viable propellant."

"But Bateman's electric *did* go farther than the steamer or the Benz," Kate pointed out.

"That's true," Charles replied. "Unfortunately, we do not have pictures of the flock of geese that caused Mr. Ponsonby to come to grief, or the stump that did in the Serpollet Steamer. And I fear, Mr. Dunstable, that we have no photographs of you, either."

"That's right, Dunstable," Dickson said, with a little laugh. "All this while you were wrapped up, shall we say, elsewhere." These words were greeted by a general snigger, and a louder guffaw from Ponsonby.

Charles raised his voice over the laughter. "We have, however, managed to apprehend the two men who packaged you." He turned and signaled to Mudd, who was standing beside the door.

"Constable Laken, sir," Mudd announced, and opened the door.

"Ah, Laken," Charles said, as the constable came in, accompanied by a very tall man in brown corduroy pants and rough jerkin and a boy barely out of his teens. Both had their hands manacled before them. "Good of you to come. And who are these gentlemen?"

"Dick Quilp," said the constable, pointing to the tall man, "and Fred Codlin."

Dunstable stared. "Yes! These are the very ones! They came on me in the alley and hit me on the head."

"Please tell the company who paid you," the constable ordered.

" 'Twas them!" said the boy, raising his fettered hands to point at Bateman and Ponsonby.

"That's ridiculous." Ponsonby pulled himself up. "I don't know what you're talking about."

"They paid us two shillin's each if we'd jump 'im," said Quilp darkly. "We didn't want t' do it, but they argued us over wi' the money."

"It's our word against the word of these knaves," Bateman growled. "They have no proof."

"I've still got th' florin ye give me," the boy said helpfully, pulling a two-shilling piece out of his pocket and holding it up.

"I drank mine," Quilp said, "but ye kin ask the barman at the Sun. 'E knows 'ow much I spent."

"This is all nonsense, of course, Harry," Bateman said nervously, to a glowering, red-faced Dunstable. "I swear on my mother's grave, I had nothing—"

Ponsonby was calmer. "Even if we did arrange a little joke," he drawled, "you ought to be grateful. If you hadn't been otherwise occupied, Harry, you would have been in the Daimler with Albrecht. You could be as dead as he is."

Dunstable was about to reply, but Charles interrupted, changing the subject and redirecting their attention with (Kate thought) a very great adroitness.

"Ah, yes, the unfortunate Herr Albrecht," Charles said soberly, and threw another slide onto the screen. "This, gentlemen, is the scene of the crash that killed him. A most appalling sight, you will agree."

Kate winced when she saw the slide, which showed Bradford's Daimler with its front end smashed against the trees, its rear end in the air, and wreckage strewn uphill behind it.

"Terrible, terrible," Dunstable muttered.

"Poor Albrecht," Batemen sighed. "To lose his life in such a way."

"Oh, Lord," whispered Dickson, white-faced.

"You see, Harry?" Ponsonby said triumphantly. "It's just as I said. If you'd been in that car when it went into the ravine, you wouldn't be sitting here right now."

"What I want to know," Rolls said in a wondering tone, "is why it didn't burn. With those hot-tube igniters and a full tank of petrol, the thing should have gone off like a deuced bomb."

"Unbelievable as it seems," Charles remarked, "Herr Albrecht failed to top off the tank. At the time of the crash, the car was virtually empty of fuel. He could not have made it past the bridge."

There was a moment's pause, as the company studied the slide on the screen, and Kate reflected with some pride on her husband's thoroughness as a detective, and with relief on the knowledge that Lawrence could be excused of any great wrongdoing.

"I understand that you have investigated the crash in some detail, Sheridan," the doctor said. "What have you been able to learn about the cause?"

"Several very interesting facts," Charles said, and signaled to Mudd again. The butler stepped out of the room, and when he returned, he was carrying three objects on a large and ornate silver tray. He put the tray on a table at the side of the room and turned up the gaslights.

Charles went to the table and picked up the leather-covered wooden brake. "I am sure you will recognize this brake block," he said, holding it up. "It comes from the left rear wheel of the ill-fated Daimler. The car crashed because someone smeared this block with grease. Albrecht was coming down the hill at a speed probably close to twenty miles an hour. When he attempted to apply the brake, the car spun out of control and went into the ravine."

"Someone smeared the brake with grease!" Dunstable exclaimed incredulously.

"Yes," Charles said. "That is what Albrecht himself said, just before he died, in Dr. Bassett's surgery." He picked up the crockery pot from the tray. "And this is the grease that was used, although it did not come from this container."

"You're speaking very positively," Dickson growled. "How do you know that?"

"I shall show you, Mr. Dickson," Charles said, and went on. "But before I do, I wish to point out that the person who applied the grease to the brake also left a smear of it on the fender." He picked up the third object, the dented fender, and displayed its dusty underside. "He left a fingerprint, as well."

"There you go again, Sheridan," said Harry Hodson, in a tone of scornful amusement, "riding your favorite hobbyhorse. Fingerprints, fingerprints, always fingerprints! Are we to hear of nothing else?"

"Sir Charles is persuaded," the doctor said, for the elucidation of the group, "that any individual in the world can be identified by his fingerprints."

"I've heard that fingerprinting can be done," Ponsonby said dubiously, "but I read in *The Pall Mall Gazette* just last week that the Yard has rejected it as a practical matter, primarily on the grounds that such evidence could not be comprehended by the average jury."

"I doubt it can even be done," said Bateman, inspecting his fingertips, "or yield any useful information." There was a rustle, as the others made the same inspection.

"Oh, but it *can* be done," Charles protested, "and with excellent practical effect." He dropped a slide into the lantern's upper optical tube, and the top half of the screen was filled with the enlarged image of a fingerprint. "This, gentlemen, is a photograph of the fingerprint on the fender."

"What a nuisance," sighed the coroner, shifting his heavy bulk in the chair. "Wake me when the lecture is over."

"I hope to keep you awake this time, Harry," Charles said. Taking a wooden pointer, he strode to the screen. "You can see, of course, that this fingerprint, like all fingerprints, is made up of lines and whorls. This particular print, however"—he pointed—"displays a rare double loop, the upper loop rotating to the left, the lower one to the right."

"Rare, is it?" asked the constable, with some interest.

"Yes, quite rare," Charles said, going back to the projector. "Let me show you several others, and you shall see that there is not a double loop among them." And leaving the image of the fingerprint at the top of the screen, he projected four prints, one after another, onto the bottom half.

"Indeed," said the coroner, sitting up straight, his eyes wide open. "Not a double loop among them."

"But what have we here?" Charles asked, as the fifth print came onto the screen. "Why, bless my soul! I believe it is a match!"

"A match?" the doctor asked. "You mean, you have found another man with the very same fingerprint?"

"No, for that would be impossible," Charles said. "Each man's fingerprints are unique. What we see here is another print made by the *same* man." He went to the screen with his pointer. "Here is the same double loop, the upper rotating to the left, the lower to the right. And here is that odd ridge, and here—" he paused. "If I am correct, I believe that there are eight principal points of comparison between the two prints. A closer study, of course, may reveal others."

"I charge you, Sir Charles," the coroner said sternly, "to reveal exactly *where* you obtained that second fingerprint."

"Indeed," exclaimed the constable. "It could reveal the identity of the man who killed Wilhelm Albrecht!"

There was a gasp, followed by much nervous shifting and muttering. Charles nodded at Mudd, who disappeared and reappeared with another tray, which he placed beside the first. This one bore nine clear crystal wine goblets.

"The print was taken from one of these goblets," Charles said, "each of which, as you can see, is labeled with a name."

"And the goblets?" the constable asked. "Where did you get them?"

"They are the goblets from which wine was drunk at last night's dinner," Charles said. "They were taken from the dining table and locked in the butler's pantry until this afternoon, when I took them to my laboratory and photographed them."

"And the print?" the coroner asked severely. "Whose is it?"

"It belongs," Charles said, "to Arthur Dickson."

"No!" Dickson cried, rising. "It isn't mine!"

"I grant you that there is a remote possibility of some mischance with the goblets," Charles agreed. He took a leather case from his pocket. "I have here a fingerprint kit, however, and it will take only a moment to obtain your prints and confirm that you are not the man."

"This is absurd!" Dickson exclaimed. "Fingerprints! I won't stand for it, d'you hear!"

"Then sit down," Dunstable growled crossly, "and don't be an ass."

"Yes," Bateman said, "do sit down and be reasonable, old chap. We all want to get to the bottom of this wretched affair so we can go about our business."

"Did you do it, Arthur?" asked Ponsonby. "If you did, best 'fess up, or they'll be hounding the rest of us until kingdom come."

"I didn't do it," Dickson said desperately.

"Then perhaps you can explain how the same red grease that appears on the brake was also found on your trousers," Charles said.

Dickson attempted a laugh. "You *are* a preposterous fellow, Sheridan! Even if you had found grease on my trousers, you can't possibly know that it was the *same* grease."

But Charles had inserted two more slides into his lantern projector. "The one on the top," he said, "is a scraping of grease taken from the Daimler's fender. On the bottom is a scraping from Mr. Dickson's tweed trousers. As you can see, this particular grease happens to contain the distinctive corpuscles of swine's blood, which are clearly evident in both samples. Here, at this point, you observe their round shapes, and here again, and here. There is no mistaking the fact that both samples come from the same source. I submit to you, gentlemen, that Mr. Dickson—"

"No!" Dickson shouted again. "And you aren't going to frighten me into a confession with this scientific hocus-pocus, Sheridan. Fingerprints and corpuscles! It's all utter nonsense. Nonsense, do you hear me?"

"I should think more seriously of this accusation, Mr. Dickson, if I were you," said the constable.

"Poppycock," Dickson muttered. "Lunacy, done up in scientific jargon. I am going back to the inn, and first thing tomorrow, to London."

The coroner looked pained. "I am sorry to tell you that I have heard enough evidence to remand you into the constable's custody, Mr. Dickson." He sighed heavily as he heaved himself to his feet. "I am even more sorry to say that the matter of Herr Albrecht's death shall have to be brought before a coroner's jury."

"A jury?" Dickson repeated scornfully. "And what makes you think that a jury of villagers would consider

such ludicrous evidence as fingerprints and corpuscles?
It's all academic nonsense!"

"Perhaps." The coroner sighed again. "But the Crown
must have a go, anyway. Shall we say, tomorrow
fortnight?"

28

"Come, Josephine, in my flying machine. Up, we go!"
—American Music Hall Ballad, 1920s

CHARLES SLUMPED IN his leather chair in the library and held up his glass. As Kate poured his sherry, she touched his shoulder.

"You'll feel better in a few days," she said sympathetically, "when the disappointment has passed."

"I am sorry to say I told you so," Harry Hodson said in a gloomy tone, "but I *did* warn you that no jury—no village jury, at any rate—would be able to understand such a complicated hocus-pocus. And I was right. Your presentation might have persuaded the Royal Academy, Charles, but the jurors were simply not able to hear it. They brought in the only verdict they knew how to bring: death by automotive mischance."

"It was the fingerprints that frightened them off," Dr. Bassett said, from the window where he stood looking out. "Perhaps if you had ended your presentation with the corpuscles and the red grease on Dickson's trousers—"

"But that was only half the evidence," Charles protested. "And by far the less interesting half."

"The more comprehensible half," Bassett rejoined. "It will be decades before a jury is capable of understanding fingerprint evidence. And it may never happen."

"The problem *really* was," Kate said, resuming her seat on the sofa beside Constable Laken, "that Bess Gurton's testimony couldn't be introduced. For fear of harming her reputation in the village, that is."

"But if Bess Gurton had mentioned her flying ointment," Ned replied, "the jury would have dismissed it just as they did the fingerprints and the corpuscles—as so much magical nonsense."

"However, seen from another point of view," Hodson went on, as if no one else had spoken, "the Crown didn't lose much."

"That's right," Laken said. "Practically speaking, even had Dickson been bound over, the prosecution could not have proved that he intended to murder Albrecht. All that could have been argued was that he meant to cause mischief in the operation of the motorcar in which he thought Dunstable would be riding, as a way of getting even for the injuries he had suffered at the man's hands. Dickson could not have anticipated that Dunstable would spend the day in the dung heap, or that Albrecht would impale himself upon the broken tiller."

Charles roused himself. "I suppose you are right, but it is frustrating to know that science cannot assure that justice is done."

Kate entirely concurred with Charles. If this had been one of Beryl Bardwell's crime stories, the plot would have been tied up much more neatly: the culprit apprehended, summoned to the bar, and punished. If his conviction could have been managed by no other means, the novelist would have arranged a confession, appropriately dramatic, of course, or even a suicide. Right and justice would have triumphed in the end, and the world been restored to order and normalcy under the law. To have events turn out otherwise was deeply frustrating.

The doctor came away from the window and sat down. "It is a mistake to assume that justice will not be done," he said. "There is more than one way to skin a cat, you know?"

"Oh?" Kate asked.

"I heard from Marsden today. Ponsonby and Dunstable have apparently forged a temporary alliance for the purpose of ruining poor Dickson. They have been busy in Threadneedle Street, buying up Dickson's notes so that they can call them in. Coming on top of the expenses of the patent litigation against which the man must defend himself, this will utterly ruin him."

The coroner chuckled dryly. "Poor Dickson, indeed! Appropriate punishment, I should say. A civil penalty, where a criminal could not be got."

Kate found herself agreeing. "Still," she said thoughtfully, "it is Dunstable who must bear most of the responsibility for what happened this weekend, don't you think? He was the one who brought those men here, and set them at one another's throats—all with the hope of making money. Not to mention that he is a particularly *odious* man."

Charles looked up from the pipe he was lighting. "I think, Kate, you will have nothing to fear concerning Dunstable. I, too, heard from Marsden. If rumor be trusted, the British Motor Car Syndicate is not long for this world. We will shortly learn of a falling out between Ponsonby and Dunstable, and Dunstable will be the next victim of Threadneedle Street. Not a moment too soon, either. We can only hope that some British inventor will emerge with a truly distinguished British vehicle, to give us parity, at least, with the German and French. Whether gas or electric or steam—"

"Do you think electric and steam have a chance?" Laken asked curiously. "After the beating those two cars took this weekend, I should say not."

"You're probably right," Charles said. "Electricity holds great promise, but must wait for the invention of a primary battery. And steam has been around long enough to have worked out the engineering problems, but people are still afraid of it."

"What about Henry Royce?" Kate asked. "He seemed to show some interest toward the end of his visit. Do you think he will take up the challenge?"

"It would be a good thing if he did," Charles said. "I daresay he would construct a motorcar that would be as reliable as a watch and as durable as the Tower of London."

"You have a great deal of faith in that gentleman, Sheridan," the doctor said. "But at least we have something to be glad for. The motorcars are gone and our village is left in silence."

"For the moment," Harry Hodson said glumly. "But they'll be back. In a few years, every man Jack will have one. It'll be worse than bicycles."

Charles laughed. "And *you* shall have one, too, Harry. Once the thing is perfected, keeping a motorcar will be much less work than keeping and driving a horse."

"I doubt it," Hodson said, frowning. He turned to Kate. "I trust, though, Kate, that you enjoyed your balloon flight."

Kate brightened, remembering the several times she had flown on Monday, after Rolls finished the repair and before the balloon was finally packed for return. "Oh, very much indeed!" she exclaimed. "Of course, the balloon was tethered, but that did not detract from the experience, for me or, I am sure, for Bess Gurton, or Miss Marsden."

The flight Kate made with Bess had been memorable. Seeing Bess's ecstatic face as she rose into the heavens, watching her enjoy the colorful autumn landscape spread out below and pick out her neighbors' houses and her own with Charles's field glasses—it had been a pure delight. "I think the vicar was equally pleased with his flights," Kate added. "I have no doubt that his sermons over the next few months will be decorated with aeronautical metaphors, and all the villagers will be eager to go up." She paused, thinking about the experience. "Do you suppose one day everyone will have flown in a balloon?"

"Not in balloons, I shouldn't think," Charles said. "They are essentially uncontrollable, which makes them fit for little other than sport. Motorized, heavier-than-air flight will soon be possible, however."

The doctor chuckled. "I'll wager a fiver that chap Rolls will be one of the first to try it. What a daredevil that fellow is! But he could not win Lady Henrietta's heart. I understand that she put an end to his friendship with Miss Marsden."

"I think Miss Marsden put an end to it herself," Kate said. "She is planning an around-the-world photographic tour, you know. A grand adventure of her own."

Harry Hodson shook his head. "I've never thought much of gallivanting young ladies, especially when they are unchaperoned. What Lady Henrietta can be thinking—" he scowled. "And of course, there is Roger Thornton. He must be beside himself at the thought of that headstrong young girl, going off God knows where—"

"I think," Kate said quietly, "that Roger Thornton has nothing to say about where Miss Marsden goes. In my opinion, her refusal to consider the match has saved them both much unhappiness."

"I quite agree," Dr. Bassett said with wry humor. "No man would want a wife who photographs his misdeeds and then shows them about."

"Speaking of photographs," Charles said, getting to his feet, "I wonder if you would like to see the X-ray photographs I made yesterday of the bones of my hand.

ROBIN PAIGE

They are really quite remarkable. Would you care to come down to the laboratory?"

The men all rose. "Ah, science," Hodson said with a half-bitter mockery. "What subtle secrets it reveals! The latent pattern of the tip of the finger, the shadow of the bone beneath the flesh."

Dr. Bassett, however, was more impressed. "The bones of the hand," he marveled. "Think of the applications in medical science. And who knows? Soon we may be able to watch the very heart as it beats."

"And soon," Kate said, rather more somberly, "we will have no secrets at all."

HISTORICAL NOTE

"Contrariwise," continued Tweedledee, "if it were so, it might be; and if it were so, it would be: but as it isn't, it ain't. That's logic."

—LEWIS CARROLL
Through the Looking Glass

YOU WILL FIND three historical personages in *Death at Devil's Bridge*: Charles Rolls, Henry Royce, and Harry Lawson (to whom we have given the name Harry Dunstable). Since you have met them early in their automotive careers, you might be interested in knowing more about them.

Charles Rolls (1877–1910) was one of the first men in England to challenge the government's restrictions on the speed and operation of motorcars. He was only nineteen when he imported a three and one-half horsepower Peugeot from France, at the time, the most powerful car in England. (Compare this to the 12-horsepower riding lawn mower you can see on sale at your local discount store.) The next year, Rolls became a member of the Automobile Club in London, and began to take part in auto races and reliability trials. In 1900, he and his 12-horsepower Panhard took first prize in the London-Edinburgh race, and over the next few years, he competed in most major European races, making a name for himself as an amateur racing-car driver. He also began selling imported cars (the New Panhard et Lavassor and Minerva were his specialties), and in 1903, went into the new- and used-car business in Brook Street, Mayfair.

Henry Royce, meanwhile, was making a different kind of history. Royce was born in 1863 and established himself, after early years of hardship, as an electrical engineer with a special genius for refining the work of others. His first such effort was an electric doorbell, but he was soon turning out an improved electric motor that earned a reputation for reliability and durability. Sometime after 1896, he became interested in automobiles and acquired a two-cylinder 10-horsepower Decauville which he rebuilt several times, finally creating the first Royce automobile.

It was at this point that Royce (the engineer and manufacturer) and Rolls (the dealer and promoter) came together. At an historic meeting in Manchester in 1904, they agreed that Rolls would have the exclusive right to sell Royce's new automobile, and that he would exhibit the forthcoming models at the Paris Salon in December, under the name Rolls-Royce. To promote the car, Rolls drove it in competition in Europe, America, and England, demonstrating its speed and dependability. In only a few years, the Rolls-Royce was England's premier automobile.

Rolls's daredevil streak showed itself not only on the ground but in the air, and as his interest in flight grew, his fascination with automobiles diminished. He was an eager participant in ballooning, making over 170 ascents. His first documented balloon-auto chase took place in 1902, some years after the event at Bishop's Keep, from which he no doubt took the idea. But with the coming of heavier-than-air flight he abandoned balloons for the aeroplane. In 1908, he went to France to study Wilbur Wright's new biplane, and bought one. He was soon an expert aviator. In June 1910, he made a record crossing of the Channel by flying nonstop from Dover to Calais and back in ninety minutes. The next month, he was flying in a restricted-landing contest in Bournemouth when the overstressed tail of his plane collapsed. He was killed almost instantly, the first Englishman to die while piloting a plane. Five years later, the Rolls-Royce company was faced with financial ruin when the luxury car market collapsed at the onset of the Great War. To save itself, it turned to the production of aircraft engines, for which it gained world renown.

Harry John Lawson's story is less laudable, but opens an interesting window onto early automotive history in England. From all reports, Lawson seems to have possessed the promoter's brassy business expertise and extroverted self-confidence. He started in the bicycle business in 1876. From bicycles, he moved into company promotions, buying up valuable patents, launching high-sounding companies, and getting out before the bubble burst. In 1895, he began to take over the infant motorcar industry. For over two years, his market manipulations and refusals to manufacture (why make cars when one could make more money by merely selling stock?) virtually blocked the development of the industry. But in 1897, his elaborate edifice began to crack, and by the end of that year, it was gone, and with it the stockholders' money. In 1904, Lawson was prosecuted for fraud and went to jail for twelve months at hard labor.

REFERENCES

We use both primary and secondary documents in our research for this mystery series. Here are a few books that we found most helpful in creating *Death at Devil's Bridge*.

Beasley, David. *The Suppression of the Automobile: Skulduggery at the Crossroads.* London: Greenwood Press, 1988.

Mrs. Beeton's *Book of Household Management.* S. O. Beeton, 1861.

Bird, Anthony and Hallows, Ian. *The Rolls-Royce Motor-Car.* New York: Crown Publishers, 1972.

The British Journal Photographic Almanac & Photographer's Daily Companion. London: Henry Greenwood, 1895, 1896, 1897, and 1898.

Cottrell, Leonard. *Up in a Balloon.* London: World Wide Ltd, 1970.

Cummins, C. Lyle, et al. *A History of the Automotive Internal Combustion Engine.* Warrendale, Pa.: The Society of Automotive Engineers, 1976.

Davies, Jennifer. *The Victorian Kitchen.* London: BBC Books, 1989.

Eves, Edward. *Rolls-Royce: 75 Years of Motoring Excellence.* London: Eldorado Books, 1979.

Morgan, Jerome J., Ph.D. *A Textbook of American Gas Practice.* Lancaster, Pa.: Lancaster Press, Inc., 1925.

Nicholson, T. R. *The Last Battle: The Birth of the British Motor Car*, *Vol. 3.* London: Macmillan, 1982.

Rolt, L. T. C. *The Aeronauts: A History of Ballooning, 1783–1903.* New York: Walker & Company, 1966.